Books by Peter De Vries

The Cat's Pajamas & Witch's Milk

The
Cat's Pajamas
& Witch's Milk

TWO NOVELS

by Peter De Vries

Little, Brown and Company • Boston • Toronto

LIBRARY OF CONGRESS CATALOG CARD NO. 68–30874

FIRST EDITION

*Published simultaneously in Canada
by Little, Brown & Company (Canada) Limited*

PRINTED IN THE UNITED STATES OF AMERICA

I believe that humanity has but one objective: to suffer.

—FLAUBERT

People have more fun than anybody.

—COLONEL STOOPNAGLE

Contents

1
The Cat's Pajamas

1

The Cat's Pajamas

one

TATTERSALL'S most embarrassing moment was one
for which any newspaper running such a feature would
probably have paid the standard fee, but which he himself would gladly have given his life's savings to have
been spared. It was the autumn Homecoming at his
college, Chichester. He was attending an afternoon
musicale, one of the campus events arranged for the
weekend, when he became annoyed by a woman whispering behind him. He turned and glared over his shoulder at her — to find himself looking straight into the eye
of an old flame.

He did not immediately recognize her, nor she him.
The ghost of Lucy Stiles the undergraduate was a moment in emerging from the fleshed-out cheeks and scrolls
of tinted hair in which in the intervening decade it had
become, if not obliterated, at least grievously smothered
and entangled. Her own mouth opening in an audible
gasp when she recognized her censor completed the
sensation that was, for Tattersall, like falling through ice
into boiling water. A lunatic assortment of expressions
crossed his face by way of: surprise (shot-up eyebrows),

3

acknowledgment (bit of a nod), self-deprecation (hunched shoulders and sleazy-rug-merchant spread of hands), and, finally, apology, more or less recorded in the mangled grin with which he turned around again, still mugging.

Such an episode is bound to be especially gruesome at a reunion, where every acquaintance glimpsed is reminder enough of what time has done to all, each face lurking behind the lifted glass or the lowered teacup a threat to what remains of your composure. Tattersall disliked and even feared reunions on that account, but he now taught at Chichester, so there was nothing he could do about it. The reunions came to him. They sought him out as such remorseless personifications of Time that he had come to think of them as the Furies themselves, stalking him from year to year, ready to spring at a moment of their own contriving. He seemed hardly to have exaggerated.

So then Lucy Stiles had become a gilded chatterbox who had to be shushed at concerts, and he a shusher of such women. But he was not! There was not a shred of proof for such a charge, save this fluke of a split second utterly without precedent in his thirty-three years, so utterly unlike him that if Lucy thought she recognized him, very well: he himself did not. He refused to make the identification. Let them adduce fingerprints, dental impressions, cephalic measurements and any other data said to hold up in court, and he would decline to authenticate the result. Let them add to these exhibits a motion picture of the scene just enacted, and he would deny he was its principal. It was the work of the Furies. They had cooked it up with someone masquerading as him, some imp or impostor lurking unsuspected in his veins, biding his time for three decades, genetically instructed to pop from hiding at the moment precisely calculated to do him in, wearing his guise, before as swiftly disappearing from view, never to be seen again, let's hope.

All this ran through Tattersall's mind as he sat with his hands digging into his knees, convinced that if his temperature were taken just then with a sickroom thermometer it would be found to be well over a hundred. He believed that mortification ran you a fever. He cursed his luck through gritted teeth. This was not one of those things at which you would laugh six months from now. No, six months from now, six years, you would still, as tonight, draw the pillow across your face and groan.

His hands had begun to enact covert unwitting gestures as, still mugging, he rehearsed the protestation that he did not go about looking daggers at people. This was an exception, a momentary lapse of urbanity — or as the jargon of the hour had it, loss of cool — not even explained by his wanting to hear the music. Far from it! If it was chamber music, it was torture chamber music. The quartet of aliens sawing away up there themselves constituted a public nuisance hard enough to bear without other distractions. Two minutes ago, if queried in an audience reaction poll, he would have said: "I'll take fingernails run across a blackboard, thank you, or the shriek of automobile tires. Not the cats from whose entrails these sounds are drawn produced in their lifetimes anything like it." Now he wished this hideous music would never end. Not, at least, till he had worked out some plan of action for the awful confrontation that awaited him the instant that it did.

His nerves were shot anyway. A long and intensifying period of self-review had left Tattersall on edge. A habit of rigorously scrutinizing his conduct and its motives (so that any disclaimer that he ever gave people dirty looks could be taken at face value) had of late entered a new phase. He had always roughly cast these exercises in honesty into words. Now he put the words down on paper. Tattersall had taken to writing himself abusive and even threatening letters. "Dear Tattersall," this other self would tap out on his office typewriter, this familiar, this Doppelgänger who hovered perpetually overhead like a prosecuting muse, "has it ever occurred to you that this open-mindedness on which you pride yourself may very well be the mask for a kind of, oh, lazy malleability, an evasion of elementary Commitment traceable — here we come, boy — throughout *your entire life?* (And don't smile at the italics as earmarks of your moral square.) Take for example your habit of 'conscientiously' 'weighing' both sides of an issue until it is no longer an issue and can be discerningly fingered in the museum of human action known as history. Are you within sight of an opinion about relaxing the rules for women visitors in the men's dormitories, or are we afraid of being a square here too, perhaps planning a chest cold the day it comes up for vote at the faculty meeting from which we shall therefore be absent . . . ?" Later he would find these letters in the pigeonhole where he got his mail. Proving that, though the unexamined life may not be worth living, the examined one is no bed of roses either.

6

The abrasive score offered an all too appropriate musical background for the memories that now deluged Tattersall.

He remembered how twelve years before, in a rowboat, on a stream clogged with water lilies, he had undertaken to explain to Lucy Stiles the meaning of the line, "I have seen the eternal Footman hold my coat and snicker," in Eliot's *Prufrock*. "Who is the eternal Footman, Hank?" — trailing a hand among the lilies. "I want to know."

Oars had had to be tucked up into the boat for the exegesis, and he had thrust his straw hat back an inch with his thumb as he began:

"Well, he's an, oh, a sort of personification of the force that seems to urge us along even as it ridicules us, don't you know, Luce. Life egging us ever onward even as it mocks us. Encourages us to keep on making fools of ourselves. Something of that sort." An apt recollection, wouldn't you say! He was still smarting under the memory when another brought down its lash. "Your eyes are the soft, gentle brown of these button mushrooms." Those liberally sprinkling the steaks over which they held hands at Tony's later.

And now he had just told this woman in pantomime to zip her lip.

These fires the Devil personally stoked. Lucy had sprung into his car one autumn evening wearing a bright blue woolen throw, or shrug, around her shoulders. She had bought it at Garfinckel's on a recent trip to Washington. She reported having been a half hour deciding from among a selection so beautiful she had wanted them all. By chance he had spent the next weekend in Washington himself, and hotfooted it up to Garfinckel's. There, sure enough, was a display in the window, with a sign reading: BRIGHTEN YOUR WINTER WITH A GARFINCKEL THROW. He had bought her a red one, over which she had squealed with such delight that he had gone home and written her a poem — *The Girl in the Garfinckel Throw*. Then to the words he had composed a tune. He sang the song to her, accompanying himself on the piano. "You have your throw, let's have our fling . . ." One last twist of the knife: she might very well have a copy of the song around.

What the Transylvanians continued implacably to fiddle was indeed music of the kind we love to hate, and several people walked out in protest. One man's exit was somewhat diluted by his happening to march up the aisle in step with the rhythms being deplored, swinging his hat in his hand. Tattersall could have taken flight under cover of such a withdrawal. The speculation shot into his mind. But the intrinsic discrepancy of it would have been just too much. Walking out on music you have just shushed somebody so you could hear it would have reduced his position to absolute idiocy. Besides, there would be no end to the mail he was going to get without giving the Doppelgänger an opening like that. The Doppelgänger was already hard at it: "Let's not pride ourselves too readily on 'sticking,' or 'taking our medicine like a man,' shall we, when the construction might as easily be put on matters that you hadn't the *guts* to flee. You just sat there. The coward has been defined as someone who in an emergency thinks with his feet. What you thought with I shall leave to your no doubt ample . . ."

8

The room seemed hot, its occupants to swim together in a mist, like the special effects in the avant-garde film to which they had been treated by the Drama Department the evening before. Tattersall felt a constriction in his chest, as though invisible hands had hitched his trouser belt up around his armpits and were tightening it with commendable stealth. He thought he must be turning purple. A timely heart attack, that's the ticket. To be sped feet-first out of this mess, and out of all human mortification forever. But no such dramatic salvation was to be vouchsafed him, and the convicts trying to saw their way out of Schönberg went on into their fourth and final movement, marked *allegro vivace*.

If only he could brazen it out, greet Lucy with a breezy laugh of the kind your unmitigated-gall types brought off with no trouble whatsoever, all over the world. You saw them everywhere, blandly inserting themselves into ticket queues instead of going to the end, butting in ahead of you at supermarket check-out counters without so much as a by-your-leave, and what's more getting away with it, too. To resemble them in the least Tattersall would have to step away out of character, as in fact he sometimes tried to when up against a situation to which they were vastly more suited. One of his tricks for negotiating a complication for which he was himself miscast was to select some person of his acquaintance whom it was less likely to throw, and pretend to be that person. He did so now. He quickly sorted through a list of eligible candidates for the job of greeting Lucy as though nothing were amiss and came to — Repulski. Of course! At once handsome and hulking, with a kind of loping animal ease, the suave Slav, as he was known around campus, was a natural for this mess. That hovering, half-oblivious chocolate-brown gaze, and that agreeably brassy grin could handle anything. Besides, as head of the Music Department he was in a way responsible for it. The performance of this work during Homecoming could only be explained by the fact that its composer was a friend of Repulski's. And fond as Tattersall was of music, he was here only out of friendship for Repulski too. So it was no more than fair that Repulski help get him out of it with a whole hide, vicariously speaking.

Having mentally donned Repulski's guise, then, he hastily tried to imagine a remark of the sort Repulski might be counted on to toss the whole contretemps off with (and given Tattersall's lack of stomach for frontier-forging twelve-toners). "Well, Lucy, the last time I saw you I believe you were talking about having your ears pierced. Now you won't have to. Mbahahaha!"

Oh, Christ, no, that's no *good*. The familiarity of it would be much too crude; it would be coming on too strong at far too short notice (however typical of Repulski on one level). Something in another vein, hurry. Something more impersonal as far as Lucy herself is concerned, and bearing in mind that slight buzz of an accent he has, though of course not including it in the impersonation. "Well, I thought zot quite an interestink experiment. Having all four musicians play different compositions at vunce."

He saw that Repulski had been a mistake, and seeing it, felt a spasm of irritation with the man. He could not carry it off, even leaning on his furled umbrella, the ferrule sinking slowly into the wet November sod. The first sally was precisely the kind the mesomorph would have made, which should have told Tattersall this was not up his alley. He would have to see it through himself, and his best bet was to pretend as blithely as possible, as equably as he, himself, could, that nothing was amiss. He had assumed the whisperer behind him to be deprecating the music, and had turned to agree with her. Of course! That must be his line. The scowl had been for the music, not her. *They* were kindred spirits. Capital! Thank God Sherry wasn't here. Was Lucy's husband? What the devil was her married name again? He'd seen it once in an alumni bulletin. Hurlbutt, Halliburton . . .

Pulling himself together, Tattersall bowed his head as if in prayer, actually to spend the moments remaining to him in mentally rehearsing a few remarks suitable for a greeting predicated on those lines, and in spiritually preparing himself to deliver them. "Gawd," he would say, rolling his eyes as he wheeled without an instant's hesitation, on the audience's arising, "I'm glad that's over. I know what you were going through. Well, Lucy, I must say the years have been kind to you."

No, leave the years out of it. They'll do you no good whatever. Just the pleasantry without the allusion to time. All right. Then the rest would have to be played by ear as, chatting beside her while they drifted slowly toward the exits, he would reconvene the scattered elements of such intelligence and charm as she must be presumed to have seen in him back in the days when, afloat on the gold and green of a Sunday afternoon, he had elucidated Prufrockian unease from such obvious firsthand knowledge.

The composition drew to a close and with it the

concert. The audience applauded and rose. Tattersall turned around.

"Well, Hank Tattersall, you haven't changed a bit."

Lucy flicked him across the chin with a program rolled into a tube. She smiled under a small blue hat, around whose edges curled the tips of her bronzed hair, remembered as of an auburn persuasion, and hanging to her shoulders and below.

"Well, actually —"

"Not a single bit."

"You're looking very well yourself, Lucy."

"You know Mayo, my niece, of course. I don't know whether you realized she was my niece. Therefore that I was her aunt."

The nineteen-year-old Gioconda standing at Lucy's side was a student in his creative writing class. For all her ethereality, he wanted to wash her typewriter out with soap. It was not for him to say whether the novel on which she was at work showed any substantial talent or not; he only knew that its jolting content and jarring language, taken in conjunction with her genteel New England rearing, put him off, as did the not quite expressionless Mona Lisa gaze with which she heard out his "criticism" in personal conference; so that he jabbered away, fell all over himself in his attempt to seem to know his business while protesting ignorance of the milieu under delineation. What did this child know of junkies and kooks and death warmed over? And by what demon was she driven to write about them in the first-person vernacular? "Write about what you know," he had said, and for his pains was reminded that she had spent two summers working as a volunteer in a Massachusetts snake pit. She spoke in a hurried whisper, and with a hint of quietly watchful amusement. She always seemed to be smiling secretly, as though she had something on you which qualified the validity of anything else you did or said. What she had on him, along with the rest of the class, was that he believed in something once called esthetic pleasure, and that it was the function of literature to furnish it in some measure, and not to beat you over the head with buzzard guts.

Inching up the aisle between this creature and her aunt, Tattersall had the sense of being caught in a web of female complicity finer than gossamer yet tough as steel, a sacrificial victim, a poor sonofabitch held for a moment in polite suspension before being delivered over to their laughter the minute his back was turned. How would the gossip go? Would his being an old beau make Aunt Lucy go easy on him in instinctive defense of her own taste? Or would it be one of those "to think I nearly married him" things?

"Mayo's been turning out some bang-up stuff," he said as they pressed forward in the crowd. He felt as though they were caught in a clogged meat grinder.

"I wish he'd tell me that," Mayo eagerly whispered.

"She says very good things about you too, Hank," Lucy said. "She thinks you're fine."

"Why don't we all have a drink and develop the point? God knows we need it after that music," Tattersall said, beginning to recover his composure.

Such an interval would have a twofold merit. It would delay the women's own certain klatsch, while giving him the opportunity to recover some more lost ground. After all, chewing the rag was one of the arts at which he was most adept, given reasonable odds.

"Oh, I'm sorry I can't," Lucy said. "Harry's going to speak at this banquet tonight, you know, and I'll have to see his dinner clothes are in shape, and maybe let him try out his speech on me, and what have you. Are you going?"

"Certainly," Tattersall said, and, winding up this encounter as gracefully as he could with a hasty, "See you there," hightailed it across the campus to the Administration Building to find out from program headquarters what and where this banquet was, and try to get tickets. He hated banquets worse than anything on earth, with the possible exception of benefit balls, and caught fleeting glimpses of himself climbing into a boxcar, after one or another, dressed in dinner clothes, and disappearing from the knowledge of men.

He still could not remember her married name. "Waterhouse, Weyerhauser, Winkleman," he panted to himself as he galloped across the grass. He was now sure it began with a W. A Calendar of Events tacked to the bulletin board identified both the banquet and the speaker when the name Wurlitzer shot off the page at him. Harry T. Wurlitzer, of course, of the Wurlitzer and Wise advertising agency, was to speak on "Advertising — the Fifth Estate" at a dinner sponsored by the Department of Economics. Reservations were closed, but by pulling some wires Tattersall managed to scrounge up a pair of tickets, after hastily telephoning his wife to make sure she was agreeable to going. "You like to eat out," he reminded her. Then he galloped homeward through the falling dusk.

Sherry did everything he wanted. She left the cellar, where he had found her coping with a faulty washing machine, and flew effortlessly about the house checking on his clothes as well as her own. She had no problems and no complications. She was a miracle of amenability who gave Tattersall no cause for complaint, except for a sometimes irritating view that the sun rose and set on him. She was a bright finch of a woman without moods, or any lapses of animation save those ordained by fatigue or bad news, which would have been wearing were it not for a certain resilience that went with it, an instinctive recognition that other people's tempos varied, that their natures periodically called for withdrawal or silence. His report that the speaker was married to an old flame into whom he had just run she took in stride, and made his curiosity her own, while sparing him hers.

Their seats were naturally not very good. They were put at a corner table for ten, of which the other eight were a close-knit group unfamiliar to them and who, happily, paid them no mind. Their discourtesy soothed rather than riled Tattersall's detestation of banquets. Lucy and Mayo, sitting together, were closer to the speakers' dais, but by chance visible. Mellowed by a couple of cocktails and some dinner wine, Tattersall led his shimmering little wife over during coffee and presented her. He tried to give the term "classmate" a deliberately jocose connotation when introducing Lucy, by his laugh freely conveying implications of water picnics, of bottles of Chianti slowly consumed, of dormitories entered long after lights-out. "Why we'd . . ." Here Tattersall, who had drunk his share tonight, made a latticework of his fingers in a manner suggestive of boosting another through an open window in the small hours, glancing in spite of himself at Mayo as he did so. "Your dormitory's been torn down, Lucy, but the river's still there."

"And running downhill like all of us."

"Swell," Sherry said, and exemplifying by her manner one of the adjectives which he forbade his students to use, "chipper," towed him back to their table. Yes, she was chipper. He was married to a chipper woman, he observed as he tripped along in her wake. They resumed their seats in time to hear the president of the Economics Club rapping his water goblet with a spoon. The speeches were about to begin.

Tattersall had correctly picked out Wurlitzer as the broad-shouldered man with the thinning blond hair seated on the toastmaster's right. His pulse began suddenly to race when Wurlitzer rose to speak. Wurlitzer cleared his throat into his fist, and then grasped the lectern at diagonal corners in the manner of dynamic speakers everywhere. The thick-framed glasses he donned before beginning gave him a look of explosive efficacy even before he opened his mouth.

"The proper study of mankind," he began, "is still, as it always has been, man. Modern man has carried this injunction farther than all previous generations combined, but all the good it's done him in the way of peace of mind. The discoveries of psychology, augmented by the illuminations of literature, have left us little to admire in ourselves," he went on, as the fear gripped Tattersall that he was going to be good. "Self-scrutiny has certainly not conduced to complacency. It's now reached a point where no self-respecting man has any use for himself."

Tattersall swallowed dryly as he tried to join in the general laughter, and he clapped with moist palms. Perhaps Wurlitzer had a writer. He seemed to be more glued to his manuscript than a man would have to be who had written it himself . . .

"Why is all this? I think it's because our self-concern has become too individual. Literature from Proust and Joyce on to nine out of ten current novels deals with the vertical exploration of interior man rather than his horizontal connection with others — the mankind Pope meant. Fiction is unilateral. Poetry, God knows, is unilateral. Even dancing, the first of the social rituals, is. Young people don't even touch each other any more on the dance floor. They just bounce around in one another's general vicinity. We hear a great deal today about the malaise of modern man . . ."

Yes, Tattersall thought, and so let's not hear any more about it tonight, shall we? Because I'll tell you what the malaise of modern man is, Buster. The malaise of modern man is that he's no goddam better than he ever was, while the slings and arrows haven't let up none either. But go on. Give us the bit about not communicating. Get to that. It's after ten.

"Man has isolated himself because of the narcissistic turn his self-concern has taken. Advertising, I fear I must confess, is tarred with the same stick. Am *I* attractive, am *I* dainty, fresh all day, graying, carrying enough insurance, well enough groomed, or able to get into this or that club. Well, damn the clubs! What I want to know is, *what's happened to the front porch!*"

17

Swell. Great. Then this citizen was going to be all the ass he could have hoped, and in so doing restore to Tattersall some of his competitive dignity, so sorely damaged. On balance, he would come out looking better by comparison. Lucy mightn't see it — why should she? — but Mayo would. This speech must certainly be bringing out the Gioconda smile.

"The front porch is gone because we've all gone inside and shut the door, there to pursue the first person singular that has replaced the third person plural poets once meant by mankind." The tie-in with advertising was so predictable that Tattersall wondered how he could possibly have failed to anticipate it. "We don't really want anything to do with one another any more, and this precisely at a time when mass conformity is the bugbear. With the character in Edna Millay, we love humanity but we hate people." Yes, he had a writer. He himself would not have known the source of the quotation, which was cropping up everywhere and without credit on the sweatshirts young people were slopping around in. "We don't want anything to do with one another any more. Houses are no longer built with front porches. There's the patio instead, in back, and screened from our neighbors the better to sip cocktails in solitude on it, or at best with a few chosen friends. The open, neighborly *gemütlichkeit* of yesteryear as typified by that institution known as the front porch is gone. The neighborhood is gone! . . ."

Tattersall stole a glance at Mayo, who was known to slip into New York for weekends in the Village, and was rumored to smoke pot, sending back his own counterpart of the Gioconda smile: a deadpan telegraph of kinship no more in need of actual facial expression than of words. Overt amusement here was out: humor itself barred it. Taste did not smack its lips. It knew instinctively what was not fair game. Sensing all this, Tattersall leaned back to enjoy in a relaxed manner the half-hour of banality that lay ahead.

The result was to overmellow him, and thus lay him open once more to disaster.

The wish to square himself with Lucy had made him get over to the dinner, and it now motivated the close, even fulsome attention he paid her husband. He laughed at all his jokes, and in the serious portions hung on every word, sometimes going so far as to give curt nods of agreement, as if by way of silent "Bravos!", always trusting that Lucy took note, though careful not to glance in her direction to see that she did, content that she could see him. Once in a while Wurlitzer gave cause for alarm, threatening again to be good, but the danger swiftly passed. This was a good bad speech, not a bad good one. "I think you found a better assortment of *individuals* on that front porch where nobody cared about status than you do now on that pernickety patio designed to make us see as little as possible of the neighbors we do our damnedest to be as much as possible like!" There was another burst of applause here in which Tattersall gratefully joined. He continued to be big about it all by sitting spellbound through the peroration.

"The kind of man who truly respects his neighbor will stand up to him when the occasion arises, and will let his neighbor see that he gives him the same right. We are now talking about pride, not vanity; character, not personality; individuality, not ego. And I say to you," Wurlitzer went on, wagging a finger in the air, "that no man is worthy of the name, either personally or profession- ally, who has not at one time gambled everything, or will not when the need arises gamble everything — but every- thing — on what he knows to be right. Who has not the guts to go for broke on the win-or-lose, red-or-black spin of the wheel of fortune if that commitment is called for. Beware of safety, beware of security — *and hang your 'image.'* "

Just then there was a slight disturbance down the line of tables to Tattersall's right — a clatter of dishes and a buzz of voices. He leaned forward, and craning his neck to look past the rows of intervening guests, sent a scowl in the direction of the offenders. "Shhh!" he even said. He then did glance over toward Lucy, but she had apparently not noticed either the commotion or the action taken on her husband's behalf to quell it. Only Mayo did, and she lowered her eyes into her lap and smiled.

two

*T*ATTERSALL lost no time in trying to square himself with Mayo. He seized the first opportunity to rehabilitate his image in that quarter, now opened up against him like a second front. After all, he saw more of her than he did of Lucy.

He caught sight of her running up the library steps the following Monday afternoon, her long legs flashing and her black hair bouncing on her shoulders, and decided to wait in the street for her to come out again. He was carrying a brown leather attaché case, filled, at the moment, with washing machine parts, and wearing a blue blazer with a white shirt open at the throat. An ascot had been removed and pocketed since leaving the house, in a moment of self-doubt. This was more Gioconda-phobia, which might be a name for the fear of being laughed at (or, what is worse, smiled at) especially by women. Even women fear the derision of their own sex more than that of men.

No such vacillation, in any event, attended the contents of the attaché case. Tattersall made no bones about liking to tinker with his hands, of plain liking to do his own repairwork, whether of machinery or furniture. He had dismantled Sherry's broken Kitchen King and was carting some of its smaller organs down to Mr. Tompkins's sales agency, for scrutiny and possible replacement, doing so on foot since Sherry needed the car to take the wash to the coin laundry. He not only did not mind such errands. He enjoyed them. Like many husbands, Tattersall liked those aspects of domesticity that got him out of the house.

The attaché case was heavy, and he set it down while he waited. He more or less hid behind a tree from which he could keep an eye on the library without being seen himself. He had decided to give it five minutes. If Mayo did not emerge by then it meant she had gone in to study, not merely to return or draw books. Five minutes did go by, but he gave it a few more. He was debating whether to light a cigarette when the door opened and she tripped down the stairs to the sidewalk. He snatched up the attaché case and ran across the street after her.

"Well, good afternoon, Mayo," he said, trying not to pant too heavily as he slowed to draw abreast of her, for she had settled down to a normal stride herself. "How did you like your uncle's talk? I didn't get a chance to see you afterward. I thought he did a bang-up job."

"It was all right as far as those things, you know, go," she answered in her rapid, gliding whisper. "I just don't know much about conformity."

Mayo's speech was heavily studded with you-knows, a habit Tattersall found intensely irksome as a general rule. You-knowers, in fact, put him on edge. You waited for the next one, clocking them almost. Mayo you-knowed you to death. She even incorporated the expression into other expressions. "He's a hail, you know, fellow well met," she might have said of her uncle.

"It's what you expect at a dinner like that, I guess," she whispered, hooking her leather bag over her shoulder. "I wouldn't know. I never, you know, go to them."

Mayo had the tendency of many people, particularly young people of a certain stamp, of preening themselves on their ignorance of those areas of life familiarity with which would stigmatize them as commonplace. The realities of bourgeois existence fell especially in that category, gaps in their comprehension of which was deemed commendable, to be preserved if at all possible — almost a form of perception. She knew nothing about Big League baseball or Little League baseball, she knew nothing about the PTA, or about banquets at which establishment platitudes were rained on the unresisting.

Then this was all he got for his pains. To be as much as told that he had rebuked a boor on behalf of balderdash of which she took an even dimmer view than he did. He longed to say it wasn't a world he made either, to tell those watchfully innocent, gently ridiculing doe's eyes, "Don't give me that Mona Lisa gaze, my dear. I didn't come out of the Dodge Rebellion owning two cars. This is a satchelful of built-in ob, you know, selescence that I'm at least waging a little war on by doing my own repairwork, and not letting every contraption I buy give up the ghost when the manufacturer wants it to. Oh, no! What's your generation doing?"

The take-over generation spawned like smelts, they swarmed like bees. Why did they then not take over? Why had they not already done so? Were there still some few not quite of the voting age at which they could elect, as threatened, the representatives who would legalize not only pot but LSD itself? They would take that till they were forty, when they would be ready for Medicare and candidates for relief — guests from then on of the square society. Guiltily shoving the ascot farther down in his pocket, Tattersall changed the subject.

"How did you like the music? The concert the other afternoon."

"All right of its kind. I just don't think the quartet was very good. So the composer didn't get a fair, you know, shake."

"There's an even farther out concert this afternoon. The German composer Witkopf? He's demonstrating some of his electronic music in the Student Center lounge. I'm on my way to it," he fabricated. "Care to come along?"

"Oh . . ." She frowned uncertainly at the Tower clock.

"It starts at two, and it's an easy place to sneak out of. I know, I've lectured there. We've just time to make it."

"We should certainly be out by half-past three," Mayo whispered.

Tattersall's spirits rose as he struck out across the campus beside this enchanting creature, swinging the heavy briefcase as though there were nothing in it. He held a forefinger against the lid to secure it, since one of the catches was sprung and he was afraid the other might not hold the weight of all the hardware by itself. Here it was again, the eternal second chance, the opportunity to sparkle on a subject in which, music being a kind of hobby with him, he was passably versed, and as they hurried under falling leaves, yet through the warm November sunshine, he briefed his young charge on what they were about to hear.

The innovation that awaited them in this instance was something known as "plaid music." The coinage, Witkopf's own, was intended to emphasize the separate but equal themes running at right angles to one another, or visualizable as such, like the patterns in a fabric. The result was best grasped by being imagined as music standing on end (like a plaid garment hung on a line), with a vertical theme, a melody in the sense of its being composed of notes going up and down the scale, interwoven with a sound principally harmonic, a single sustained noise varying in volume and depth but with little use for pitch, so that in its persistence it could be imagined as fixedly horizontal.

"Or you can think of it as warp and woof," Tattersall panted as they sprinted up the stairs to the lounge. "I don't care. It's more legitimate than might at first appear. It's basically quite rooted in tradition, when you think of arpeggios against held notes, say, which runs through the history of musical . . ."

They slipped into the last two seats left, one of them available only after an elderly gentleman had removed his hat from it and set it on his lap. Tattersall sat with his thirty pounds of hardware on his. Repulski rose to introduce Witkopf, who in turn gave a short introductory talk about what he was driving at. The composition they were about to hear was a recording of a symphony of his made in Stuttgart the summer before. The comments being rather technical, Mayo drew a small notebook and pencil from her bag, and after a few moments of inconvenient scribbling on her knee, leaned toward Tattersall and whispered, "May I use your briefcase?"

"What?" he said, looking away.

"Your briefcase. To write on."

"There's no paper in it," he whispered back, pretending to misunderstand.

"No, to write *on*. For a desk." She wrote in the air to illustrate.

Feeling for the third time in as many days that malevolent agencies were conspiring to keep the back of his neck roasted, Tattersall picked up the attaché case in both hands and transferred it from his knees to Mayo's. Then he looked away again, trying to do so in a negligent manner, but he knew perfectly well she was turning to gape at him.

"What in God's name have you got in here?"

"Another chapter of Oxenfelt's novel."

An old lady in a black hat turned around to glare at them, the forerunner of many another scowl from various directions. These Tattersall welcomed, as they put a necessary end to Mayo's interrogation. They all again concentrated their full attention on Witkopf.

Witkopf refuted most of what Tattersall had said in defense of his music. It had no roots in tradition whatsoever, according to him. It owed nothing to anybody, living or dead. It was a revolution overturning the form of government, indeed government as such, and not merely offering another change of administration such as even such radical innovators as Stravinsky and Schönberg had done. Conventional instruments themselves were dispensed with except insofar as they might offer their electronic contribution to those of picks and shovels, saws, vacuum cleaners, running faucets, and anything else at hand. For all sound was to be regarded as music, and the sequences, or modalities, to follow on recording, often unplanned and unexpected, were improvised out of what painters and sculptors, too, called "available materials." A basic reverence for reality, in short, permeated it all. There was one effect achieved by using a violin to beat a rug, another by blowing a flute underwater. The human voice was employed, but in arrangements and to purposes arbitrarily chosen by the composer, often on the spur of the moment, actually as the conductor. Thus the music was in part aleatoric, that is, the product of chance, hence replete with random turns and unexpected developments to which Witkopf urged his audience to listen with closed eyes, the better to keep an open mind, and simply give themselves to what they heard without prejudice or predilection. There would be "loud hushes" interspersing the rhythmic and arhythmic sections, in which they might recompose their minds and await the next "duration." They must feel perfectly at liberty to hiss, but in so doing they would be only aleatorically contributing to the whole. That ought to be borne in mind. It was only fair to remind them.

Tattersall abandoned the horse blanket he had planned to keep in mind as an aid to comprehension, and instead let the succession of noises that followed have their way with him, though not precisely in a manner envisioned by the composer. What he did was dwell freely on whatever they suggested to him in the way of physical objects. The tradition of composers who painted musical pictures was vast, self-justifying. Tattersall made no effort to find logical or even emotional order in the tonal happenstances they were now served — to which he did not take too kindly now that their originator had undercut his defense of them — but simply converted the squeaks, rasps, buzzes, gurgles, murmurs and rumbles into their, for him, optical counterparts, and as arbitrarily as Witkopf dished them up. Thus he "heard": chicken livers, a glass of blood, pancakes revolving on a phonograph turntable and maple syrup poured on records, a public fountain plashing motor oil, medical capsules filled with tiny multi-colored shot made to explode at staggered intervals, prolonging repose or excitement in the swallower. That kind of thing. In the climaxes of the music, which issued from four huge amplifiers stationed in the four corners of the room, he imagined all of these objects as being fed into an enormous Disposall, in which they were assimilated at inconceivable temperatures and extruded at the other end in the form of long, pure sheets of metal known as Silence. The audience was at long last put into it, everyone, including the old lady in the black hat sitting directly in front of him. There was a faint, final grinding as she went, a delicate crunch of bones, shoes, jewelry, corset stays, the works.

Tattersall momentarily gave off this reverie to glance about him. Many heeded the composer's admonition to close their eyes, though one or two used their fingers to stop up something else. A fragment of Repulski's profile indicated his brown jawbreaker eyeballs to be shut in meditation, exemplifying the passivity required by a fair surrender to this medium. A long silence of the kind promised by the author, for the digestion of received impressions and the preparation of the spirit for a fresh course of effects, fostered the sense of legitimate trance among the listeners.

It was then he felt the point of Mayo's elbow gently prodding his ribs. He turned. Silently, she indicated that she was finished with the attaché case and would appreciate having its great weight removed from her lap back to his. Tattersall nodded. He reached both hands over and, grasping the handle with one and bracing a corner with the other, began to lift it off of her knees onto his own. It was then that the next modality occurred — all that could have been asked in the way of a random sequence with available materials.

Either Mayo accidentally unlatched the single good clasp, or it had also now broken under the strain. With nothing to hold it shut, the lid fell back under a sudden shift in the contents of the briefcase, which also simultaneously made the briefcase slide off of Tattersall's knee. A misguided attempt on Mayo's part to help was partly responsible for the awkward angle at which it tilted. When the lid flopped open, everything spilled out on the floor. The objects included a pump, a hose, a timer, a solenoid (a contrivance which transmits instructions from the timer to the rest of the wash machine) and an elbow-shaped pipe assembly. In addition there was an assortment of incidental mechanical giblets such as nuts, bolts, gaskets and lock washers.

The cascade of hardware was followed by the crash of the attaché case itself, which slipped out of both their hands. Instinctively, Tattersall moved to retrieve the articles and put them back. But the folding chairs on which they sat were too closely crowded for such a tidying up, which would have necessitated getting down on all fours — not to mention prolonging the disturbance with more racket and to-do. So he got back into his chair as quietly as he could. The last thing he saw before folding his arms and closing his eyes was a twisting sea of faces. Everyone was turning to glare at him, with the exception of the composer.

three

AS Tattersall walked down the driveway to his house, the attaché case now containing some purchased replacements along with the old parts, his wife pulled in with the load of wash from the coin laundry. She slowed to a stop beside him with her head out the window, like a passing motorist about to offer him a lift the remaining twenty feet. "Any luck?"

"I think we can get that piece of action sculpture going again," he answered with his consumer-consumed irony. He quickened his pace to keep abreast of her, like a secret serviceman guarding a presidential car. "One part they didn't have and I had to order it. So it won't be today," he puffed, trotting beside her.

"Swell."

Never had the principle of repairwork seemed so apt a metaphorical concept for human relations as now. They were always breaking down and having to be patched up. They were always in the shop. He had just begun to make some strides toward getting Mayo Stiles to see that he was not a poop, fink, drag, pill, blip, blob, or whatever — but *fun* — when now this. That the mishap had

had a kind of grotesque relevance to it, amounting to an act of deliberate satire had he wished so to claim it, was beside the point, as was the fact that the accident was also partly Mayo's fault. It had occurred, and an intricate piece of personal relationship was again on the fritz, like the washing machine itself. How would he get it back into running order? God alone knew. How would he face Mayo in class? Perhaps he would write her a song. Something in his own inimitable Cole Porter style, with deft multiple rhymes making light of her mortification and his. He might be himself. That sometimes worked, though less often than was generally supposed, and always with some confusion as to what precisely that was, at least on one's own part. But it was all, all repairwork. It was all maintenance. That went for love as well as friendship, and no doubt for parenthood as well as love. A misunderstanding was like a broken spring. Apologies were like draining out old oil, with all its filthy sludge and slime, and pouring in new. In the end you had to scrap the old model for a new anyway, a whack at another friendship, a fresh mate — and then the ear cocked again for mechanical defects as you tooled precariously down the superhighway of life. His friendship for Repulski could be presumed in the junkyard. He had managed to duck away without seeing him, thank God, but Repulski could be counted on to track down the cause of the commotion. Fear of encountering him, not to mention Witkopf, had made Tattersall hastily gather up the fallen truck and beat it, with only the barest explanation to Mayo. A mumble identifying the available materials to be wash machine giblets, and how he fought the central powers by doing his own repairwork. "Because neither Detroit . . ." All this while on all fours, and casting wildly about among the accusing feet for a length of cord to secure the attaché case with, if not a scourge of cords, to use as it once was used upon the defilers of the temple. He often saw himself as Christ beating the be-Jesus out of everybody in sight. He now carried the attaché case under his arm, taking no more chances, though the second latch proved not to have been sprung after all. Mayo had accidentally opened it.

"How do you do it?" Sherry made a kissing noise of appreciation at him as she came walking toward the house, the basket of laundry riding on one hip.

Another nerve was set vibrating. Surely a man should be able to flee the world's poor opinion without coming home to a woman who thought he was the greatest thing that ever come down the pike. He instantly repented these thoughts, and to make amends said, "Look like a moom pitcha wife," as he held the door open for her. Even now she was as neat as a pin, with the basket of laundry on her hip and dragging on a fag, as though making some effort to adhere to the concept of the slatternly housewife. It was a generously molded flank for one her size. She was of the feminine order known as "petite," another word Tattersall detested and strictly forbade his students the use of, along with "intriguing," "contact" as a verb, and "feel" in the sense of think. He plucked the cigarette from her lips and took a last drag on it himself before pitching it away for her. He concluded the ritual by giving her a kiss. All, all maintenance. "All's to do again," Housman had rightly said, of the eternally repeated makeshifts of men themselves the most ramshackle of instruments, in a universe now clearly defined as a mechanism speeding inexorably toward the cosmic junk heap.

She sensed his mood. Too bad he couldn't get to work on the washing machine right now, because this was a frame of mind often soothed by tinkering. She was always glad when he was seen going downstairs into the basement, and there heard addressing his tools to mechanical objects that seemed by turns defenseless and perverse, like himself. But he liked equally to operate machinery. Among the chores he especially enjoyed was ironing with their electric mangle. He now put the fresh basket of laundry through it while Sherry worked on the bank statement and the monthly bills, with which they had little trouble keeping abreast thanks to a small inheritance from her father's side.

Clean linen has restorative properties in its very nature. Watching bedsheets come out immaculate as newly fallen snow under one's hand is almost as satisfying as slipping between them when one is tired. Tattersall sat like an organist at his instrument, erect, a pleasurable glaze over his eyes. For an hour he managed to make the world go away. Trying to cut a figure in it is beset with hazards often as great as those that threaten mountain climbers and hewers of paths through wildernesses. Like the single stone that starts an avalanche, the slightest mischance may bring down around one's ears the supposition that one is hot stuff. But he tried to forget the mass of rubble out of which he must now dig himself by throwing himself into his ironing. He began to hum, then sing the words of an old hymn that came half-consciously to mind as he worked. "Though your sins be as scarlet, they shall be as white as snow . . ."

When he thought of the electronics concert again, it was to imagine that the fabrics rolling spotlessly out of the mangle were photographed by a motion picture camera whose exposed film was then, in turn, converted by computer into its equivalent in sound. The result would have more esthetic validity than the aural garbage to which they had been subjected that afternoon. Plaid music indeed! He mentally drafted a few comments on what they had heard for class delivery tomorrow, for the benefit of those of his students who might have attended the Witkopf affair besides Mayo, and even for the delectation of those who hadn't. He would not use terms like "aural garbage." Far from it. He was foxier than to fall that easily into the hands of kids watching like hawks for the chance to tag you as an establishment poop. No, he would make them fall into his by the much subtler method of defending the far-out *in principle*, the better to let the product collapse of itself.

"Now, these people like Cage, and other people who use the random and the fortuitous, are perfectly right in their assumption that 'everything we do is music.' All right. We have all closed our eyes and sat with our head back on a train, after we've finished our paper, and just listened to the sounds all around us. Just gave ourselves to them. The coach door opening and shutting, scraps of murmured conversation, the rustle of other newspapers, the rhythmic rumble of the wheels with the clatter of tracks and switches underneath, and then the sudden rich silences during station stops, and other noises mingled in turn with them. Or lain awake in a hotel room listening to their equivalent in elevator doors, footsteps in the corridor, keys turned in locks. Oh, keys

35

turned in locks! A woman's laughter, the thrum of traffic in the street below, the random punctuation of automobile horns (whether of motors that will or will not bring Sweeney to Mrs. Porter in the spring), a doorman's whistle. There's nothing that doesn't have this suggestive poetry to it — *experienced at first hand as part of reality itself*. Put on a record in the name of art it's dead. A drag. So kindly don't give me an album of railroad or hotel noises for Christmas. I'd rather get on a coach, or check in at the Waldorf."

This position roughly hammered out, Tattersall again tried to forget the two concerts and the banquet in between, and enjoy his ironing. "Though they be red as crimson," he sang in his rich, rough tenor, "they shall be as wool . . ."

Sherry had come downstairs, and she stood a moment watching him from behind. She may have been reminded of the scene in *The Phantom of the Opera* in which the girl steals up behind the monster as he plays the organ and snatches off his mask. No such dramatic potential lurked at the heart of this marriage — she thought.

A lull in his singing made a slight motion on her part audible to Tattersall, and he halfway turned his head in acknowledgment of her arrival.

"Hi," she said with that unflagging cordiality that made Tattersall by turns grit his teeth and congratulate himself upon his luck. "We're in extra good shape this month. And the fifteenth we clip another five hundred dollars interest off the Fanny May bonds."

"What are they again?" he asked, an intellectual to be accredited as such by the gaps in his knowledge. "What are Fanny May bonds?" he would say. "Who is Leonard Lyons?" he would ask, to show he was educated. "Who are Simon and Garfinkle? Who are Mia Farrow and Baby Jane Holstein? Who are all these people?"

"Federal Mortgage Association. No, Federal National Mortgage Association. Someone nicknamed them Fanny Mays."

"Ah, yes." He was a good provider, and they could trade their car in or buy another washing machine any time he damn pleased. They were the only people he knew who owned a mangle. They could squander a bit now and then too. He had liked a still life hanging in the Student Art Show, of which he now spoke. "I was thinking we might buy it. It's only thirty-five dollars. It's a gouache of an artichoke."

"Oh, I don't like artichokes." She came in farther and sat down on a camp stool to keep him company, like an intellectual companion. "But if you've got your heart set on it, why, go ahead. What took you? Getting the parts I mean."

"I stopped in at that concert of electronic music. For my sins."

"What do you go out of your way to listen to stuff that irritates you for?"

"Well, I ran into Mayo Stiles. I try to keep up with what these kids like. If I don't dig them, how can I grade what they write?"

"I think you put yourself out too much, Hank. That's all over and above the call of duty. It's like putting in overtime nobody pays you for."

Tattersall smiled as he winced. He groaned at his good fortune. Her trusting responses were, as far as their verbal content was concerned, precisely the ones some-one would make who was dishing out irony. Anyone overhearing this exchange without knowledge of its prin-cipals would have thought that here was a woman giving her lout of a hubby the wittiest what-for. Her implicit confidence in him seemed at times a kind of deficiency in a mate, almost as though she wasn't doing her share in the war between the sexes.

The attaché case was within reach of her, and she bent forward and pulled it toward her across the floor without getting off the camp stool. She opened it between her feet, and sat gazing down at its contents with her elbows on her knees. Once she glanced over at the disabled, and now disemboweled, washing machine. She sighed. Then she lit a cigarette. Tattersall laughed.

"What's so funny?"

"Nothing."

Tattersall had not been amused so much as delighted with an idea for an advertising series that hit him like a ton of bricks. There is a Freudian claim that the work of the wit is done principally by the subconscious. Certainly this brainstorm came to him instantly and with no conscious mental effort. It just hit him.

There would be a woman sitting in a laundry room, or utility room, with a weary and harried expression, and the line: "Are you tired of detergents that don't get your wash really white? Light up a Kent." Or a Winston, or whatever cigarette bought the idea — or whatever cola, chewing gum, or candy bar. It would be a twisteroo catching the reader (or listener) by surprise — a pleas-ant surprise. All that was needed was some sponsor sophisticated enough to see the possibilities inherent in non sequitur, in an adroit application of the principle of defeat. For make no mistake about it, these would be the first commercials of the Absurd.

He could see Wurlitzer being so struck with the idea that he would implore Tattersall to give up teaching and come to work for Wurlitzer and Wise at thirty thou a year, with annual increases and full fringe benefits. For it was a notion secretly dear to Tattersall that when it came to the agency crowd, and all those birds who looked down on teachers for their low salaries, he could outshine them at their own game any day he had a mind to. All their pretense at being "creatively" engaged in "communications," all their jargon about identification and images, were but masks for rankling self-doubt. He chuckled to himself again, shaking his head in delight. "Do you despair of ever finding a wax that will get your linoleum floor the way you really want it? Are you sick of inferior cleansers and their lavish claims? Pick yourself up with a Snickers."

His obsession with impressing the Wurlitzers abruptly recalled his reasons for wanting to. Just as Lucy had probably told her husband about the incident at the concert, it was a cinch Mayo had told them both about the repetition of his conduct at the banquet and would now go on to relate the debacle at the electronics recital. The portrait of an ass was emerging at breathtaking speed.

Suddenly he found himself telling Sherry the story, in a rush, but affecting a straightforward, offhand amusement, a nothing-to-it attitude which he hoped her own reaction would validate. We all tend to exaggerate a secret. It becomes like a worm gnawing us hollow inside.

Sharing it with someone who in the nature of the case will be more objective helps us to recover our own perspective. It was by way of shopping for this reassurance that, continuing matter-of-factly to iron, he related: "I was sitting at that concert the other afternoon, you see, and there was this woman whispering behind me. It *was* rather annoying, to some others around there too, I could tell. Well anyway . . ."

In a moment he had told her the whole story, and was relieved to find her laughing freely.

"I know that feeling," she said. "Something like it happened to me. Driving the car, remember? I must have told you. Somebody made a stupid move passing me, and I don't snap at people as a general rule, so it must have been pretty bad. Not that I snapped, exactly, but I did turn and give him a dirty look as he went by, and who should it be but Jerry Freeland. I was so mortified — well, we both were —"

"Of course I remember!" Tattersall said, prolonging his laughter to impress on himself the molehill out of which he was making a mountain. The sense of deliverance was so great that he took her out to dinner, made love when they got home, and then fell into a deep sleep.

But he awoke from one of those dreams in which we are naked in public, and he groaned into his pillow. "It's not the same thing. Traffic is not a reunion, and Jerry Freeland is not an old flame." And he spent the next black hours substantiating Mark Twain's observation that we are none of us quite sane at night. This was the hook on which Mark Twain writhed in his hotel room after making an ass of *him*self at the Whittier birthday dinner.

Sherry spent a few days with her mother, out of town, leaving Tattersall to turn himself steadily on the lathe of self-torment. He avoided Mayo's eye in class, save for a few glances which confirmed that she was avoiding his. That Friday afternoon, she was scheduled for a personal conference. They tried to talk about her work as though nothing had happened. Then he made another move. Locked in those gambler's toils in which we are driven to take ever greater risks to recoup ever heavier losses, he prolonged the conference to the point where he could glance at his wristwatch and say, "Hm. After five. Time to be thinking about dinner. Can you join me, by any chance?"

"Oh, I don't think I should, Mr. Tattersall."

"My wife's out of town."

Bleeding Christ, what was he saying! Had he gone completely off his chump? His throat was now dry, and though he was only a chap asking for one more second chance, to show he was great gas and not a clod, poop, fink, blob, fog, drizzle or gink, he knew his eyes were being taken for the eyes of a rebuffed old lech. Those were the eyes her eyes told his eyes her eyes thought they were looking at. Or, rather, again avoiding.

Bending a paper knife in his hands, as an alternative to slitting his throat with it, he said, "I only meant otherwise I'll have to dine alone, and that's no fun. I miss my wife when she's gone. We could talk about your work a little more. I may not have made myself clear. That a substandard, illiterate narrator *imposes extra disciplines on a writer* — it does not relax them."

"You make yourself clear, all right. And I think I

ought to go home and work on that, you know, molesta-
tion scene tonight," Mayo whispered.

Tattersall stumbled across the campus, his skin again
feeling as though it were on inside out, and all his nerves
seething like a crock of boiled worms. Now would be a
good time to nip home and test his theory that you ran a
temperature when mortified. There was definitely the
skin-on-wrongside-out sensation that went with fever. But
he was in no mood for clinical investigation. He wanted
to jump into the Chichester, and would have done, had
not the Everlasting fix'd his canon 'gainst self-slaughter.
There were voices, "He asked you to dinner, really? Said
his wife was away? Hm. Turned out to be quite a chaser.
Glad I passed him up." No! It's just the eternal Footman
holding my coat and snickering, don't you see, Lucy, as I
tried to explain to you in the rowboat long ago —.
"Sometimes when men reach a certain —" Nonsense!
Nothing of the sort at all. Simply trying to recover my
self-respect, groping and threshing blindly about for it,
like a man stumbling about for his trousers in the dark,
knowing they're there somewhere. Can't respect yourself
beyond the point where other people's respect for you
stops. Self-esteem is what others think of you, no use in
denying that.

So what's a good plan of action?

Because proving to Lucy Wurlitzer what a catch he
had been became now the consuming passion of his life.
After debating several possible courses, he thought, Got
it. Call the Wurlitzers on some pretext or other, and
then *you* toss in something about asking Mayo to dine
with you. Anything, so long as you get there first. Ounce
of prevention idea. Our Lady of Prophylaxis. Throw

yourself on her mercy. But the important thing is to be casual about it, as though you have nothing to hide. That ought to defuse it. Phone booth behind the physics lab. You've got the two dimes it costs to call the city. Around the stone bench dedicated by the class whose thews no longer hustle them about, past the sundial that records only sunny hours, and thank God there's a city directory in there. Where did Lucy say they lived? East 79th Street.

"Hello, Lucy? Hank Tattersall. Glad I caught you in. Look, I find I've got to whip into town for something and I was wondering if you and your husband were free this evening. Could possibly even rip a chop with me."

Briefest possible moment of hesitation?

"Why, Savannah already has dinner going here. Why don't you come up? We'll be alone."

"Wouldn't think of barging in. No, this was just an impromptu notion of mine. Happen to find myself alone — wife-visiting-her-mother type bachelor — and I was hoping Mayo might join us. Well, maybe she's footloose for the evening. Perhaps some other time then. It seems ridiculous we never see each other, living so close. So let's take a raincheck on it when Sherry gets back."

Tattersall stood outside the phone booth breathing heavily, and with a sense of having tucked another strand of entrail back through an emotional hernia he seemed to be springing. "Phew," he said with relief. But it had been a narrow squeak, and the struggle to pull himself together and set things to rights had only begun. He needed some food, to say nothing of the drinks to precede it, and so he headed for a restaurant — Tony's, to convince himself that his and Lucy's old steakhouse housed no ghosts of which he need stand in fear.

Instead of checking his attaché case, he carried it to the table with him, and there in a corner he sat reading and grading the week's papers over a whiskey and water. From Oxenfelt another chapter of the predictable anti-hero, an alienated Brooklynite depicted in black adventures in which the time sense was deliberately distorted in order to emphasize modern fragmentation. "Two can play at that game," Tattersall thought, and, smiling over his drink, tried to think up something a little more light-hearted than the average pedagogical comment. A very amusing whim seized him. He reversed the pages so that they read backwards, and on the margin of the last one, now the top, he scribbled, "Real impact. Genuinely shocking and galvanizing. But I tink it packs an eem greater wallop dis way," and signed himself "Anti-reader."

Anti-reader soon had three whiskeys under his belt, and was warming to the lark. He found both the fancy and courage to do what, he realized, he had vaguely been wanting to do for a long time — namely pay these kids back in their own kind. If the English language was no longer the coin of the realm, then he would cash his in for what was. If the slob was in, he would join whom he could not lick. He was by now so used to narration by goons that he was beginning to think like them anyway. And they would all have more fun this way. He could already hear it bruited about the campus what a gas that Tattersall really was.

"Jeez," he jotted on a section of Mayo's novel that she had revised, "din't none a dese characters eem git into de foist grade, dat not eem one a dem can talk United

States? And how about character *development?* Dis wino a yours, he gits put troo a series a episodes so bloodtoisty it musta done sumpm to him by dis time — at least make him woise. I mean he's bein put troo de wringer fa Chrissake. But I must say de deliberate confusion of reality wit illusion in de guy's mind is most adroitly done. B–"

Tattersall had entered into a state of near exhilaration. His mellow frame of mind made him do something else he had not done in a long time — grade the submissions. When after dinner he drove across the bridge for an evening in the part of town where Chichester's modest version of the lower depths was to be found — the "tough" section — the mood engendered by the narrators, not to mention his own self-intoxicating parodies of them, was still upon him. Shouldering his way between two men standing at one of the representative bars, one in a turtleneck sweater and the other in a blue denim shirt and lumberjacket, he ordered a beer and began shooting off his big mouth.

"I says fa Chrissakes if you don't know how to drive a car, get de hell out from behind de wheel and leave de road to people who do," he related, rather expansively. "He turns to look at me, and I'm a sumbitch if it ain't some guy I know. Was I mortified, you."

The two listeners took in Tattersall's tweed jacket a little dubiously at first, but as the evening wore on and liquor blurred particular impressions they forgot it, engrossed as they became in his tale. It was largely fabrication, but based at several points on fact, minor incidents that had befallen people he knew if not always himself personally, and of no consequence in themselves, but

45

woven into a single night's odyssey, and with no especial regard for time sense, they packed a good deal of punch, of the sex-and-violence kind in vogue.

"So de sumbitch says I'll git out from behind de wheel all right, Buster, provided you do too. Get what I mean? And I'll knock dose teet so far down ya troat you'll tink you're eatin popcorn. So I says Oh, a master a irony, huh?"

"Of what?" the turtleneck asked.

"Some friggin expression he used. I don't know." Tattersall took a pull of his beer and wiped his mouth with the back of his hand. "He says dere's ways a buttonin up lips like yours fa good, ya know. And I says you stink on ice. And he says you jist gonna sit dere wit only your head stickin out, like a cuckoo clock, or you wanna git out all de way and try to back up dem fancy words wit a little action. Well, dere was nuttin to do but oblige dis gink. So I climbs outa de car and we starts mixin it up in de middle a de street. And I mean he had a right like a mule. I got in de way of it a coupla times dat I din't care much for, I'll admit, but den I commences gittin in a few myself. We hung a mouse on each odda, is about de size of it. I don't know how it woulda come out. Because a squad car arrives and starts pullin us apart like a coupla refs. Well in de course of nearly bein booked, me and my opponent get so peed off wit de fuzz dat we turns friends. How's dat fa motivation, pal?"

"For what?"

"How de hell do I know? So anyways, when de fuzz finely lets us go we shakes hands and has a beer on it. We're buddies now, and starts combin de town fa gash. We finely picked up a couple plums at anodda bar, and

46

went up to one a dem's place wit a bag a delicatessen stuff and some more cold beer and tied one on. I'll never forget it. Finely dis one plum says she's got to woik de next day and would like to hit de sack early, and we says dat's fine wit us, let's hit it, and we all roars. Laugh, we thought de plums was gonna bust a gut. Well," Tattersall continued after another gulp, and a dramatic pause, "dere was a slight confusion about who was wit who — know what I mean? It seemed we bot' had our eye on de same plum, namely de one who wanted to hit de sack early, and by Christ what wit one ting and anodda if we don't wind up where we started — fightin! How do ya like dem potatoes?"

Both his companions shook their heads in appreciative acknowledgment of the dramatic power inherent in this development. The one in the lumberjacket, a short powerfully built man with coal-black hair, said, "The way it happens. Then what happened?"

Tattersall had been settling himself against the bar in ever more raffish attitudes. Now he leaned with his back to it, propped on his elbows. He surveyed the premises with a sinister boredom, as though debating whether to go on with this saga or start a fresh chapter of another with a brawl here.

"What *happened?*" He took another slug of beer, stalling till the wheels of improvisation had accommodated another shift of gears. "We mixed it up agin while de ceiling and walls got pounded on by different tenants. Jealousy is one a da strongest a human emotions, nest pa? My old pal was now so mad because it looked as dough de plum was not goin fa him dat he goes fa me, wit a bottle dat is. He lets me have it over de head, and dat's what might of saved my life. Because I passed out cold, and de sight of me layin dere made him so contrite wit remorse dat it sobered him up and brang him to his senses. So it was beddy-bye witout no gash, always a letdown, nest pa? Because when I woke up de plum was dressed and on her way to woik . . ."

In this way Tattersall held forth far into the night, grooming his diction as well as the style it served. When he got home, about one o'clock, he went straight to bed and fell asleep. He awoke with a headache it took most of the morning and several aspirin to make a dent in. He got through his two classes somehow, mostly by letting the students read their stuff aloud for general criticism, and then giving them their heads while he sat holding his as inconspicuously as possible. It wasn't until he had put away a good breakfast — at lunchtime — that he could pull himself together enough to read what he had written on the papers. He had only the foggiest memory of the happy inspiration that had overtaken him the evening before, here in the same restaurant.

"Sweet Christ in the morning, what have you done now?"

He breathed this in such an audible gasp that the waiter came over to ask whether he wanted something. He shook his head politely. The waiter left.

Tattersall drew a thermometer from his pocket, shook it down, and poked it under his tongue. Something had made him that morning take it from the medicine chest and clip it, in its case, to the inside breast pocket of his coat, where he carried it like a fountain pen. Now was as good a time as any to test his theory that you ran a slight fever in moments of intense chagrin. This was probably now his most embarrassing moment, superseding the one that had precipitated this series of events, which was like a chain reaction he seemed powerless to check. It made you believe in the Greek idea of Nemesis. The fact that his embarrassment now was private rather than public did not make it any the less scalding an experience. Yes, he was sure he had a fever. He put his palms to his cheeks. They were burning with shame.

With the thermometer in his mouth, he got out an eraser and tried to rub out some of the comments, particularly the one on Mayo's manuscript. But they were in ink, and resisted deletion short of making tatters of the entire page. He gave this off, and, while waiting for the thermometer to register, sat chin in hand, reviewing the present stage of his general predicament, and sorting out alternatives for trying to extricate himself from it.

His mistake had been in not writing preliminary drafts of his remarks on separate sheets of paper, and waiting to see how they looked in the morning before entering them permanently on the manuscripts themselves. It was too late for that now. He tried to recapture, or at least clearly remember, the spontaneous impulse to which he had so irrevocably yielded, but he could not do so. It must have seemed to possess a valid gaiety at the moment, but that did him no good now. It did not survive cold reappraisal by daylight. He could scarcely now quite believe that he had written those words on Mayo's manuscript, yet there they were, in a bold scrawl running diagonally across the top of the page above a chapter heading. Of course he could retype the page, but not without detection. Mayo's type style differed from both that of his typewriter at home and the one in his office. Even if he rented one that matched hers, the ribbon she used was some strange purplish color he would probably have trouble duplicating. He might even have to run in to New York for it.

He pulled the thermometer out of his mouth and looked at it. Not even ninety-eight. Which showed the shape he was in. People in a bad way are often subnormal, owing to lack of energy. His blood had certainly been running cold for the past five minutes. His actual temperature was probably more like ninety-seven and a half. Chagrin had sent it up half a degree.

He clipped the thermometer back into his pocket, beside his fountain pen, and then put the manuscripts back into the attaché case with the decision to try to forget them for the time being. He was known to keep submissions for a week or more, by which time Sherry would be home and he could try his comments out on her. He often showed her his remarks, for her opinion. Perhaps she would reassure him as she had the last time he had tried something out on her for size, namely the story of the original incident at the musicale. She was level-headed if anybody was.

He showed her Mayo's the instant she got home, almost before she could get her coat off. He made her sit down and read it in the living room, and as she did he watched her anxiously from another chair. It turned out that she was quite genuinely amused. In fact his comment finally had her in hysterics, he was overjoyed to see. "This is a scream, Hank," she said. "Teachers ought to do this sort of thing more. Unbend."

"You don't think it's too strong?"

"Nah! For Pete's sake, if a student can't stand a little

ribbing he just hasn't any sense of humor, and shouldn't be writing."

"You understand it's parody."

"Of course I do. And a darn nifty one. Let me read some more. Have you got some more?"

Nevertheless, Tattersall doctored the comment before returning the paper, in a manner calculated to soften it. He worked on it long and painstakingly, this time using preliminary drafts in order to get it as right as he could. In its original form it ended, "de deliberate confusion of reality wit illusion in de guy's mind is most adroitly done." He changed the period after "done" to a comma, and added, for there was room, "and presents a most effective use of the surrealist technique applied to fiction. You could be one of those successfully effecting a transfer of the Absurd from the theater to the novel." And he changed the B− to a B+.

He stood at his desk when he had handed it back to Mayo, after class, watching her walk out of the room and through the doorway into the corridor. She was halfway to the building exit when he saw her stop to read it. She stood a moment with her head down, doing so. Then she suddenly stiffened, squared her shoulders and marched rapidly away.

"Maaw!" he bleated like a stricken sheep, throwing his head back. "Maaw!"

Whenever he saw her in the next few days, he searched her face eagerly for some ameliorating sign, but it betrayed nothing. In averting her gaze to avoid his, as she seemed to, she appeared to be giving him a grade even farther below passing than he had feared — than a cold stare would have done. He got a few of those from

51

the other students, but also a lot of good-natured laughs of appreciation from the less thin-skinned. But they didn't essentially matter. And it came to Tattersall that, quite apart from the emotional turmoil he was going through, Mayo was one of those people, periodically encountered in the course of a lifetime, whose approval we must absolutely have. It had been her habit to stop occasionally at his desk after a classroom session, to chat of this or that or to air a point. Now she no longer did. "Maaw!" he silently bleated to himself every time she walked by and on out.

At last he could stand it no longer. He ran to overtake her in the hall.

"What did you think of my little effort, Mayo? I mean did you think it, you know, came off?"

"I know you don't think much of my work, Mr. Tattersall," she answered, lowering her eyes to the books cradled in her arm and not slowing her pace.

"That's not true," he said, pattering along at her side. "We all tend to exaggerate things. To fail to take them in the spirit in which they were meant. And just because this was done as a bit of burlesque . . . My wife . . ."

Groaning savior, not that again.

"Is she still away?"

"Oh, my God, no! She's back. Her mother hasn't been at all well. And now she, poor thing, has to go visit *her* mother, because, believe it or not, Mrs. Tattersall's grandmother is still alive at ninety — a victim of geriatrics!" he cried out in helpless indignation as he watched her stride down the stairs to the exit. It was only a moment that he thus struck a tableau of all dumb despair, all immedicable human pain and outrage, before again taking off after her. "What didn't you like in particular about my little pastiche? My poor little tara-diddle? Some of the other students were most —"

She stopped, and they stood together in an impeding eddy of hurrying students as Mayo softly chided, "You must have realized how harsh it was by the fact that you changed it. The afterthought you put in was written with another pen, because the ink is different. So is the line that goes up and down in the plus sign. It was a B minus first."

"I see we've got to talk this thing out. Can you have lunch?"

"I've had lunch. After all, it's half past two. You must have eaten yourself."

He stood watching her pass through the revolving door and vanish down the walk. He was not sure what to think, or even what he was thinking. Perhaps he should say what he was feeling, since it was physical sensations, rather than thoughts, of which he was being dealt this numbing and contradictory jumble. Mingled with them was a suddenly unbearable curiosity about Mayo's emotions — at the moment, of course, the critical factor. Had she a right to this extreme reaction, or was it the result of the same subjectivity that had all along been making him exaggerate his own plight? How did matters stand as of the moment? How bad was this, really? He reached wildly for his thermometer, but it was in the pocket of another coat.

four

A ND so I thought it would be nice if we could all have dinner and get to know one another a little better," Tattersall told the Wurlitzers.

He was revising his tactics. He had decided to pull back from the second front, represented by Mayo Stiles, and shift his forces for a concentrated effort again on the first. This involved starting from scratch, of course; indeed it entailed a fresh hazard to the image he was trying to clear. Since it had been he who had taken the initiative, calling the Wurlitzers twice more to enlist their interest in such a foursome as had now materialized, the absurdity of its doing so in their uptown apartment was not lost on Tattersall. He was even momentarily the ass again, but only momentarily. Counterbalancing impressions were being swiftly mobilized to reverse the effect. Pre-dinner cocktail in hand, an arm hooked negligently around the back of his chair, he was doing his sociable best to make the Wurlitzers feel at home with him in this, to him, somewhat glacial duplex. It had been "done," as poor Lucy had predictably put it, by a disciple of Mies van der Rohe. "And that crowd think less is more, as you know," Wurlitzer said. Yes, Tattersall knew, and also that the aphorism originated with Browning, and not with the crop of architects who had merely appropriated it for a rallying cry. It killed him not to be able to correct his host, but he could not have done so without incurring a graver charge than that of ignorance.

So principally, now, he was getting on with the business of making Lucy see after all and in spite of everything what she *had* passed up for some rather wide neckties and some rather wet cigars. But in courting Lucy all over again, he had also to sell himself to Wurlitzer. The twain were one flesh, and would discuss him in their bedroom after he was gone. He told Wurlitzer how much he had enjoyed his speech, particularly the sections lamenting the passing of the old front porch. He, too, had noticed the disappearance of that institution with all its implicit values from the American scene. He was getting quite a front porch himself, Wurlitzer.

"These kids today," Tattersall said, to assure his forty-year-old host that he considered him a contemporary though he was almost as much older than Tattersall as Tattersall was than the students toward whom he so graciously viewed them as sharing an age disadvantage. "They do mean all their protests, they mean them a hundred percent. They're a lot more anti-bourgeoisie than we were. But all the same, it'll be interesting to watch," he added with an engaging laugh as he adjusted his hammerlock on the Scandinavian chair upon which he had been deposited, "when they get their fill of alienation and cut for the establishment bread."

"You make yourself out quite a fuddy-duddy, Hank,"

Wurlitzer said, returning his laugh. His ruddy face beamed up clear along his scalp, which showed through his dwindling yellow hair. Always chunky, judging from college photographs on the piano showing him bursting his blazers even then, the decades of which Tattersall had so amiably knocked off one were expanding him swiftly, though a faithful regimen of workouts at a midtown athletic club kept the fat to muscle as far as possible. Tattersall had heard that he liked to play Santa Claus at office Christmas parties. He was said to enter wearing a St. Nicholas costume and shouldering a sack, from which he drew the bonus checks for the year and flung them to the employees in turn as he called out their names. This struck Tattersall as having a faintly sinister, even sadistic, tinge. He was sorry he had thought of it since it cast a damp on his determination that they make an evening of it with the girls and hit it off as one Joe to another.

"Well, I hope I'm not a fuddy-duddy, but I don't regard myself as any stormy petrel either," he said.

"Of which the academic world has its share, evidently, Hank."

"What do you mean, Harry?"

"Have you noticed how at odds your scholastic community is with our foreign policy, just for one thing? Obviously the health of a democracy depends on dissent, but they're way out of line with public opinion this time, me buckaroo. I mean conspicuously more than in recent memory. Now I think in recent times, say two generations, you've had a public opinion that's fairly liberal. Academic thinking is now to the left even of that. Therefore it stands to reason that it's radical."

"Then I must be radical too, because I'm opposed to our foreign policy."

"Oh, let's don't get into politics so *early*," Lucy prettily wailed, with a glance in Sherry's direction.

It was then that Lucy's habit of frowning when she laughed came back to him with a jerk. In a recent dream he had cast her as a Circuit Court judge rapping for order with a croquet mallet, wearing that expression as she entangled herself in juridical robes. Many women knit their brows when they laugh, but they are women above a certain income and social level. A peasant housewife could not be imagined with such an idiosyncrasy. This voyeurism was presently transferred to his wife. Sherry's oblivion to any menace lurking in the turn the conversation had taken recalled again the question at what point innocence ceased to be commendable, or indiscriminate deference to one's husband. Her thinking the sun rose and set on him, when he had his own number, gave him a fresh twinge of vexation. As for Wurlitzer, his talk continued such a predictable rehash of what "the business community" thought, as against the "intellectual community," that by the time they were through dinner and into their brandies all Tattersall could think of was how he'd like to work for this clod, just long enough to show him what "impractical" intellectuals could do in a jungle to whose rigors they were thought unequal. It was in this spirit that he tossed off his idea for the commercial.

They had just caught a television show handled by the Wurlitzer and Wise agency, of which the advertisements featured a chorus of singing and dancing soup cans famous for scurrying into line just in time to spell out

57

the name of the product. Wurlitzer had shut the set off
with some murmured notation about planned improve-
ments. Tattersall was lolling back in his chair with his
legs crossed. All the good food and wine, served by an
immaculate maid, gave him a pleasantly blurred sense of
having wandered into some kind of power structure
against whose criteria it might be amusing to pit himself.
Borrowing a mannerism from a sybaritic acquaintance
given to gesturing with his feet, he twitched a toe in the
direction of the Magnavox and said, "I've had a notion
for a series of commercials for that thing."

"What thing?"

"That one. The television medium."

"We're always looking for new ideas, Hank."

They were all ears, and also all eyes as he swirled the
brandy in his snifter and took a sip before beginning.

"Are you tired of detergents that never get your wash
really white? Light up a Salem."

They were if anything even more attentive. He had
them in his grip, there was no doubt about that. They
waited for him to go on. Lucy, leaning forward on a
white leather hassock, or pouf, with her elbows on her
knees and the fingernails of one hand along her teeth,
was typical of their breathless regard.

"Are you sick of the performance of your present car?
Does it burn so much oil you're beginning to think the
damn thing is part Diesel? Is there so much sludge in your
crankcase you can hear the bearings groan inside it?
Pour yourself a drink of Cutty Sark, the man's Scotch.
Or have a Pepsi. Or a stick of Juicy Fruit, or a glass of
Manischewitz wine," he continued sharply, like a teacher
to a classroom full of dolts. "Whatever the sponsor

would be. The whole thing is a non sequitur, you see," he continued, as though threatening to explain even what that meant if they did not shape up.

You could have heard a pin drop. He slid up in his chair and took another drink of the brandy. The fingers of his free hand had crept to his inside breast pocket, where they felt along the tops of the pen and pencil to the sickroom thermometer clipped there.

"The two things have no connection, don't you see. The whole thing *has no bearing on the product what . . . so . . . ever*. It cuts through the humbug about solutions by honestly admitting that there are none, in the end, and in that respect I suppose you could call it Existentialist, or the commercial of the Absurd. The plug, at last, has come of age."

Wurlitzer did not seem to be looking Tattersall in the eye. Rather he was directing his gaze at his head, where dwelt such thoughts. In other words, none other than the teeming and fecund old coco. Our greatest natural resource. Tattersall resumed running it up the flagpole, trusting they would not make it necessary for him to point out that his influences were Beckett and Ionesco. His arms and legs twitched and flew in all directions.

"You would show the woman with the husband's work pants and their irremediable stubborn stains, or the oven no scouring powder gets lamb-fat spatter out of. Or the man with the mountain of bills no loan company has managed to get him out from under in conveniently arranged installments, or the flashlight with inferior batteries that he's sick of, and then wham" — he smacked his palms together, shooting one hand two or three lengths ahead of the other — "you hit them with the

59

unexpected switch. There is nothing to be done about these things in any final sense. They are simply the cares that infest the day. They are part of the human condition. So have a smoke, or a snort, or a Peter Paul Mounds, goddam it!"

"I understand," Wurlitzer said, sympathetically. He was not unimpressed at all. His face expressed that gravity professionals experience when confronted with an original concept calling for an abrupt readjustment of their entire mode of thinking. "It's fabulous. Of course it requires a sophisticated sponsor. I mean somebody who can take something heretical and run with it. And has humor. That's a lot of specifications. Sponsors who meet them are few and far between. For every Avis and Benson and Hedges there's a thousand of the other kind. Because this goes a step beyond just kidding the product. It kids everything, even the medium. Even the art form itself. It's not just avant-garde. It's positively . . ."

"Nihilistic?" Tattersall said, sensing Wurlitzer to be groping for a word.

"Yes. It's nihilistic. It's Existentialist, if you will. How the hell did you ever think of that, Hank?"

Tattersall shrugged and murmured something modest. He knew that Lucy was watching him with some version or degree of the awe prolonged in Wurlitzer's regard. Sherry smiled with her perpetual pleased deference. She would be wearing the same expression if he had laid an egg.

"Do you toss off ideas like this all the time?" Wurlitzer asked. "If so I can see a great future for you in the advertising game, God forbid." He now did laugh, and, throwing Lucy a glance, jerked his head at Tattersall.

"Put him in with crazy Gascoyne. What a fabulous team they'd make. He's our far-outer," he explained to Tattersall, who nodded. "He believes in an irrational universe too, which expands and contracts at intervals of, if I'm not mistaken, eighty-two billion years. How much do you want for this brainstorm?"

"You're welcome to it," Tattersall said, flinging a hand carelessly into the air.

"Well, any time you get tired of teaching."

The evening was like a tonic that exhilarated his teaching. He postively shimmered in class. He lectured brilliantly, especially to the advanced group. He devoted several sessions to humor, which many of them seemed to be writing, however black. He discoursed on the Aristotelian view of laughter as being provoked in man by something that falls just short of that which would have excited pain, and emphasized the perilous line at which the law of diminishing returns sets in and amusement is reversed — or rather goes on to its reverse.

"And so we see that comedy deals with that portion of our suffering that is exempt from tragedy," he concluded. "For with what does humor deal save with that which isn't funny. Or at least isn't funny at the time: broken bones, broken machinery, bad food, hangovers. Husbands. Wives. Brats. There is no comic mileage in good health, an excellent dinner, harmonious unions and well-behaved children."

Their pencils flew. Not a word was to be missed. Except in the case of Mayo. She either sucked her pencil or used it in a curious flamboyant manner about which his suspicions were confirmed when he could manage to

61

sidle around for a closer look at her notebook. She was doodling.

"For one cheek of this old world is always in shadow whilst the other twinkles in full sunlight," he continued undaunted, passing her desk as though he had seen nothing. "We no less than the stars in their courses swing in our eternal orbit of contradictions: love and hate, hot and cold, birth and death, yes and no. This principle of contrariety is built into the very bricks of the universe. It whizzes in the merry molecules, it boils in the unthinkable vats of galactic space. Peer into the microscope and you will find it. Gaze out through the telescope and it is there. If you take the wings of the morning and fly to the uttermost parts of the earth, lo, it is there. You eat it and you drink it, you sneeze it and you sweat it. Socrates rightly said that the talent for tragedy was the same as the talent for comedy. Tragedy and comedy have a common root, whose name at last I think I know. Desperation. A man with his secretary in trouble is funny, if he shoots her it is tragic, but he is scarcely less desperate in the one case than the other. Mirth and grief have a common manifestation, the convulsion, and of course they share your tear ducts, like good neighbors sharing a well. This is the army of unalterable law, standing, rank on rank, behind us no less than behind Prince Lucifer himself in starlight. The whole cosmos is a contradiction balanced as delicately as a stick on a clown's nose. The thing anything is most closely wedded to is its opposite. The relativity scientists of the day tell us that the quality that most nearly resembles Everything is — Nothing. That is why this life is always half promise and half threat. It is like Walter Cronkite giving us fair notice that he will be back with more news in a moment . . ."

As he was chucking paraphernalia back into his attaché case, someone stopped at his desk, and, looking up, he was surprised to see that this time it was Mayo. "Hello, stranger," he said. He learned the secret that had kept her wrapped in that faraway gaze. The Satyr Press was interested in publishing her novel, and had offered her an advance on the strength of the first chapters, including the one that had excited Tattersall's powers of pastiche. *Maaw!* Moreover, what they had seen was a version prior to the revisions on which Tattersall had so strongly insisted. *Maaw!* Nor did the editor with whom she would henceforth deal agree in the slightest with certain cuts and rearrangements recommended by Tattersall in the interest of unity. *He* saw that the unity was emotional rather than logical. It was a contemporary work, written in a prevailingly Existentialist climate.

"Now I think I'll let you buy me that drink," she whispered with the gentle smile.

He had not offered to buy her a drink at all. He had invited her to dinner, then lunch, a progressive scaling down to be completed by the Coke which was all the drink he could buy her on the campus in any case, certainly at this hour of the day.

To be reduced to a Sad Sack on the one front while fresh from triumphs on another was proof, indeed, of the principle on which he had just been lecturing. That kind of corroboration who needs? Glumly sucking his pop in a booth at the Sugar Jar, he mused on the evening of riot now definitely ahead of him. Oh, indubitably. "Are you fed up with the galling contrariety of existence? Does it

63

seem as though the eternal Footman will never stop holding your coat and snickering? Have a double bourbon on the rocks." Don't think he wouldn't! Dusk came, night fell, and, in a unity emotional rather than logical, he headed across the river after dinner and made for the same bar in which he had taken refuge in another identity not so long ago.

"I'm standin on de corner mindin my own beeswax," he told a clutch of good listeners, "when some gazebo wit a clipboard buttonholes me wit some questions fa motivational resoich dey call it. Find out what people like so dey can make de product accordingly? More invasion a privacy you ast me, so I gives dis gink short shrift, bleeme. He's collectin statistics on some make of car. What do you want above all in an automobile? he inquires of me, and I says a twenty-year-old blonde witout no scruples."

They all roared like hell. He continued, a completely realized character.

"So anyway, I lets him question away, cause I got curiosity a my own I want to satisfy, know what I mean? All de while I got dis gink under observation myself. Dat suddenly seems more important dan gittin rid a him. One ting led to anodda, and I finely asts him what make a car he's data-scroungin fa. He told me, and I says your product chews out loud, mista. He says I'm glad to hear you think so, because we pride ourself on caterin to a particular clientele. And I says Ah you stink on ice. Den I walks away. I'm sick a all dis brain pickin. It's de bane a our society. What do you guys tink?"

When he got home, Sherry was reading in bed.
"Out with the boys?" she said.

64

"None a ya business," he said. "I support ya, feed ya, and I treat ya right when I'm home. Where I am when I ain't is non a ya business. All as I'll say is, I don't do no tomcattin. Fa da rest, my life is my own, and ya better git dat troo ya head, macushla."

She laughed, a single lazy chuckle that made the book bob on her stomach. She had for so many years made a point of being amused by his kicks — English toff, Russian peasant, now American mug — that response had become second nature to her. They were simply chief among their domestic jokes.

But this one showed no signs of letting up. It went on. It went on longer than the time he'd been a professor in an Eastern college. He had found a set of false buck teeth in a dime-store display of Hallowe'en costumes, and, wearing these, with an old pepper-and-salt coat, he had shuffled absent-mindedly about mouthing bromides through the awful fixed grin. It had nearly cost him his job, for the President of the school had unexpectedly run into him shuffling through fallen leaves and muttering deprecatory remarks about the curriculum. He had made the mistake of removing his teeth when recognizing the President, thereby unmasking himself. Otherwise he might have gone undetected. He promptly stopped acting like a college teacher. A barren period had followed in which he described himself simply as a tenant-in-residence, then suddenly he was a plantation owner. "Stop picking those banjos and get out there and pick that cotton." Sherry went along with all of it, believing that a man should be himself.

But this was different. The persistence of this present mood finally began to cause her a little concern. It was still on him some days later when he answered the phone to hear a voice say: "This is radio station WRTZ, Mr. Tattersall. Your number has been dialed after being selected at random from the book. If you can correctly answer the following question, having to do with American history, you are eligible for our drawing on an all-expense trip to Bermuda. Are you ready?"

"Yes."

"What American President is known as the father of his country?"

"Duh, Abraham Lincoln?"

"Oh, I'm sorry. It's George Washington. Thanks for being a good sport though and trying, and as a consolation prize we're sending you absolutely free a carton of Embassy cigarettes."

"Dey chew out loud."

"They have the new filter almost as long as the tobacco unit itself. No other cigarette can make that statement."

"Kin Embassies?"

"Can Embassies what?"

"Make statements. Kin dey talk, dese gaspers?"

"And so thank you, Mr. Tattersall, for being such a good sport, and good afternoon."

They went to a cocktail party at which someone who happened to have heard the conversation on her radio was present. She was a tiny, merry woman named Mrs. Wills, who was still in stitches over it. "I nearly called you up myself," she said, choking back her laughter, "to tell you it was one of the finest things I've ever heard."

"You mean the call was broadcast?"

"Oh, don't object. It was a blow struck."

"For what?"

"Literacy. Intelligence. All the things that matter. Somebody's got to cut through all this hokum."

Cutting through hokum had not occurred to Tattersall as part of his purpose, but the implication that he was doing so seemed to give an added dimension, or resonance, to the sort of thing he was trying to do; almost a kind of crusading element. At any rate, the story, retailed as satire, made Tattersall the center of a small group whom he continued to amuse with his act. The Dean of the school was there, Dr. Shaffer. Nestled well down in his fat pelican chins, he smiled into his punch cup at the carryings on. They were a fast crowd. There was a discussion of prevailing literary trends, to some of the ranker aspects of which the Dean took modest exception. Tattersall asked him whether he would like a karate chop. "Not especially," the Dean said, looking down his vest with his apologetic smile. The tone grew rowdier and jollier there, and from across the room Sherry, already concerned about the hit Tattersall was making, happened to glance over in time to see him belt the Dean across the puss, that is, pretend to, with the classic double slap — a swipe with the back of the hand and then with the palm coming back.

"Excuse me," she said to her group. "I've got to rescue Hank."

She reached Tattersall's side in time to see him make a hammerlock of his arms and say to the Dean, "Put your head in there."

"I won't either," the Dean said, simpering at the carpet.

"Then don't talk about realism."

The conversation moved along to the topic of integrated housing. It was something for which Tattersall militantly worked on a local civic committee, but of whose appeal to middle-class sanctimony he was so well aware that, when the Dean boasted about the color-blindness of his particular neighborhood, he could not resist the opportunity to cut through a little more hokum. "Yassuh, all you need is sixty thousand dollars to buy a house there. So what do it mean dat de section is open to all colors?" he said. "Just dat some dem ladies got deeper tans dan odders."

Perhaps he had been working too hard, Sherry thought as they drove home, herself at the wheel. Well, the spring vacation would soon be here, and perhaps they could take a cruise. Or they might get married again.

They had been married three or four times in their six years together. They had been happy years, as those things went, but much of the happiness depended on the repeated nuptials his spirit required, or which his nervous system craved. It was more than the simple pleasure he took in exchanging vows. A couple of years of living with a housewife, and he felt the urge to make her a bride again. That was the longest interval he could go without feeling the need upon him again. The first time had been some twenty months after their marriage. They had been to a wedding reception for a young cousin of Sherry's, and, musing in their motel room afterward, he had worn such a wistful expression that Sherry had said, "You wish it was you, don't you?"

"Why not? We could elope this time. Where do elopers go? Isn't it Maryland where you don't need a license or anything?"

He called it "renewing the dream." She had had

qualms about its possibly being illegal in some way, but not he. And in any case, such a likelihood could only add an extra dash of flavor to the adventure. Which soon became a regular practice. When daily life had begun again to pall, off they would pop across some state line or other — once to Mexico, when they were vacationing in California — and knock up the first justice of the peace they could find to tie the knot again. When medical tests and licenses were required, they would get them, giving outmoded single identifications. Then off on the honeymoon, a fresh fortnight of champagne and caviar in some bridal suite or other, together with all the other paradisal delights apt to the occasion, including the deference inevitably showered everywhere upon newly-weds. Then home again with the sense of starting a new life, not merely resuming an old one.

The best account of what happened between now and the following spring is contained in a series of letters Tattersall got from himself in that period. For as the drug addict is unable to kick the monkey, he was unable to kick the Doppelgänger. One of the letters read:

"Dear Tattersall: First permit me to dispose of a little bit of casuistry, or hairsplitting, with which you have been trying to dispose of *me*. It might be cast in the form of a syllogism going something like this. I am a mess. But the honesty required for such ruthless self-inventory is almost unheard of. Ergo I am a gem. No. It won't wash, and I warn you that I will not be the dupe by which you use deflation as a means of blowing up your ego. The very scrounging for pride on that level forfeits the right to it — not to mention that this brand of self-castigation is also an inverted exercise in self-pity. So I'm sorry. What's always been true is true still: Thou shalt not go hence till thou hast paid the last farthing.

Now back to the order of business, and down to brass tacks.

The wish to cut a figure, my dear Tattersall, is certainly not one to which exception can be reasonably taken. Women have other ideals but that is ours — to be thought the cat's pajamas. Especially by them. The fallacy lies in supposing it to be realizable in all quarters and at all times. Pull down that vanity! Our dignity is not that foolproof, you know, or important. Somebody who has today seen us glitter when we walk will tomorrow catch sight of us chasing our hat down the street, or coming down the Grand Promenade with a loose garter dangling under a trouser cuff. Just as we may see him so running or so promenading. You know that what happened to you could happen to anybody, and that the only intelligent thing to do is forget about it. But no. The memory of such a fall is an acid so exquisitely corroding you that you won't sleep till you've redeemed yourself . . . somehow, anyhow. You had no serious interest in Lucy at all. You wouldn't have married her if she were the last woman on earth. Nevertheless what she chucked when she chucked Hank Tattersall she must now be made to see. Up, up, my peacock's tail! Out of the dust, my feathers! That takes priority over everything else on your agenda. Look to what lengths you go just to contrive opportunities to restore your image. It's not enough that you get together socially. More "exposure," as the media people say, is required. So you volunteer for some dreary alumni committee just because she's on it. Then she quits, leaving you stuck with it. Thus the long, tortuous odyssey of self-justification on which you have apparently embarked in early middle life. It is perhaps fitting, my dear Tattersall, that voyages so motivated are vexed, now by immobilizing calms, now by unexpected storms that take us onto islands more irrelevant than those to which Ulysses was swept on a more legitimate journey. Next week the students may demonstrate against dormitory regulations if the faculty votes against their further liberalization, and you will have to take a stand as a member of the alumni board as well as a teacher. Well, don't expect any sympathy from me . . ."

Tattersall did not read any more just then. It could wait. He had opened the letter as soon as he had fished it out of his pigeonhole in the English Building. Now he thrust it into his pocket along with his other mail and went to his office for some relaxation exercises.

The decision to have repose is always well advised. Closing his door, he sat slumped in his swivel chair with his arms hanging limp over the sides and his mouth drooping open in an expression of total idiocy. His eyes became hooded, his tongue lolled, as he systematically affected the relaxation of which he was in search. The principle involved is a perfectly valid one psychologically — or, indeed, physiologically. An ostensible state of muscular at-ease, of torpor, communicates to the brain the information that this condition obtains. This in turn prompts the brain to send out instructions to the muscles that all is well, they may relax, and so on, setting up a kind of beneficent circle which at length results in a bona fide version of the composure that had been feigned.

In contrast to this are the isometric exercises with which those living sedentary lives try to keep their muscles from becoming flabby. Tattersall also faithfully did these. So that he spent much of his day alternately sagging and going rigid, looking now like a collapsed puppet, now like one twitched suddenly erect. He was pushing his desk through the wall when the telephone on it rang.

"Tattersall? This is Dean Shaffer."

"Oh, yes, Dean."

"There's a panty raid going on right this minute in Ida Lowe Hall."

"Do they think they'll find any?"

"I'm doing a quick run-down on some of the faculty — whoever I can find in. Tell me, do you think we should ignore it?"

"Don't even ignore it, as the fellow said."

"Right. Now, while I've got you, what about this bed stunt they're going in for. It's the latest thing. Seeing how many they can get on a bed at once, the way they used to see how many they could get into a telephone booth, remember? Michigan, or one of those midwestern universities anyway, has the record. Sixty-five or something like that. A double bed. Of course the beds break."

"Of course," said Tattersall, who had never heard of this craze, but who did not want to seem not to be keeping abreast of prevailing academic trends. He even had a reefer in his drawer. "If you're asking my opinion again, I'd say ignore that too, but make them pay for the beds."

"Ah. That ought to make them think twice. A good idea. Now I want your thinking on one more thing." The Dean was breathing heavily, as though he had run up a flight of stairs to answer the phone instead of having done the calling, or perhaps had been himself shinnying up drainpipes in quest of undergarments. "Do you suspect all this is tuning up for something more serious next week if we don't relax the parietal rules?"

"I think it may very well be."

"Now I'm taking an informal poll on how the faculty is likely to vote on that. Do you mind telling me how you feel?"

"I think the regulations should be liberalized. Extend the visiting time to eleven o'clock, with, say, a two A.M. curfew weekends."

"Thanks. That's all I want to know now. Have to ring off. Do you expect you'll look in on the panty raid?"

"Oh, I think I'll just rummage through a few of my wife's things."

"All right."

Tattersall felt suddenly distraught, and the urge again seized him to live in another key. It was a mood not assuaged by reading Oosterman's latest piece of fiction, a complex psychological study of a neurotic business secretary who habitually stole into her boss's office and filled his fountain pen with vichyssoise. "Excellent," Tattersall scribbled on it, "and a welcome relief from stories full of all those damned Freudian symbols." Oosterman would laugh. He was all right.

As he was jotting the comment, some train of association deposited in Tattersall's head the suspicion that it was Oosterman who had put the reefer on his desk. That half the class smoked marijuana was plain from their defense of it in a discussion that had developed, in a session about three weeks ago when a story dealing with it came up for general criticism. But Oosterman had been much the most vocal on the subject. He preached that pot was not habit-forming, did not lead to drugs, left you with no hangover, and was patently better for you than tobacco or alcohol. The next day Tattersall had found on his classroom desk an envelope containing a reefer and a note reading, "Try it." He had pocketed it, put it in his office desk, and forgotten it. Now he took it out again, slipped it into his pocket, and headed for home.

"You remember that reefer I told you one of my students gave me?" he said to Sherry at dinner. "Here it is."

"Oh, let me see it. I've never seen one. Not much to look at, are they?"

"I suppose most of them are homemade." He watched her examine it as he had, with a gingerly curiosity. "They're quite harmless, apparently. You just get high and that's all. No aftereffects. And better for you than liquor. Care to try it?"

"Well, I don't know," she answered with a nervous giggle. "Are you game?"

"Why not?"

The giggle proved prophetic of the experience in store for them. For the result was mainly a laughing jag that went on all evening, and half the night. They sat smoking together on the couch, passing the cigarette back and forth between them and sucking in as much air as possible with each drag, which debauchees were said to do in order to derive maximum benefit from the smoke. Holding the last of the cigarette by a toothpick thrust into it, they managed to consume every scrap. By that time Sherry had begun to bite him on the nose and ears, laughing all the while. The toothpick seemed to amuse Tattersall. He held it up to open derision for some time before discarding it in an ashtray.

He carried Sherry upstairs to the bedroom, where he turned on a light and proceeded to scrutinize every naked inch of her with a relish that consisted in the most intense and concentrated appreciation of geometric forms. He traced the arcs, curves, parabolas, the concavities and convexities of which her figure seemed the supreme embodiment. He had an especially exaggerated eye for the triangulations which she suddenly struck him as possessing in the most inexhaustible profusion. There was a triangle of imaginary lines drawn between her hips and feet when they were together, reversed when the legs were spread and the lines were drawn between her parted feet and her navel. The fleece beneath was triangular. There was a triangle of which that was a point, and the other two formed by the breasts, also, themselves, vaguely triune. "Turn over," Tattersall ordered, and, rolling her onto her stomach, continued his pursuit of the trinities on the dorsal plane. Long after Sherry's amusement had, in sexual satiety, subsided to a series of contented grunts, Tattersall remained in full sway. Everything excited his mirth. She found him laughing at a door hinge, and when she asked from the bed what was so funny, he worked the door a few times by way of demonstration, pointing derisively at it. He turned back into the room.

"Do you know what broke Schopenhauer up?" he said.

"Gee, you mean he ever laughed at anything? Beside women's hips?"

"A tangent. It's a fact. He thought a tangent was funny. I'm serious. To understand why, you have to know what his hypotenuse — Jesus, hypothesis of humor was. That laughter — now listen carefully — laughter is our sudden perception of the incongruity between an abstract concept and the actual reality. A tangent is an example. Turn over on your stomach again."

He picked up a book and held it against her rump.

"This forms what is known as an ordinary tangent. Right? A straight line in this relation to a curve. Now what made Schopenhauer smile every time he saw one was, he said, the incongruity between our abstract knowledge that a straight line and a curved one can never, never form an angle, and the fact that such an angle lies visibly before us on paper."

"What a price to pay for genius."

"You're beautiful. Marry me."

"Oh, not again. It's such a nasty night out."

"All right, later in the week then. I thought we might try Connecticut this time. We can get the blood test and license by the weekend. We can decide on the honeymoon later."

"If you insist, but I don't know why so soon again. It isn't as though this marriage isn't working out. I think it's working out beautifully. Better than most of the rest, don't you think?"

Tattersall said he agreed, but it wasn't a question of that. It wasn't a matter of how old or how successful the marriage was. *He* had undergone experiences of so radically transforming a nature that he could not be considered the same person as he had been. Nor, he thought, could she. They were two different people, in need of fresh partners. In short, a new union.

"I'll make you happier, too," he said. "I feel I can do anything for you. Swim the highest mountain, climb the deepest ocean. Make us rich overnight by inventing some new kind of computer, or getting control of an industrial corporation by winning a proxy fight. Anything but teach!" he suddenly and unexpectedly blurted out in conclusion.

That was the thing that worried Sherry — the suspicion that he was spoiling for a new identity, not just a change in the old one, or a temporary variation of it. It cast a shadow on her forthcoming marriage.

They were married in Greenwich and honeymooned in the Motel On the Mountain, off the New York State Thruway. He padded barefoot toward his virgin. "What a lovely breast," he said, fondling one. "So soft and sweet, yet so firm. Oh, and you've another right next to it. Excellent."

Word soon spread that they were newlyweds. A party at another table in the dining room sent over a bottle of wine when they were having dinner.

"This is the part I feel guilty about," Sherry whispered, after they had raised their glasses in a salute of acknowledgment to the donors. "I don't feel right about it."

"Nonsense. It gives people pleasure. Look at the host beam. And there's nothing you can do about it. It's one of those things. So enjoy yourself. The end of all good hunting is closer than you think. I aim to. I'll soon enough have to go back to the campus and all those damned problems again."

"How are you going to vote on the dormitory rules?"

"The way I feel *now?*" Tattersall pressed her hand with a suggestive grin. "Probably to repeal them altogether."

"You want to lose your job, don't you?" Sherry said, returning his smile by darting him an anxious glance.

"Oh, come on. This lobster is terrific."

"All the same I'm worried."

She was a simple woman, and it was just like her to know him better than he knew himself.

five

TATTERSALL watched the demonstration from a distance. Several hundred students were marching in a steady circle around the Administration Building chanting "No curfew on weekends!", the slogan also emblazoned on several of the placards they shouldered or held aloft. Some posters were embellished with drawings depicting boys and girls disposed in unobjectionable arrangements, such as playing cards under bright floor lamps, or sitting on the floor in protectively large numbers, listening to records and drinking nothing stronger than beer. There was nothing to suggest that the quarters for which liberalized regulations were demanded were dormitory rooms, or that boys were asking permission to entertain girls without chaperones behind closed doors, if they so wished.

The demonstration was being staged to coincide with Reunion Week, and now visiting alumni of various ages stood in groups around the fountain near which Tattersall had paused. There were a number of seniors among the onlookers; more than among the participants, since they were about to graduate and leave, and had little or no interest in the subject now. They had more curiosity about the alumni which they were on the brink of becoming. The old grads soon had their fill and returned, by contrast, to more nostalgic concerns, swapping reminiscences, exchanging gossip, and in at least one case, striking up a song or two. The music mingled with the sound of the chanting, which though persistent was restrained and systematic, in keeping with the admonition to "orderly milling." "Orderly Milling," Tattersall thought to himself. "It sounds like a hospital employee. Hello, Orderly Milling? Send up another tank of oxygen to Room 312."

"Hello, Hank." Wurlitzer, after a spell of harmonizing, had strolled to his side.

For Wurlitzer was a graduate of Chichester too, making the final, nagging configuration to a mind prey to triangles. He attended college functions with a special fervor since meeting Lucy at another spring reunion here — her seventh and his fourteenth, as Tattersall rather churlishly noted in a new-math calculation which he chose to believe made Wurlitzer twice Lucy's and his age. It gave him, that is, twice their adult life. Thus Wurlitzer and Lucy had met as alumni, he and Lucy as classmates, but this did not deprive Wurlitzer of the fancy that he had "beaten Tattersall out" — such at least was the conviction corroding Tattersall now. Lucy had upon their graduation suggested they not correspond, as letters might delusively foster and protract a relationship best regarded as a schoolday fling over and done with. She had taken the words out of Tattersall's mouth, but he had quixotically not told her so — which left him, in retrospect, a suitor refused. Feminine vanity would inevitably make it so; masculine ego, as typified by Wurlitzer, lay the flattering unction to its heart as well. The assumption that he lived in left field was too much for Tattersall. The sense that he and Wurlitzer were rivals fed at him like a canker worm.

"How do you feel about it?" With a nod Wurlitzer indicated the demonstration to which his question applied.

Tattersall understood it to be Wurlitzer's view that young people "went too far," "demanded too much," and were "getting out of hand." Which was just enough to congeal a latent sympathy with their cause into formal support on Tattersall's part. It was all he needed.

"I think they're right," he said.

"You do?"

"Yes. We're here to give them an education. Not regulate their private lives."

"Then why aren't you in there marching with them?"

Wurlitzer had spoken it facetiously, even with a discernible laugh. But Tattersall answered, "Why not indeed?" and strode over and joined the line.

He was rather surprised to find himself there, since he was also a member of the discipline committee. The demonstrators marched three and four abreast, and he tramped rhythmically along to the right of a youth in a black turtleneck sweater, on whose left was a girl in a plaid skirt and maroon cardigan. That they ignored Tattersall pleased him, since it meant they saw nothing unusual in his participation by reason of age or appearance. In his tweed coat and black knit tie he could easily pass for one of Wurlitzer's crazy mixed-up kids. Braced by these deductions, he threw his shoulders back and lustily joined in chanting, "No curfew Saturday! Curfew shall not ring on Saturday!"

For all the rhythmic shouting and stomping, quite blood-rousing in its way, the line steadily circling the Administration Building was indeed an orderly one. It recalled prisoners being exercised in a yard. The half-dozen or so cops one passed at their successive posts, standing with feet planted apart and nursing their sticks behind their backs, heightened this resemblance to an orbiting contingent of inmates in stir. Was that how the term had originated? They quite resembled a vast porridge being stirred by an invisible authoritative ladle. On one circuit he saw President Mattock and Dean Shaffer posing with the student ringleaders for some newspaper photographs. They smiled in a simulated tableau of amicably Hearing the Young People Out, and as if in balanced rejection of any implication that youth was Going to the Dogs. One of the ringleaders was not too fortunate a spokesman for the cause, having, in a way, compromised it.

Bats Hartack was a junior majoring in architecture, who had violated every rule concerning girls and dormitories except one — the eleven o'clock Lights Out rule. His lights were always out well before that time. On that score there could be no complaints. Since the present expanding agitation had started, some few months before, he had been found with a girl in his bed. Opinion was divided as to whether this prejudiced the cause or performed the service of bringing it into clear and dramatic focus. Some such debate was presumed to be going forward now between the principals, judging by the way reporters took notes, now on what one side said,

82

now the other. All this was orderly too. Then suddenly the scene was given a different and quite galvanizing emphasis. Tattersall was recognized. Another minute and he would have been safely past the front of the building. But one of the ringleaders spotted him and instantly made capital of it. "There's Mr. Tattersall!" he shouted, pointing, and Tattersall was led captive through the roaring mob.

His statement was straightforward and terse. It began with what he had pithily told Wurlitzer, that they were there to educate the students, not regulate their private lives. "Parietal rules, as we call these campus regulations, can only be partial and therefore hypocritical in any case," he said, as pencils flew and cameras clicked. "The rules themselves mean nothing. Whether you have a two A.M. curfew or a ten o'clock one, there are still twenty-four hours in a day. And nobody checks the rooms anyway, except in the most desultory and sporadic fashion. The possibility of what you may find in them makes such espionage more disagreeable than the offenses they uncover."

"Then how was Hartack caught?" a reporter asked.

"By someone not looking for that at all. He'd heard there was something stronger than beer in the room, and happened to find something stronger than whiskey."

"What are your views on that? As a member of the discipline committee, would you expel a student for drinking bourbon on campus?"

"Yes."

"Why, if not for the other?"

"Because in that case he's breaking a state law, and worse, a gentlemen's agreement. There's a delicate truce between us and the local authorities, by which they connive at beer and wine in return for our cracking down on whiskey. It's not perfect, any more than anything in this world is, but it's one way of solving this whole tricky and complex problem of college drinking. And it works. It's an honor thing, if you will, and so if I found Hartack drinking whiskey, yes, I'd kick him out. His sex life is his own business. That does not involve what you could accurately call a gentlemen's agreement." The laughter was such that Tattersall could enjoy having to hold his hand up for quiet. "We don't interfere with the sex life of students living off campus. They sleep together in one another's apartments all over town and everyone knows it. That's what I mean about its all being hypocritical. The parietal rules *are not honest.*"

The President's face, which looked like a pot of tomatoes the best of times, now positively blazed, as though it had caught fire, while the Dean simply looked at the ground with his crapkicking smile, as though it was he who had been caught with the girl, and was a devil.

"Do you have a statement to make about all this?" one of the reporters asked the President.

"Just that there will be an emergency meeting of the discipline committee in my office in exactly one hour," the President said, and turned on his heel and strode away.

As a member of it, Tattersall scurried conscientiously about in preparation for the meeting. He sought Hartack out immediately after the demonstration and ordered him to appear without fail at the emergency session. He had a plan which he hoped would put an end to this whole sordid muddle, and marching in unexpectedly with Bats Hartack by his side served his strategy by catching the President unawares. The President was engaged in preliminary consultation with the two other members of the committee: the Dean, and Edmonds of the History Department, a man who sucked on curved pipes and weighed both sides before making a judgment.

"What is the meaning of bringing Hartack in on this, Tattersall?" the President demanded, looking up.

"I thought that's what you meant. That he be summoned. Else what's the meeting for?"

"To consider you! As you very well know. Your insubordination — which I make no bones about calling it. This is real malfeasance. What right have you to march in a demonstration aimed at a committee of which you are a member? Up to now anyway," the President added darkly. If one might not more accurately say brightly, for his face glowed dangerously again. He ground his teeth wretchedly a moment, and then said, "Do you march against yourself, man!"

"I don't look at it that way. I took the demonstration to be just what the term implies. A public declaration of opinion. No more, no less. There are some students who oppose liberalizing the parietal rules, and they were given their right to heckle. Conversely some faculty members favor it, and by the same token share in the right to speak up and say what they think. Or so I assume, unless free speech is a one-way street."

The President looked to Edmonds for his view on this thinking, and in so doing riveted all eyes upon him. Edmonds nodded thoughtfully, puffing on his pipe, and at last said through a cloud of smoke which obscured him personally, as Jehovah was said to obscure himself in making pronouncements, "I think Tattersall has a point. It's a piece of casuistry, granted, but valid in its way. He's compromised us as a committee in one sense. But in another he's certified us before the world as honestly accommodating dissent, thereby laying claim for us to a confidence which the student body is now in all conscience obliged to give."

"What do you think, Dean?"

"I'm in agreement."

"With whom — Edmonds and Tattersall, or me?"

This was hard on the Dean, who tried to take both sides of every question, not merely, like Edmonds, weigh them with a view to selecting one. The fence-straddling was in turn hard on the President. It was an open secret that the Dean's definite maybes were chief among the factors undermining the President's health; that another mouthful of mush would kill him, by bringing on another duodenal crisis.

"I agree with you absolutely that Tattersall's action was imprudent from one point of view," the Dean said, "but that by sheer luck it may turn out in our favor." While the President sat magisterially trying to hear everyone out before deciding whether to release unto them Barabbas or another, the Dean, his chins making him look more than ever like a pelican, took the opportunity to glance at Hartack as someone to whom plain disapproval could be safely directed. "Once we know what in the world Hartack is doing here."

That worthy (as such types were called in the fiction Tattersall knew full well the Dean still read) had all this while been standing, as, indeed, had Tattersall. After waving them to chairs, the President acidly asked Tattersall to enlighten them on the point the Dean had raised. That made the Dean's thrust seem to have been directed at Tattersall, causing the Dean guiltily to drop his eyes again.

"I can only assume," Tattersall began, "that if action was to be taken on my participation in the rally, it would consist either in a request for my resignation, or, if the milder line were adopted for which I would have to thank my good friend Edmonds, in some kind of statement of censure which would force me to tender it anyway."

"A distinct possibility," the President said to his desk blotter.

"In that case," Tattersall said slowly, "there would be a student revolt."

"So that's your little game, is it? Blackmail!"

"No. Not in the least. The fact is that I have decided to tender my resignation anyway. Not over this, or as a member of the committee. As a teacher. I have another offer of employment open to me, in another profession, which I have decided to accept. That ought to cut this Gordian knot for us all."

There were murmurs of protestation and reassurance. "Quit teaching? Why would you want to do a thing like that?" the President said, scarcely able to conceal his joy.

"I just think I'm ripe for a change, that's all. Nothing more to it than that. Well, to get back to the business at hand. I thought one reason Hartack's presence would be valuable is that he can hear for himself that my resignation is not being asked for, and so testify to the student body. That way there'll be no misunderstanding, no needless hoopla over nothing. Certainly no wasteful and destructive student revolt." After they had all breathed a sigh of relief, Tattersall turned to Hartack. "Now let's put a few questions to the prisoner while we have him here, shall we? Does anyone mind if I conduct the interrogation?"

"Not at all," said the President, only too tickled that this was to be Tattersall's swan song.

They were loosely ranged around the desk at which the President himself sat. Tattersall now twitched his chair about so as to be facing Hartack more squarely. Hartack, a stocky blond with a crew cut, did not look like a firebrand now that he was actually before the tribunal that would decide his fate. The sudden fear of expulsion, or even of a suspension that would in effect lose him a whole semester since they were within so few days of its end, brought beads of perspiraton to his brow, and made him clear his throat nervously. He agreed to come clean when Tattersall warned him it would be wise to do so, and not deny facts of which he had the evidence — evidence, Tattersall added, that he had gone to the trouble of personally collecting.

"The truth is that you were only caught in bed once with this girl, but that you have really been taking her into your room regularly. Is that correct?"

"Yes, sir," Hartack said, wetting his lips. "I guess that's right."

"You guess. How many times would you say you violated the rule?"

"I can't say."

"Because they were so many. It might be easier to state the period of time over which you have been doing so, rather than enumerate individual instances. How long would you say? All semester? All year?"

"All year."

"Last year too?"

"Yes, sir."

"And the year before that."

"Yes, sir."

There was a silence in the room. It continued for some time. The committee members could all be heard breathing heavily. When they had drunk their fill of implication, Tattersall turned slowly from Hartack to them.

"You've heard the whole story, gentlemen," he said. "the full facts. And I wish to submit to you, gentlemen, that these are extenuating circumstances. This is obviously not a superficial relationship, but a deep and serious one. This girl is not a pickup, nor is this your short-order sex, a case of popping in and out of the sack such as we know to be going on everywhere, not only here but all around, anywhere you can name. These young people are going steady in the fullest sense of the term, not shacking up in the shabby and superficial one. *This man has been pulling the wool over our eyes for four years.* Clearer proof of his intentions could not be asked. In view of all this, gentlemen, I think it would be regrettable to make an example of someone who might more properly be held up as one."

"Hear, hear!" they said.

That was how they voted too, not only clearing Hartack of the charge, by the simple device of dropping it, but shaking his hand by way of commending a meaningful bond such as could only refresh their faith in an age of promiscuity. "There are marriages that don't last that long," Edmonds said from within a dense cloud of smoke.

Having excused Hartack, they settled down to the larger issue, that of overhauling the regulations in general. Tattersall again stressed the point that students on campus were being cracked down on for what those living off it got away with scot-free. The President protested fatigue with that argument. The obvious impracticability of policing the entire city didn't absolve them from the responsibility of governing the part they could. "If a cop is giving you a ticket for speeding," he said, "the fact that cars are whizzing by at eighty miles an hour while he is doing so is no ground for complaining that you're being discriminated against. He can't be everywhere at once. And if they're having such meaningful relationships, let them prove it by contending with a few obstacles!"

Then the Dean, having just murmured that there was something in what Tattersall said, now agreed with the President also, picking lint from his knee with his crap-kicking smile. Then he made a joke. He remarked that infractions were hard to be sure about in any case, if you found two people in bed together, because nowadays you couldn't tell the boys from the girls. Then Tattersall, who had made that observation himself years back when it wasn't so common, said, "Maybe they *like* to resemble each other, the young people. Maybe that's very loving and sexual, rather than hermaphroditic." Then the Dean backed down a little and said, "There's something in what you say." Whereupon Tattersall had one of his twinges of remorse for jumping on him, and to make amends, cited a cartoon contradicting his own position and supporting the Dean's. It showed just such an androgynous youth as they were talking about, with dungarees and long hair, standing at a mailbox reading a letter which began, "Dear sir or madam . . ." Then the Dean said, "I see what you mean," lowering his eyes to the floor while Tattersall rolled his to the ceiling in an expression of absolutely giving up.

Not even Edmonds could summarize, or "recap," these bandied and qualification-tormented observations, or resolve their contradictions by pointing out with his pipestem the truth that lay somewhere in between. So they came to no decision about what to recommend, but tabled the matter till another meeting, which meant another term. Which was perhaps just as well. But in rolling his eyes to the ceiling, Tattersall had noted a wide and rapidly spreading wet spot in the plaster there. Thus a serious leak in the plumbing was detected, in time to save the school hundreds, possibly thousands, of dollars in repair expense, and making them all feel that something worthwhile had been accomplished by this meeting.

They adjourned on a generally happy, or at least hopeful, note. The President was so glad that Tattersall was leaving that he begged him to stay. But Tattersall was adamant. He needed a change. All he had to do now was reveal his decision to his wife, who was not surprised, and then set out in search of Wurlitzer to tell him he was accepting his offer of a job at the agency. He found him at the fountain, harmonizing with some of his cronies.

six

TATTERSALL was about two months into his new career when, through the half-open door of his cubicle at Wurlitzer and Wise, he caught a glimpse of a long-legged girl who looked familiar. He saw her from the back just as she turned a corner of the corridor and disappeared in the direction of the wing in which the agency brass were quartered. She slipped along with a rapid gliding walk, as though about to break into a trot toward or away from something. She carried a leather shoulder bag, and her head was tilted to one side in a manner that rang a bell, even though the black hair remembered as hanging straight down was now done up in a large biscuit.

Tattersall rolled aside the typewriter stand behind which he had been working and shot on tiptoe down the hallway to the corner where she had turned, and peered around it just in time to see her vanish again, this time into the complex of executive lairs which included Wurlitzer's own. It was Mayo Stiles all right. Another leap brought him to a water cooler where, standing with his back to the closed double door, he could listen to what went on behind it with a paper cup in his hand. He heard the receptionist's typewriter stop, and then Mayo's voice asking to be announced to Wurlitzer. "He's expecting me," she said.

Tattersall remained at the otherwise deserted water cooler a few minutes, reviewing the general situation and trying to sort out the possibilities inherent in it. The one that made most sense was that Mayo was seeing her uncle about a job herself. She had graduated and now wanted to write, with the problem of a livelihood classically embedded in that wish. The Satyr Press could not have advanced her much. He knocked back several paper cupfuls of water during this train of thought and bleated "Maaw," a few times, although, truth to tell, he was as much excited as nonplussed by the speculation. A buzzer sounded behind him, and the receptionist told Mayo to go in. The typewriter there resumed its tattoo, and Tattersall returned to his, assuming the dramatic crouch he had come to develop here, like that of a hard-pressed jockey pressing on, in turn, his mount.

Working with the door partway open enabled him both to see into the hall and be seen by anyone approaching down it, banging away at his copy or glaring at what he had written with that grim and bitter self-evaluation that went with creative standards. Orders were to regard Tattersall as offbeat, special, to give him his head and let him incubate his own ideas in his own good time. The previous resident sport, Gascoyne, with whom Wurlitzer had once mentioned his possibly collaborating, was no longer with the firm; regrettably, accordingly to Wurlitzer, who considered him "a real pro" despite his Off-Broadway copy. He was now working for another agency.

Wurlitzer wanted a minimum of twenty "are you sick of's" before he would even think of showing the series to the one client for whose blood Tattersall might not be too rich. He was too rich for the average sponsor's blood, that they all knew. This one was a manufacturer of a line of soft drinks still lacking a "cola," and who was about to launch one, to be called Kickola.

"Are you sick of batteries that go dead when you need your car most?" he had been writing when he had glimpsed Mayo in the passage. This wouldn't work, since failures of ignition were likely to be at their most vexing to commuters who had just inadequately breakfasted and must be off for their train, or in the dead of winter when the thing to hit the spot is a cup of hot coffee or cocoa, not a cold bottle of Kickola, even supposing one were available. Tattersall twisted the sheet of paper out of the roller, but instead of discarding it cross-filed it under headings such as Coffee, Cocoa, Gums, Mints and Antacid Lozenges, as well as other products conceivable as ameliorants in the crisis postulated. The complex variety of factors that had to be taken into account in this venture had by now been borne in on Tattersall. He had so far submitted a hundred and eleven "are you sick of's" to the front office, where superiors of an almost Kafkaesque anonymity and elusiveness had accepted ten and rejected the other hundred and one. Moreover, they refused for obscure bureaucratic reasons to return the rejections. They considered them killed, unaware of the swelling limbo in which Tattersall was cross-filing carbons. If whatever plugs finally made the grade here met the same rate of extermination at the hands of sponsors to whom they were in turn submitted by the

94

agency, Tattersall estimated, he would be several hundred years old before the show got on the road. Here they wanted the "are you" vignettes to be both dramatic and commonplace — something listeners could identify with. Thus one could not be fed up with oil furnaces exploding, since such things did not recur with a sufficient frequency in everyday life, nor with fabrics to which lint easily adhered, since such experiences lay at the other extreme, below the threshold of exasperation. Neither, in any case, called for a Kickola. But Tattersall knew one thing. Neither the strains of composition nor the obstacles flung up by the front office against the end product would make him ever compromise the original integrity of his conception. These plugs were going to express a dignified resignation to life.

He was sitting with his elbows on his knees and his hands folded under his chin, scrutinizing what was in his typewriter, when he became aware of two people coming down the corridor. Without raising his eyes he knew them to be Wurlitzer and Mayo. He was hammering away again when they stopped in his doorway.

"Hank?"

It was not till he paused once more in his fusillade that he looked up, with a start of interrupted concentration.

"Oh, hello, Harry, I'm sorry I — Mayo! What a pleasant surprise. What brings you here?" He wheeled the typewriter aside again and scrambled around it to greet her. "You're looking fine."

It fell out that she was going to get married. Her young man was a medical student whose remaining few years of study and internship necessitated her working

95

for a while to help make both ends meet. Her novel would be published some time next year, but would not be expected to bring in any money to speak of. She was taking a job here at Double W, as the agency was called, in the copy department. So they would be seeing a lot of one another again.

"I was surprised to hear you quit teaching," Mayo whispered. "Whatever made you do that?"

"Oh, I wanted a change. The real world, you know. I found myself beginning to think about tenure, that old placenta." Shifting his weight to another foot, he adjusted this esoteric metaphor downward to Wurlitzer's level. "That old cocoon. And that's a danger signal. When things get too safe and snug, flee for your life."

"I think Hank felt the academic world was too secloistered for a man of his restless nature." Had Wurlitzer really said that? Secloistered. Tattersall hoped he had heard right. A glance at Mayo revealed nothing to indicate that she had caught any such malapropism.

"You can say that again," Tattersall said.

"He's turning out to be a real pro, anyway," Wurlitzer said. Tattersall would have found the testimonial more bracing had he not heard it in frequent requiems for the departed Gascoyne. Still, it was a term of praise Wurlitzer used for everybody. He would have called a prostitute a real pro.

"Care to join us for lunch?" Wurlitzer said.

Tattersall had more sense than to accept such an invitation. He declined it by pleading something in the pressure cooker, glancing at the typewriter as he responded with this bit of agency slang.

He told Sherry the day's news when he got home, not

neglecting the malapropism his ear had chosen to pick up whether it had been uttered or not. He was determined that Wurlitzer had said it. "A regular Joyce. Secloistered. A great composite word for secluded, cloistered and sequestered," he said as he shook up the cocktail with which to unwind. He admired the cotton print in which she sat, neat and fresh, waiting for her drink. "You might go all the way and make it seclustered. To mean all those clammy little cliques you get into on campus, you know, and that you're damn well out of!" He was not sure he should have left.

It was an odd aspect of academic life for a loner like Hank Tattersall to express no regrets about, Sherry thought, humid fraternization being among the tendencies to which he was least prone. She wished again that he erred in the direction about which other wives could by contrast complain; that he bowled, golfed, played poker or even drank with cronies. She thought about that again after dinner as, drawing on her gloves, she prepared to go out for an evening of committee work for some charitable organization. He was playing the piano, with the same rapt expression he wore sitting at the mangle. His fingers picked out a popular song, into the words of which he then flung himself. He had a really good amateur tenor, with a certain rough sweetness to it. If he would only join a singing group somewhere. She could see him in a glee club, standing tall and straight in a grove of shirtfronts, singing *Brown October Ale* and *Shipmates o' Mine* and *Where My Caravan Has Rested*. But he couldn't see himself that way. He had joined in the singing around the fountain where he had found Harry Wurlitzer the night he hit him for the job, but only for diplomatic reasons, and it had gone against his grain. He preferred belting a song out on his own. She could hear him as she entered the elevator (they had moved into a city apartment of course) and knew that was how he would spend the evening. When he had the house to himself he would let go for hours at a time, either accompanying himself at the piano or singing along with phonograph records. In that case he would harmonize with other soloists, or with quartets or other vocal groups of some distinction, without having to go out through the wet and the drear to attend rehearsals.

When she got back about a quarter to eleven, he was sitting in his armchair smoking a cigar, surrounded by sheet music and unreplaced record albums. She brewed them some tea, and as they sipped it he talked again about Mayo, wondering what her young man was like, and how soon they were going to get married. Sherry went to bed, but after a sleepless hour came in again to find him still sitting where she'd left him, staring into space and wreathed in the smoke of still another cigar.

"Would you like to get married again?" she said.

"Well, we *are* two different people. This is a new life. Up to now I've been a teacher, you a faculty wife. Now I'm an organization man and you're a company wife. We might make a better go of such a marriage."

"I'm not going to make a big production of it. Another license and all that red tape."

"Don't you think it's worth it?"

"Yes, but we've got a *file* of marriage licenses by this time — all probably illegal. And bothering ministers and getting justices of the peace out of bed and all. I just feel guilty. Why can't we just slip into an empty chapel somewhere and exchange the vows by ourselves. Pretend there's someone officiating. It comes to the same thing. God, I know the ceremony by heart by this time."

"How would you like to elope this time?" he asked, half turning his head with an engaging grin.

"But nobody's objecting to the match! Except me, a little."

"We've never done that before. That's why — you might like running away."

"From whom? You have no parents, and I've got one arthritic mother."

"She objected to me when she first met me."

"She's gotten over it by now."

"I doubt it. Deep down, I sense a persisting grain of hostility. She disapproves of the match and so we have to run away and get married. We've never given it that feel yet. It might be just the thing we need. That final dash of reckless romance, of first fine careless rapture the unions have hitherto lacked. I knew there was something missing in all the other marriages. That's it."

Sherry came farther into the room and sat down in a chair facing his.

"Look. You can't elope any more. You're living in the past. You're dreaming. Almost every state around here has got a waiting period after you get the license — just to prevent this impulsive kind of thing — and even where they haven't you've got to wait for your blood test. In other words, couples don't go popping off to Maryland anymore, or wherever it was they eloped to, after having a few."

"You've solved that with your suggestion about slipping into a chapel and exchanging our 'I do's' without benefit of clergy. Then it doesn't make any difference where we go."

"So if you accept that it's just the feel of the thing, we don't even have to do that. If it's the feel of a honeymoon we want, of being newlyweds and having people think so, all we have to do is register at a hotel and *say* we are. Pick up the phone and ask for some bridal suite."

He did not reply to the point directly, but sat dreaming again. At last he said:

"The super's got a ladder which I'm sure he'll let me use. I'll prop it under your window, and hold it while you precariously descend in a new blue suit, an orchid in the lapel, clutching a valise. As I help you down the last rung, my hand will inadvertently slip up your leg and along your bare flank, for this is our wedding night. The raptures of the nuptial couch await us!"

"Or a hospital room, unless I can get safely off the garage roof you'd have to prop the ladder under. I'd rather descend five floors in an elevator, thank you. Just ring twice for a signal and I'll meet you in the lobby."

They had scarcely returned from their honeymoon when there was a telephone call from Lucy, asking them to a small dinner party for Mayo and her fiancé — quite uncannily bearing out Tattersall's statement that Sherry had entered upon a new existence as a corporation wife. So closely was protocol followed that, when Tattersall answered the phone, Lucy asked to speak to Sherry, in order that the social invitation might be extended to her. Tattersall's part in the mosaic was given a much more dramatic definition a few days later.

The very afternoon of the party, Wurlitzer trotted excitedly into Tattersall's office with some news he knew would interest him. Tony Lumpkin, president of the company they had in mind for Tattersall's idea, was in town from Chicago, and they were inviting him to dinner at the last minute, so that they might all meet.

"We'll get him good and sozzled up, and then hit him with it," Wurlitzer said. "I've found that's much the best way with Tony. He tends to freeze and stiffen up at formal presentations of ideas, but around the old piano —"

"Piano?"

"Yes. Haven't I told you about Tony? He likes to sing. Nothing fancy. Just barbershop stuff. I heard you around the fountain, and you're not such a slouch in that department yourself. So while the ladies are powdering their noses maybe we can get in a little caterwauling. And when the moment seems right, wham."

"You mean I'll have to sing?"

"For your supper, why not?" Wurlitzer said with a jolly laugh. "We all have to do it. Way of the world."

"I thought you wanted more specimens."

"For a formal presentation, yes. But over the old brandy bottle, which is where a lot of business is transacted after all, it's a different matter. Just try it on him for size the way you did with me. And Hank?"

"Yes."

"Good luck. You know I want you to make good here."

seven

HOW Wurlitzer's prime prospect for an advertising idea as offbeat as the one at stake could also be a barber-shop quartet buff was a puzzle on which Tattersall did not dwell, beyond the question's naturally crossing his mind. He spent more time wondering what Mayo's fiancé was going to be like.

He turned out to be an earnest young man with a blond mustache and pale blue eyes, named Barry Met-calf. Without looking in the least like Mayo, he re-sembled her for reasons Tattersall put his finger on almost instantly. He shared her habit of listening with lowered eyes to what you were saying, smiling faintly the while, as though internally weighing fallacies in your statements, or as though there was something about your clothing to which it would have been impolite to call attention. Tattersall experienced a familiar urge to rush off and examine himself in the nearest available mirror — the damned Giocondaphobia again. They were in dinner jackets, and Tattersall sensed that he and Met-calf, at any rate, shared the characteristic of being more at ease in tweed coats, without this recognition of a personal bond between them alleviating his half of the discomfiture. He was glad when, during cocktails, Wurlitzer grasped his arm and hauled him through the crowd of some twenty guests over to meet Lumpkin.

Here was a different breed of cat. He was a man who struck Tattersall immediately as a recognizable type, the like of which, however, he could not remember having run into before. Perhaps one had been able with intuitive accuracy to imagine the Lumpkins of this world prevailing in segments of it which one had not hitherto trod. Enormous without being exactly fat, he gave the impression of keeping his weight down by the sheer physical exertion involved in laughter. He was always laughing. Wurlitzer had to delay his introduction for several minutes while Lumpkin listened to a funny story someone was telling him. He laughed all through the exposition, not nervously as people will who are afraid of missing the point, but heartily, relishing every moment of it for its own sake and only slightly less than he did the payoff, which he greeted with a final roar of delight. The fact that it was a shaggy dog story fortified Tattersall's damaged faith in his capacity for special humor. At last Tattersall was presented, and Lumpkin said, "Harry tells me you're the new ball of fire there," and laughed like hell again. His tycoon's genius for "drawing people out" made Tattersall positively shrink inside himself. He classified Lumpkin with those self-made millionaires, midwestern and Texan, who with wealth amassed on commonplace and even embarrassing products proceed to buy up eastern publishing houses, whose heads they then get on the long-distance telephone at hours like eight in the morning, though it is only six or seven o'clock in Chicago or Fort Worth, or wherever they are.

"Harry tells me you sing," he said.

"No, no. Only as a ham."

"That's what I mean. We don't want to get mixed up with stars from the Met," Lumpkin laughed. "What do you sing?"

"Songs."

"What kind?"

"Oh, I don't know. I never really gave it any thought. Just anything." Tattersall tried frantically to think of some titles that might conceivably interest Lumpkin, and finally said, "*Santa Lucia, That Old Gang of Mine.* Things like that."

"No, I mean what part?"

"Oh, tenor. You could call it that."

"First or second?"

"Second."

"Good. Somebody who can carry the melody. I'm bass and Harry's baritone, as you know. So if we can scare up a first tenor maybe we can line out a few after dinner."

Being so committed hardly added to Tattersall's enjoyment of his food. He found himself seated near both Lumpkin and Mayo. A full half-hour of travel talk in which he was lost, never having been abroad, much less to any of the exotic places whose names were being bandied about with the easy profusion of the air age, put him further out of sorts. He found himself growing unhappy, even hostile. What finally got him was the lavish celebration of obscure places and primitive scales of living in which all the globe-trotters engaged, with no apparent realization of the inherent absurdity of their position. At last he cleared his throat angrily, and, having done so, found people turning to him expectantly, as though he had intended to speak, though nothing was farther from his mind. Even Lucy looked over from the end of the table where she reigned, a lull having fallen in the conversation there. It was now quite necessary to say something. What? He had always wanted to tell gadabouts who left you with a mouth full of teeth to shut their tourist traps. He came within an inch of blurting it now, or the demon itching to destroy him did. Instead he managed a more rational response.

"I mean I can't quite figure out the way of life we're developing here," he said, toying with his dessert fork though they were still eating roast lamb. "Do you really want the donkey carts and mud hovels you can only get to in three hours by jet?"

Lumpkin threw his head back and roared, leading off a burst of laughter that took Tattersall by surprise. He had been satirizing them. Now their frankly amused reaction made him smile himself, quickly restored his spirits, and encouraged him to develop his point.

"I mean if we really want to slow down, get back to a really easy pace, why, board a supersonic plane and *zzt*, be zipped through space at a thousand miles an hour by all means. In a twinkling we're back to lazy days on rutted back roads, where the tempo of human life has not changed in five thousand years. Soon, they say, fifteen minutes in a rocket will get you all the natives you want in two-wheeled carts, flicking flies from the rumps of water buffaloes."

Lumpkin nearly choked. "That's rich. Of course he's absolutely — It is a crazy — I mean just flying here from Chi makes me — And then all these other —" He gave off, simply pointing helplessly to Tattersall with tears in his eyes.

Tattersall became the hit of the table. Even Mayo's fiancé, he was pleased to see, caught her eye and exchanged smiles of amusement with her. By the time they were through coffee and the ladies had climbed the stairway for half an hour in Lucy's sitting room, he was even resigned to the harmonizing scheduled to follow.

Tattersall had no basic objection to men raising their voices in song, provided they did not link arms, or engage in any of the more oppressive forms of camaraderie. He had done that sort of thing once, the time around the fountain, of course, when he had burned his academic bridges behind him. He could stand it once more if he had to in order to make progress on the road taken. One had to play ball, to butter people up in any profession. He preempted the piano as a means of partially detaching himself from the group, which included, besides himself and Wurlitzer and Lumpkin, a man named Matthews who permitted himself to be recruited as a first tenor in default of anything better. He stood behind Tattersall and to the right, Wurlitzer and Lumpkin behind him and to his left, in that order, thus conforming to the traditional positions of the male quartet.

They sang *Danny Boy, The World Is Waiting for the Sunrise, You're the Cream in My Coffee, Rose of the Rio Grande,* and other such favorites. After listening dutifully for a bit, the other male guests unobtrusively began a card game, so that the singers were more or less left to themselves. That made them more relaxed, with better and more pleasing results. Lumpkin commented on "that lyric tenor" also tickling the ivories, humorously but with detectable appreciation. He organized an arrangement of *My Baby Just Cares for Me* more or less around Tattersall. Tattersall took the air while the others wove in a "bum bum ba bum" background, pulling on their noses to obtain a humming effect — an extreme from which Tattersall was at least exempt since his hands were otherwise occupied. "We'll walk it in, nice and easy, and you sort of walk the piano in under yourself, Hank," Lumpkin said. They practiced it several times, pausing here and there to polish it up, or over some passage in which Lumpkin spotted a chance for one of those luscious minor chords that are the barbershop quartet's special joy. Then they ran through it without interruption. They were rewarded with a round of applause for which they were not prepared, for the ladies had returned and were listening.

"You do have a nice voice," Lumpkin told Tattersall in his own booming bass, when at last they disbanded and plucked their brandies from the piano.

"For the bathtub."

"That's just what I'm talking about. Just what's good about it. Great for this stuff that we've been singing, which is at its best when it has an amateur quality about it. And you know what? I think television's ripe for a program of old-fashioned barbershop harmony. This whole camp fad proves it. It shows a nostalgia for corn that people won't admit in this sophisticated day and age, so they smuggle it in the side door. I hate that. If you've got heart, come out and say so! Don't you?"

"Sure," Tattersall said, backing off an inch as he cast an eye at Wurlitzer.

"Or maybe something like the Street Singer would go again. Remember him on the radio years ago, Harry?"

"I certainly do," Wurlitzer said. "Arthur Tracy. I can hear his theme song now. *Martha.* How it used to get them. Here." He laid a palm unequivocally on his midriff.

"I'd like to hear that right now. Hank, how about it?"

There was nothing for Tattersall to do but permit himself to be coaxed back to the piano. "Martha, rambling rose of the wildwood . . ." he sang, throwing his head back and gazing at the far ceiling. A lock of his black hair dangled over his forehead. "Martha, with your fragrance divine . . ."

When the applause was finished, it was still Lumpkin who held the stage. The subject was evidently an obsession with him.

"That's what I'd like to hear on television," he said, pointing a fat thumb sideways in the direction of Tattersall, who was attempting another retreat. "Hell, we could even call it the Street Singer again. Or the Hurdy-gurdy Man, or the Peanut Vendor. He pauses every block or so with his pushcart and sings his heart out, gazing up at the windows out of which people are leaning, throwing dimes and quarters into the street. Or coming down to buy his peanuts, or whatever. I've even thought of a theme song I'd like. *There's a Long, Long Trail A-winding.* Do you know that one, Hank?"

By the time he had obliged with that, Tattersall thought he had earned a hearing for his idea. Without further preliminary he pinned Lumpkin into a corner behind the piano and, finishing off his brandy, said he wished to propose a commercial series. Lumpkin thought he meant a series of programs which would have commercial appeal, and Tattersall had first to straighten that out. When he did, Lumpkin said, "Oh, I see what you mean. OK. Shoot."

Tattersall cleared his throat in preparation for the opening sample, and, mimicking an announcer's voice, said:

"Are you sick of scouring powders that *say* they'll get your oven clean but don't?"

"Yeh-heh-heh," Lumpkin laughed.

"Wait. That's not the punchline." He started over again. "Are you sick of scouring powders that say they'll get your oven clean but don't? Or those pots and pans, to say nothing of that grimy, filthy sink? Is your whole kitchen an absolute and utter mess? Have a Kickola."

In a pause Lumpkin took to be pregnant, but which Tattersall knew to be barren, Lumpkin waited, his eyes shining expectantly. His eyes seemed to enlarge in anticipations of this sort, his ruddy face to grow redder. His brow glistened as he nodded. It was a good job that his mouth was only moderate size, as it was flung wide in flights of mirth, and even stood open in moments of readiness for them.

Tattersall sighed, and said, "That's it. If that's the way the whole house looks, when it seems as though you'll never catch up, it's a losing battle, we recommend that that's the time to reach for a bottle of good old, ever-reliable Kickola."

"But it's not a kitchen aid. We don't handle them at all. It's a soft drink."

"I know."

"But the two have no connection."

"That's just it. That's the whole point. It's the Absurd applied to advertising. The despair thing, you see, man in an irrational universe, deaf to his pleas, indifferent to his needs. Not merely the acceptance, but the very adoption, of absolute and total pointlessness. I think we're ready for adult plugs."

"Me too . . ." Lumpkin's gaze began to wander, and his face suddenly went slack, as though, numbed by an evening of fellowship, he could not for the moment be expected to cope with subtleties. Tattersall shot another accusing glance at Wurlitzer, but he was busy talking to some women. Tattersall plowed doggedly ahead, as though he were plodding through a bog in a dream. His legs suddenly felt tired. He sighed again, his hands in his trouser pockets.

"Have all brands of cigarettes let you down? Doesn't any you've ever tried have that rewarding, satisfying, deep-down flavor you've been looking for? Forget it and have a Kickola instead."

Lumpkin nodded. "I think I get it now, but —"

"Are you tired of coffees that don't really pick you up?" Tattersall's tone abruptly changed. His voice took on a shrill edge, and he removed at least one hand from his pocket to seize Lumpkin by the lapel when Lumpkin threatened to wander off in the direction his gaze had. "Have you got your belly full of fountain pens that leak," he continued grimly through his teeth, "not only staining your fingers but causing smudges on your letters, so that you have to write them all over again? Treat yourself to a refreshing Kickola, now in the convenient, no-deposit, throwaway tin cans with the flip top."

"Yeh-heh-heh," Lumpkin laughed nervously. He pinched his large red nose and gazed down at the carpet. At the end of a pause intended by Tattersall to enable what he was saying to sink in, Lumpkin looked up again, to find Tattersall staring at his cranium. Lumpkin gave him the sort of smile meant to humor a dangerous man. "Uh —"

"Or if we want to go into complete surrealism, as we probably will later, once we've educated the public this far — more doctors drink Kickola than any other soft drink. *The two have no connection whatever, you see.* Why is it a recommendation for a soda pop that doctors drink it? It isn't. There's a balmy irrelevance to it that gets the audience with us right away. The entire series will be like that," Tattersall told him firmly. "They will be all non sequiturs, every last bleeding goddamned — "

"Yeah, I . . . ." Though the response was affirmative in nature, Lumpkin shook his head as he muttered it, like a dazed boxer picking himself up off the floor. He seemed to have buckled under the remorseless rain of complexities to which he had been subjected. After hearing out several more sample Dadaist plugs, he said he liked the idea very much but that there were difficulties. "It's very literate. There's no doubt about that. One of the most far-out I've ever heard. But there's a twofold problem. It needs the right product as *well* as the right show. Leaving aside whether Kickola's the right product, yes or no — let's give it the benefit of the doubt and say yes — it still needs the right show. And I think you'll admit that not by any stretch of the imagination will it fit this kind of program I have in mind. You couldn't throw sophisticated commercials into a Street Singer."

"You really intend to do that?"

"Yes. The more I think of it the better I like it. I've talked myself into it tonight. I think the time is ripe, right now, for a revival of that kind of show. Or variation of it. And you may think me crazy, but you know what? I can see you in it."

"In what"

"The Street Singer."

"Why couldn't I sing the songs in the bathtub. That's my bag. I do it all the time. And the acoustics are terrific. The Bathtub Tenor."

"It wouldn't have enough mobility. It would be too confining. Plus you can't show a man in the bathtub on television."

"I see what you mean."

"But the other way, yes. I have hunches about those things." Lumpkin laughed again. He had recovered his good humor. His eyes sparkled as he appraised Tatter-sall. "But I'd want a natural voice — untrained, the way a primitive painter is untrained. That's essential. So don't go taking any lessons on me, Hank."

"There's no danger of that."

"It wouldn't kill you to try it on for size at one of the studios," Lumpkin said. "And give me a buzz if you get any more adult commercials."

eight

TATTERSALL was hammering out a black commercial. "Do you hate your very guts? Have you got a bellyful of those insides, winding in and out of one another down there in a manner for which there is no excuse, getting your excretory and reproductive organs entangled in one of the great booboos of evolution? Are you nauseated with the very universe, in, and to, whose vast, drowned depths the finest idea is no more than the entrails themselves, as the late Justice Holmes suggested? Have you, along with the late Isak Dinesen, come to see man as an exquisite instrument for converting vintage claret into urine? Do you see us as no more than a swarm of maggots proliferating a moment in 'an old chaos of the sun,' as the late Wallace Stevens put it? Late, late, they're all late! Do you wish you were late yourself? Dead and done with the whole stinking fraud . . ."

This commercial had already run to fourteen pages — roughly between forty-five hundred and five thousand words — and the end was not yet in sight. Not nearly. It would be a half-hour program in itself, interspersed with interruptions of one or two minutes of music, reversing the customary pattern. He wanted a prime time-slot for it, such as Sunday night either just preceding or directly following Ed Sullivan, with an actor of some authority reading it, like Morris Carnovsky (certainly, since his devastating Lear, one's first choice). The sponsor was not too important, but it might be the makers of Pepto-Bismol, since the emphasis was upon nausea and disgust. Their alacrity in rhyming the name of the product with "dismal" indicated the necessary resilience and maturity.

Tattersall had finished the fifteenth page and now screwed in the sixteenth.

"Do you think a man's retch should exceed his gasp?" he hammered out. "Do you sometimes think you'd like to cut out this meandering tripe with that Japanese souvenir knife your Aunt Susie —"

He saw Wurlitzer galloping down the hall toward his office door and quickly twisted the paper in the roller so what he had written was invisible. He managed to slip the rest of the manuscript into a desk drawer and slide it casually shut as Wurlitzer entered.

"Hello, Hank. I want to show you a pilot layout for a new series we're really keen about." Wurlitzer was carrying a portfolio. He set it down on the desk, and was about to open it when he turned to take Tattersall in more closely. "Christ, you look like something the cat dragged in. What's the matter?"

"My liver. It keeps secreting unmitigated gall."

"Yeah, well, nothing better than good old Carter's little pills. God, you do look like you've been pulled through a hedge backwards all right. Been working too hard?" Wurlitzer glanced down at the paper in the typewriter. In the three weeks since the party, Tattersall had had one more "are you sick of" accepted, but it had been written before the party. Since then he had entered a new period. While, admittedly, a note of pessimistic bitterness had crept into his stuff, it had also, he thought, grown in depth and resonance. "I'm sorry Lumpkin didn't cotton to the idea," Wurlitzer now said for the third or fourth time.

"It doesn't fit in with this Street Singer show he wants to do."

"No, I can see it doesn't. I told you he was sharp as a tack. Look at this."

The series of which Wurlitzer spread out a rough mockup on Tattersall's desk was one Mayo had whipped up on spec for an airline client. The central theme was a humorous, sophisticated play on the use of jet planes as a way of getting to primitive countries for relaxed holidays in a low key. One layout, which set the self-twitting tone, showed a toothless yokel grinning invitingly beside an ass-drawn vehicle of rude construction, over a caption reading, "Like to ride donkey carts? Get aboard one of our Boeing Super 707's. We'll have you on one before you know it." And so on. You were to take advantage of space travel to come by its welcome reverse, in lands where the tempo hadn't changed since the days of the Roman Empire, or even those of Belshazzar.

"That adult?" Wurlitzer said, beaming. "That an adult idea?"

"It's great," Tattersall said. "How did she ever get it?"

"God only knows. Who knows how those brainstorms hit you, what puts these bees in your bonnet? But the thing is, I wanted you to be one of the first to see it, because she's a student of yours. You can take a certain amount of pride in her."

"Yes, that's right. Well, she's coming along fine."

The only way for Tattersall to behave, after the client snapped it up, was in an adult fashion. Which meant, to say nothing. And what was there to say? If he hadn't sensed an advertising campaign in what he himself was running on about, that was nobody's funeral but his own. It certainly wasn't Mayo's. If she had the wit to spot its potential, so much the better for her. Could you say she had stolen the idea any more than Tattersall had stolen the idea he was working on from his wife, just because he had happened to see her light up a cigarette under certain circumstances? That he couldn't get his off the ground was not her fault.

He avoided her around the office, guiltily skirting corridors in which she might be encountered, slipping shamefacedly out to lunch at hours he knew would not coincide with hers. He would stand behind the now permanently closed door of his office and, his ear to the crack, listen for her in the hall. He could recognize her tread, as he could that of Wurlitzer and almost everyone of importance, and her whispering voice too. She often went out to lunch with a gay little group which included Crowley, the head of the copy department, and an older woman named Kay Corcoran, who was in charge of photography and photographic layouts. She worked in close touch with both of them now. Tattersall could sometimes hear them talking about finalizing things, or firming them up. Once about a piece of text for which someone was proposed who could subtle it up.

When glutted by these corruptions of the English language he would speed by cab to those bars where now it seemed to him to be spoken in something more like its purer form, and where he would resume his sagas to all who would listen, if only a barkeeper nodding mechanically as he wiped his glasses.

"So I says listen, wise ass, I wouldn't say dat last remark was very prudent wisdom-wise. Unless what you want is a little knuckle pie I says, revolving my fist suggestively under his kisser, if you now what I mean . . ."

These were not the Third Avenue taverns discovered and taken up by white-collar professionals pouring out of Gabardinesville at high noon and six o'clock. No. These lay in the other direction from Madison and Fifth, the far west side where they were to be found among warehouses and trailer-truck garages, just short of the dense, polyphonic clutter of the river docks. There one also roosted at lunch counters where one ordered directly in the jargon in which the waitresses passed one's wishes on into the kitchen. "Fried two sunnyside I guess, Maisie, and a pair down, no b." Or, "I'll have a b.l.t. on white toast, hold the mayo."

Back in his office, he worked on the commercial with his door shut. He felt it to be flowing beautifully. "Are you sick of being tired and tired of being sick? Get a bottle of those sedatives the French make in suppository form. Your friendly neighborhood druggist will tell you what you can do with them. A dozen should be about right." That was his ending. And, having that, he could work on the rest of it with confidence and leisure, giving himself his head. It was already ten thousand words, and he felt he could go on for another ten, twenty, fifty or a hundred thousand. It was only a question of how much time he had.

For Tattersall knew that his days were numbered here. The very extent to which he was let be proved it. No one asked to see copy any more, because they all knew the axe was going to fall, sooner or later, and till it did he was indulged. Wurlitzer he seldom saw, Wise he never had. Maybe Wise didn't even exist, except as an abstract or symbolic personification of the tedious latter-day suffix. (Tattersall could never forgive Dylan Thomas for using it in one of the most haunting lines he ever wrote: "Altarwise by owl-light in the halfway-house.")

But though he was indulged, he did not indulge himself. He now lashed himself to work as never before. He wasted not a minute of the company's time (in contrast to the agency stars who loafed away hours of it) but got there at ten on the dot and left on the stroke of six, with strictly an hour for lunch and no more. Between times, he stayed at his desk and sweat blood over the commercial. He sweat blood over it simply *because* it was no use. It became a point of honor with him. Standards hopelessly adhered to are by that very token more to be commended than those pursued in the hope of gain. Indeed, his very failure validated him as an exponent of futility, especially in this game. "I stink, therefore I am" — how much more convincing a self-postulation is that than its Cartesian original, involving, as it does, evidence so much more palpable to one's fellowmen than mere cogitation. Corroboration is wrung from them.

So Tattersall gave the doomed job his best while he

had it, after which it would be a question of what he would do next — and how long.

For he sensed that the trend of his life was irreversibly downward, and that each decline would occur in a progressively shorter cycle. He couldn't have said why, he simply had a hunch. He saw his life as a narrowing spiral, precipitated toward a point unknown but preordained by fate. Funnel-shaped, like a whirlwind or waterspout. Or put another way, the story of his life was like a book with ever shorter chapters, spinning him giddily toward its conclusion. He did not know what his end would be, or where or when, only that his failure would be flamboyant. It would possess an eloquence alien to the monochromes of achievement all around him.

One morning during the week of Thanksgiving he was taking a coffee break in a restaurant in the arcade of the building where he worked, called the Ad Lib. He was alone. In the booth behind him, Crowley, the copy head, was sitting with two or three other klatschers. Mayo was not one of them. She never went down for coffee. Unaware of Tattersall's presence, they were gossiping about him.

"Harry seems to think he's a one-shot," Crowley said. "Not that he's gotten anywhere even with that idea. It's not jelling. It's laying an egg. Which leaves him a noneshot."

"He probably belongs on a campus," Kay Corcoran said. "So they're really thinking of letting him go? I understand they had a kind of six-months' trial period in mind, which is about up."

"At the end of the year, yes. Harry says trial is the word for it, too. For everyone." They laughed. "He says he doesn't mind handing out these fellowships now and then to the ivory tower boys, but they have to come through, and they can't go on indefinitely. You can only go so far supporting intellectuals."

It was then that Tattersall resolved he must grasp the initiative himself, by executing some gesture that would show he could not be fired — he was quitting. But what kind of gesture? One that would combine in his exit a dignity of style with a content of meaningful protest. He racked his brains in vain for the answer. A last check with a little severance pay and a notice that his services were no longer required seemed the lusterless and bathetic end that awaited him here. It was just around the corner, for the holidays were approaching fast. It was the sight of decorations going up around the office that made him suddenly remember something.

He had for a long time heard about the Christmas custom at Double W. How Wurlitzer played Santa Claus with the annual bonuses by entering an improvised stage in uniform, dropping his sack before the lighted tree, and drawing from it bags containing the employees' checks, reading the names aloud and flinging them to each in turn. There were probably a few gold pieces, or some other ballast, in them to bolster the resemblance to pouches of treasure.

He recalled the instinctive distaste he had experienced when first hearing of this rite, long before coming to work here. Now his repugnance increased. Nor could he see how an underling in the corporation could fail to share it. He made a few tactful but probing inquiries, and learned that most of them did. They resented being treated like feudal serfs, having what was their due tossed to them as sops by the lord of the manor. But what could they do? He was the Boss, and clearly relished the role, which swelled his own ego in total, even though perhaps understandable, oblivion to what it was doing to theirs. The results of his canvass convinced Tattersall what he ought to do on their behalf, by way of valedictory — or rather by way of making his valedictory count — but he doubted whether he would have the courage. As saints were said to go slightly out of their minds in order to consummate acts of self-immolation, he would have to go slightly out of his.

There was certainly no want of Dutch courage at the office party in question. Everyone was well oiled by the time for the ritual — which was probably why they didn't mind it any more than they did. A bell rang, causing voices abruptly to stop and silence to reign. Wurlitzer popped from behind a drawn curtain, bent under his bag and shouting, "Ho-ho-ho!" An avuncular self-satisfaction was discernible underneath the silver whiskers. Tattersall stole a glance at Mayo, to whom he had so far managed not to speak. She stood with folded arms in the crowd, her face expressionless. He wondered whether Wurlitzer had a pillow stuffed into his costume, and if so, whether it was a bed pillow or a sofa cushion. He wanted to laugh, and yet he was also sweating. He took a nervous gulp from the glass of nearly straight bourbon in his hand. He had certainly drunk more than enough, but whether it was steeling him or not he was at a loss to know.

"Overton!" Wurlitzer called out. "Pembroke! Matthews! Crowley!" digging the little sacks from his bag and flinging one to each in turn. He had apparently located their positions with notable accuracy before-hand, perhaps by peeking through the curtain.

Tattersall emptied his glass and set it down on a windowsill. Perspiration covered his brow, and ran in rivulets down his ribs. His cheeks were flushed. The hot room swam in a mist.

At last he heard his name called. "Tattersall!"

A bag sailed through the air toward him. It went over his head, so that he had to make a leap to catch it, like an outfielder snaring a high one against the left-field wall. There was a burst of laughter at this. He held it a moment in his hand. For a second he hesitated. His courage was failing him. He couldn't act. A kind of paralysis had overcome him. Then a cherished vision flashed into his mind — Christ beating the be-Jesus out of the money changers. But even that could not motivate him. The inspiration wasn't right. It was not self-destructive enough. He had another. Samson willing to bury himself in the ruins of the temple in order to bring it down upon the heads of the Philistines. He drew back his arm, held it cocked for a split second, and hurled the bag back at Santa Claus. It caught him squarely on the right ear before landing on the floor with a flat, deflating smack, like a beanbag someone had dropped in a game of catch.

nine

LUMPKIN walked the floor of the conference room with his hands in his hip pockets. Two television network executives whom he had flown in from Chicago to consult, on getting Tattersall's long-distance telephone call, wore the same expression of thought as his. One, a man named Bester who was a producer, sat with his lower lip thrust forward, while a director called Kohler tapped his chin with his fingertips and stared at a wall. They were trying to decide whether Tattersall should be a peanut vendor or sell flowers from a cart. They wanted some such occupation, with its aura of honest labor, to lend dimension to his image, even though it would be mainly that of street singer.

At last Bester said: "Why don't we shoot him both ways and see what we think then. Let me call prop and see if they've got both."

That was the decision that was reached. The property department had a flower cart, or at least a pushcart convertible to the purpose, as well as enough wax blooms of the sort required for the effect wanted. A bona fide popcorn-and-peanut wagon would take a little digging up. But they could shoot with the flower cart any time they wanted. Stage Five was free right now. So they all rose, including Tattersall who was on hand for the conference, and trooped down to the studios. There he was turned over to costume and makeup men, and after half an hour led out onto a sound stage for a screen test.

He had been put into dark work pants and denim shirt, with bright red and blue striped suspenders. The traditional bandana kerchief was knotted around his neck. His naturally wavy, and naturally abundant, black hair had been additionally frizzed upward at the ends with a curling iron, and a set of handlebar mustaches affixed to his upper lip. Lumpkin had distinctly not wanted to see him — or, rather, hear him — in a preliminary test as himself. Whether he was photogenic as himself was not the point. He wanted to see him cold, as the character he was intended to portray. "I want an ear of corn," he frankly warned them all. "I want schmalz, though without hokum. No hokum, but honest schmalz. I want an ear of corn." He was not laughing now. This was all heart.

The opening shot was of an empty street against the rising sun. A long vista, held for a moment, with no sign of human life. It was dawn. Then against this painted backdrop Tattersall materialized dramatically into view out of a side street, rounding the corner as he sang a chorus of *Santa Lucia*, pushing a cartful of violets and potted geraniums before him, head-on into the audience. He looked from left to right and back again as he sang, as to neighborhood folk gathered at the curb to listen, or to listeners hanging from upper-story windows. "Home of fair poesy, land of pure harmony," he sang, his voice rising sweet and thrilling on the morning air. His very tones evoked the virgin clarity of sunrise. The choice of theme song had struck Lumpkin as better than his original inspiration, *There's a Long Long Trail.*

It would be twenty-four hours before they could see the rushes, but everyone watching behind the glass panel was cautiously excited. It was an excitement borne out by the result. This was a find. Only one thing persistently troubled Lumpkin — the choice of a theme song. He didn't like *Santa Lucia* any better than he did *Long, Long Trail,* or *My Little Gray Home in the West* either, for that matter. Kohler came up with a suggestion. "How about the *Neapolitan Street Song?*" he said. "After all he *is* a street singer, and with a certain Latin flavor. What could be more natural?"

They did a take on it, and it came out quite well. Again, though, Lumpkin was dubious about something. This time it was the contents of the pushcart.

"I'm not sure flowers are quite it," he said. "Neither is the peanut vendor. Simplicity but not fragility, is what I want. *Earthiness.* I want it strong."

The flowers were removed, and, almost extemporaneously, several stalks of bananas were flung onto the cart. Everyone smiled. This was it.

Thus was born the little Italian huckster known to millions who, weary of a world of strife as well as of the bewildering accumulations and accelerations of the Space Age, turned on their television sets at six o'clock every Wednesday evening for a quarter-hour's respite in his simple songs. He both came out of the dawn singing, "Napoli . . . Napoli . . ." and vanished into the sunset doing so, leaving the sense of a simple workaday's joy in between. The fadeout was a last-minute inspiration of Bester's, incorporated barely in time for the three weeks of regional trials with which the show was to be test-marketed in smaller stations in out-of-the-way places. Reactions to the pilot programs were all that the sponsors and producers had hoped. They signed Tattersall for thirteen weeks, with option to renew.

He threw himself as heartily into his new identity in real life as he did before the cameras. The day the contracts were signed he hurried home clutching a posy of violets, and nothing would do but that he and Sherry go out and celebrate. He was growing his own mustache now, training the ends upward rather than in the handlebar style. "We make lots a da mon," he said, throwing his arms around her. "We have lots a da fun."

The occasion struck him as calling for a spaghetti house of which he had heard a good deal, known as Mama Bellini's. He proposed to her in the cab going over. It was love at first sight, he said, when he saw her in a new rose-colored dress, with her hair cropped and swept back from the temples in a fresh way, and he hoped it was the same with her. "We get a married," he said. "We live a happy. This time it's a work."

Mama Bellini was a clucking, hovering maternal sort who sent over a bottle of Chianti when she learned they had just become engaged. A fiddler on duty leaned across the table and scraped out a chorus of O Sole Mio, in which Tattersall joined. "We have bambino in eight, nine months," Tattersall said, causing both Mama Bellini and Sherry to blush. Mama Bellini waddled up a flight of stairs to her flat above, and returned with a pair

126

of white booties which she pressed into Sherry's hand. She would not hear of their being refused, for, though a kind of family heirloom, they were only one of a dozen circulating pairs she had knitted in her time, as matriarch of a clan now numbering upwards of thirty grandchildren. Her husband, Guido, was dead. Looking narrowly at Sherry, she said, "You're not Italian."

"No," Tattersall answered for her. "I marry high. I marry a fancy," and gave Mama Bellini a winking nudge. He summoned the waiter and ordered *zabaglione* for two. "And I think a bottle of Asti Spumone."

"If you mean Asti Spumante, the Italian champagne, yes, we've got that cold," the waiter said.

"That will be fine."

Home again, Tattersall sat at the piano polishing up some of the songs agreed on for his repertoire. He wore a silk dressing gown and smoked a big cigar. Midway through *The Spanish Cavalier*, he happened to glance into a wall mirror and saw the reflection of Sherry sitting in a chair. Her hands were folded in her lap, and she was watching him without expression. Aware that he was returning her gaze, she rose and excused herself. "I think I'll go to bed," she said.

To say that Tattersall lost himself in the role is to mean that he found himself in it. He *became* the simple wop huckster of the side streets, flinging his melodic gold to the very rooftops. He threw himself into the songs as one might throw himself into the water, with total immersion. Till performance and actuality became one, as they often do in what is called real life. The distinction between reality and illusion vanished nicely. Around the studio, he had the flamboyance that often goes with simplicity. He became known for his outbursts of Latin temper. When warned that his singing was taking on too much art, too much conscious poise and polish, and faced with the insinuation that he was taking lessons on the sly, thereby putting his whole quality in jeopardy, he reported, "That's a big a lie! That's a false a hood!" He made a rather convincing little dago at that. It was the Celtic strain in his mixed English heritage, through which had been passed along the liquid eyes and the twisted raven locks.

Since Double W still handled the commercials for the show — simple straightforward squibs as befit its nature — he could not always avoid seeing his former associates from the agency, nor, indeed, did he try. He never encountered the Wurlitzers, either of them, but he did Crowley and Mayo. He ran into Mayo while on his way to lunch and, since she was alone, invited her to join him. She demurred at first, shifting the strap of her bag nervously on her shoulder, but sensing that his own manner was now free of constraint, she finally agreed, and permitted herself to be whisked by cab to a nearby spaghetti house which he fancied. He recommended the spaghetti Caruso there.

"How's things with the jet set?" he asked at long last, swabbing up sauce with a crust of bread. The time it had taken him to raise the point, as well as the negligent fashion in which he did, indicated how little he cared. "They still like horses and buggies?"

Mayo smiled into her virtually untouched plate, twining a few strands of spaghetti around her fork. She wore the silver-white lipstick then in vogue, almost like aluminum radiator paint, and its pallor gave her a vulnerable, even helpless look, as of one easily victimized. By shifting the subject onto her novel, through a tranquil murmur about the impossibility of ever really pinning down where your ideas came from, she gave the scene the quality of a dream they were jointly dreaming. Paying only the vaguest heed to what were in fact dwindling echoes of classroom days, Tattersall wished her luck with the book when it was finally published, at the same time trying to catch the waiter's eye. This was an implied but clear declaration that he did not in the least regret the informed civilities and behavioral restraints prevailing in the days when he had been an Anglo-Saxon. "In the end all art is, you know, autobiographical," Mayo said as he screwed about in his chair with a hand half-raised in readiness to flag the elusive waiter. Something he had completely forgotten chose that moment in which to pop curiously to mind again. In the opera, Gioconda was a street singer.

"Didn't Flaubert even say 'Emma Bovary c'est moi'?" Mayo whispered on about literary matters.

He nodded vaguely, making a chucking noise in order to dislodge something from his side teeth, at the same time brushing his verdant mustachios upward with his forefingers. He was quite right in offering himself as free of complexity now. He no longer wrote himself upbraiding letters. Those wearing analytical diatribes had ceased to encumber his mail. To the last, long screed from the Doppelgänger calling him "without a doubt the greatest single pseudo-sado-masochistic self-castigator around," he had merely tersely replied, "Sounds a great."

He made every effort to see to it that Sherry rode the crest of this wave with him. He liked to have her around for the shootings — for the show was taped — and after each one they would hurry off to one or another of the steadily proliferating "their" places for lunch or dinner, as the occasion befell. The thirteen weeks were renewed, then renewed again, making for the customary year of thirty-nine, to be followed by a summer replacement.

They spent the summer in Italy, flying to Rome and then meandering by rented car through the countryside from one fabled city to another. They spent wildly. He threw his money around. They bought lace in Naples, crystal in Venice, linens in Florence, and art objects everywhere. Their air express bill alone was staggering. Henrico developed quite a tire around his middle from all the rich food. Their lunches were dinners, their dinners banquets. They made a prolonged stay in Padua, which he had adopted as his birthplace. He remembered, from a previous incarnation long, long ago, a college musical for which he had written the lyrics. The story had loosely concerned a pair of lovers traveling with the international set, as it was then called, with episodes giving the flavor of different cities through which they passed on their madcap rounds. One had concerned Padua, and Tattersall had written patter rhymes running: "Well, here we are again in Padua. Now, darling, don't be madua back again in Padua. You should be very, very gladua with me again in Padua. How very, very badua not to be more gladua, instead of being sadua, back once again in Padua . . ." It had been pointed out to him that Cole Porter had worked in much this same vein, a rotten coincidence that had left a bad taste in his mouth and nearly put him out of sorts with the whole show. Sitting in a café now, all these years later, he could smile at the memory. Padua was their last stop but one before flying home again. There, they relived their enchanted summer unpacking the treasures they had amassed on it.

Then as suddenly as it had all sprung up the whole thing collapsed. It burst like a bubble.

Henrico, as he was called, went on the air again late that September, along with all the returning fall shows and all the new ones. But from the very first broadcasts there was a noticeable, indeed a marked, drop in his Trendex. He laid it partly to stupidity in the choice of his summer replacement, namely a quartet of the barbershop variety dear to Lumpkin, so close in essential feeling to the Singing Huckster that, when he went back on, it was to face a public suddenly glutted with heart, with folk art, with nostalgic innocence. They were sick to death of the peddler and his *Neapolitan Street Song*. They were sick of his pushcart and the humble streets down which he trundled it where the heart of humanity beat. They were sick of the sight of him and the sound of him. His Trendex skidded and slid like a boulder bouncing down a mountainside. His contract was canceled. He was out on the street.

He and Sherry had saved very little when they were riding high, and soon found themselves trying to live on her money, a precarious existence at best. Bitterness with his summary dismissal rankled. He had forgotten there was a clause in the contract giving his sponsors the right to cancel it; not renewing was the worst he had thought they could do. Flareups of Mediterranean temper were frequent, though no longer of any avail in the circumstances. They did not even serve to relieve his own feelings of resentment, which deepened and festered inside him. He tried to reach Lumpkin whenever he heard he was in town, and even once or twice by long-distance telephone at his Chicago office, without success. Lumpkin was always "out" once the secretary was onto who was calling. He was in conference, or auditioning a Swiss yodeler, or a family of German bellringers. In the end Lumpkin signed on a Gospel singer for eleven in the morning, whose theme song was *Beulah Land*. By that time Tattersall had already returned to coping with the problem of making a living.

On being fired, he had been given the pushcart as a souvenir. It was his to keep. One morning he rose early and trundled it to a nearby produce market. He filled it with fruits and vegetables and set off among the back streets.

The first few days he fared poorly. He laid it to his lack of experience, the time it naturally takes to get the hang of anything — until he remembered something he had learned in his days in show biz. It is that you can't confuse people. He made the mistake of continuing to sing. This made him both a singer and a vendor — therefore neither. Those who might have thrown him a coin or two for his songs refrained from doing so because they assumed he made his living as a huckster. Housewives who might otherwise have emerged to haggle in a neigh-borly fashion with him over his wares could not take him seriously, or rather had no faith in merchandise he ap-parently needed to throw in songs to sell. On the air he had been clearly a singer — the good folk seen buying his produce were not real, merely atmospheric. In real life he must be one or the other. So he stopped singing, except to bawl out "Bananas, string beans, sweet corn! Get your fresh fruits and vegetables here!" in his rich voice, to announce his approach in the peddler's immemorial cry.

He soon learned the neighborhoods in which he could most lucratively ply his trade, where there were fewer stores in competition, where the housewives liked him best, and he them, and so on. There are always streets and alleys up which the hawker does better than others, and his route readily crystallized around them. One street skirted a large university campus, and under its shady maples Tattersall loved to pause. He grew fond of the students who stopped to buy an apple or a banana, or a few figs, or, in the case of girls who were married and did their own cooking, more substantial provisions. Many would stop to chat, having grown fond of the little immigrant from Padua. He amused them with his stories, and talked often about his beloved birthplace nestled among the vine-clad hills of northern Italy. Particularly, they found his salty, straightforward blend of quaintness and assertiveness much to their taste. His unfamiliarity with the American idiom especially endeared him to the young students. "I like to stop with da kids and chew a da cloth," he would say, provoking gales of affectionate laughter from them.

Tattersall's ability to sustain this level was not matched by his wife, or appreciated by her. Loyally as she exemplified the breed of woman who lives absolutely in and for her husband, the number and variety of identities with which she was called upon to amalgamate her own became finally too much. He came home one afternoon to find her soberly having a drink.

"I had lunch with Lucy today to talk about you. She called me, actually, to discuss it. She's been discussing it with Mayo, of course Harry, and lots of others. They're all pretty much agreed. They've got a theory that it's all an act."

"Act?"

"Yes. Some kind of put-on. A devastating satire aimed at all of them, in which you're trying to say they're all hucksters. Or we're all hucksters."

"Well, I wouldn't know about those literary a symbolism."

Devastating, at any rate, was the sequel to the exchange, introduced by Sherry as preparation for her plan. She said the next day: "I think I should go see my mother again. She's not well, so probably I'll stay a little longer this time." She took most of her clothes and drove off in the car, which was in her name.

Her departure brought Tattersall up with a start. He quite appreciated her point of view, and saw the necessity of digging his heels in and arresting the long decline that had led to it, and then of reversing it. In a decision aimed at winning her back, he quit peddling, sold the pushcart, shaved off his mustache and got his hair cut, and resolved henceforth to accept only white-collar jobs.

A friend in the state highway department got him work writing safety slogans for use on turnpikes and parkways. "Anxious to get there? Slow down," was an example of the maxims he coined in that capacity — a short-lived one since the demand was naturally limited and the pay slight, the work being assumed on a free-

lance basis. On the same basis he next turned out witticisms for the Standard Oil people. These were the
humorous one- or two-line pleasantries that greet patrons
and passing motorists from the bulletin boards of filling
stations throughout the country. Tattersall's aphorisms
were a cut above what is usually found there, but unsuit-
able on other grounds, or perhaps for that reason. A
typical sample was, "Marriage is for two people who
want each other the worst way" — a tone somewhat
more sardonic than the traffic would bear, at least the
traffic typified by average American Sunday drivers — to
say nothing of refinery executives. A warning, in effect
putting him "on probation," only served to sharpen the
cynicism and deepen the pessimism with which the
epigrams were already imbued. They grew in blackness
and obliquity both, as had the commercials before them.
The author was judged as harboring too bitter a vision of
reality for the Standard Oil people, and he was let go.
The last straw was: "Your Casanova type doesn't really
like women. Screw them all is in effect his motto." It
was really the last shot, fired in the knowledge that he
was going to be fired.

These two intervals of relative elevation in his lot
arrested only briefly its downward course, now precipi-
tately resumed. He took what he could get. He hired out
as a day laborer for a landscape gardener named Horvath. He knew from his own days as a home owner the
difficulty of getting landscape men to come, and that it
was readily translatable into their own trouble finding
decent help. So it was no surprise to Tattersall that
Horvath took him on without any experience. "Anybody
can pull op weeds and cot graz," Horvath said when

Tattersall, accosting two men coming out of a diner and heading for a parked truck, asked whether one of them were the boss. "Jomp on tailgate."

A smile twisted Tattersall's features as he did so, signaling a subtle change in his reaction to his fortunes, to his accelerating rhythm as an outcast. Each time he was out on his ear, now, or mucked something up, a kind of secret elation seized him. He was *glad*. It was a sensation he was powerless to resist. He was glad as he rode on the tailgate, onto which he had hoisted himself by the heels of his hands in a deft backward motion. To be a misfit in a tale told by an idiot is after all hardly the worst of fates. He swung his legs under him as they bounced along toward their next job, which was at a large Greek revival house set back among obviously long-neglected flower beds. He and the other helper, a silent Hungarian refugee named Barzack, were dropped off there together with a power mower and a wheelbarrow. Barzack was to cut the grass while Tattersall weeded in beds Horvath indicated, before rattling away again in the truck with the shouted warning that he would be back in a couple of hours.

Tattersall got on his knees and set to work.

The ground was soft from recent rains, and the plants easy to uproot. He worked with gusto, pulling weeds up and dropping them into the wheelbarrow by the hand-ful. He tried to remember their names from a brief and all too sketchy background as a Sunday putterer. Plan-tain, dock, purslane . . . And dandelion of course. The place was thick with dandelion.

He moved slowly through the bed on all fours. The sun was pleasant on his back, not too hot. A late morning sun. Creeping alone one edge of the bed, he saw that the crevices in a flagstone walk leading from a nearby back door had become overgrown with grass and other greenery, and he conscientiously pulled that up also.

In the midst of this attentive little digression, the screen door twanged open and the mistress of the house came running up the walk, waving her arms and shouting like a crazy woman.

"My herbs! Those are herbs you're pulling up for God's sake stop!"

On his knees, he grinned vacantly up. "Please?"

"Those aren't weeds — they're herbs. Precious herbs I've been cultivating carefully for five years, man!"

"Nix verstehen," Tattersall said, still smiling deferentially as he climbed to his feet. He spanked the dirt from his knees. "Nix sprechen der English . . ." He shrugged philosophically, taking the adversity in stride.

"Oh, my God," the woman moaned to herself, rolling her eyes. "Another foreigner. The help you have to . . ."

"Ja," Tattersall agreed.

She became patient, explaining in the broken English which for some reason we adopt in the attempt to communicate with aliens. "*Herbs. Herben.* You've upgepulled some — Here."

She stooped and crumbled a fragment of the uprooted treasures in her fingers, sniffed it, and held it out for Tattersall to do the same, which he obediently did. He inhaled the fragrance, nodding appreciatively.

"Ja, ja, stinken sie schön."

"So, herbs. Rosemary, basil —"

"Ah, Kinder? You kleine Kinder?"

"No, not children. *Plants,*" she said, pointing doggedly to the shambles at her feet. She began again. "Basil, tarragon, sage, thyme . . . ."

"Please?"

"Thyme, thyme!"

"Ah!" he nodded, understanding now, and pulled from his pocket a large watch which he held out by its cord for her to consult.

"No, no. Ich mean —" Her attempts to explain the ravages to the flagstone walk were interrupted by her discovery of similar havoc wreaked in the flower bed. "My Michaelmas daisies! My nicotiana! And oh my God, the evening primrose!" she shrieked. She fished several broad-leafed stalks from the heap in the wheelbarrow. "Can't you tell flowers from weeds when they're not in bloom? This is nicotiana. This — oh, what's the use. You obviously haven't had any experience. Never mind that now." She thrust some plants into his hands and pointed to the flower bed. "We've got to put them back, quick, there's not a moment to lose. Before it's too late. *In.* Sticken sie back in der — in der Erde."

"Oh, ja, ja," he said, nodding emphatically again to show he comprehended now. "Der Erde."

She had illustrated her order with a brisk pantomime about which there could be no mistake, and with which he as briskly complied. Getting back on his knees on der Erde, he replanted all the flowers she was able to sort out from among the weeds that still had roots on them. He watered them with a sprinkling can she fetched and filled herself, running as fast as she could in her ruffed mules.

That done as best it could be, she hauled a chair over

from the terrace and set it grimly down beside the bed on which he was at work, and in which she supervised him with the aid of a walking stick she went inside to get. She silently pointed it at each weed to be uprooted, waiting till Tattersall had disposed of it in the wheelbarrow before indicating the next. She was an elderly woman with a crown of white hair and a straight mouth. Tattersall's mute compliances were supplemented by an obliging, at times hangdog, smile, from which she would try to keep her gaze averted. Once in a while he would point inquiringly to a plant to show he wanted to learn, like a pupil eager to show his teacher he was doing his best, and she would nod agreement. Yes, he had identified a weed, correctly distinguished it from a flower. Sometimes she would shake her head. "No, that happens to be a trillium, just not in bloom now. A very, very schön, uh, Blumchen, very hard to grow, so lieber Gott touchen Sie him nicht." There were, conversely, plants with flowers which he was ordered *to* uproot, much to the bafflement of the simple kraut. "Maar sie got Blumen," he would say. "Nevertheless they're weeds," she would answer. "*In.*" And she would point to the wheelbarrow. One of these semantic victims was a tiny blue flower over which he pouted sympathetically before plucking it up and handing it as an offering to the grand lady, with the same humble smile. "Oh, my God," she said, looking away. "Talk about a will to fail."

Unable to carry on in this vein any longer after the bed had been weeded and another selected for attack, or at least uninclined to, the woman rose and walked around to the front where Barzack was cutting grass. He was not so beyond communication as not to grasp her wish, conveyed through more pantomime, that he change jobs with Tattersall till Horvath could be reached for consultation. So the Hungarian weeded while Tattersall spent the remainder of the morning wandering pleasantly behind the power mower.

Horvath put in an appearance shortly after noon, and following a brief conference with the woman carted Tattersall away to another job a couple of miles away. "Jomp on tailgate," he ordered with a weary sigh. They stopped at a small grocery store to let Tattersall pick up a bag of fruit and some cheese and sausage for his lunch.

The new mistress was an attractive young widow who was clearly of the class of Bored Women driven by the emptiness and ennui of existence to seek thrills in the form of affairs with their chauffeurs. The lean, tense stride and the restlessly darted glances bespoke suppressed sexual energy if anything did. The brief appraising look she shot at Tattersall as she crossed the patio told him everything he needed to know. Here the displaced and bumbling kraut could be dropped for a handsome buck nigger, exulting in the noonday of his manhood as he felled trees and pulled up boulders with his bare hands. He took off his shirt and tossed it onto a picket fence. His white teeth flashed as he worked. His naked biceps were like coiled serpents, and he walked with the fluid grace of the panther.

He flung himself under an elm to eat his lunch. Lying on his back, his legs spread in their tight jeans, he sank his teeth into an apple. From where he lounged, he could see an upstairs bedroom window, from which of course he was visible himself. A palm thrust negligently under his belt, he gazed up into the sunlit boughs as he chewed the juicy pulp of the fruit, spitting the pips with a lazy, animal ease — a sight to stir the most jaded female blood.

His belly full, he closed his eyes, the better to drink in the voluptuous warmth of the day. An arm flung across his brow, he dreamed on the darkening bronze of his skin, rejoicing in it. It would deepen through the long summer months, till the muscles rippling under it were indeed like a nest of coppery reptiles in whose toils any woman worth the name would love to find herself helpless caught. The very thought made her faint with bliss. A breeze from time to time fluttered the checkered shade in which he lay, and sent secret, liquid highlights slipping across his naked flesh. His mother bore him in the southern wild. He was sprung from hot jungle loins, and his blood had drunk the ichor of the sun.

A soft rustle different from that of the wind in the boughs was heard overhead. Like that of a shade being raised, or a curtain furtively parted. He was being watched, covertly savored above.

Carelessly, and with the same unconscious animal ease, he sat up. He stretched till his muscles nearly burst their glistening skin, his white teeth gleaming as he yawned. He could not resist a look, but he made his upward glance an accidental one. Sure enough, there was a silken form between the pale curtains, withdrawn as he looked. He rose and resumed his labors, now alert to any sound from the house. A quivering excitement had taken hold of him, but he did not look when he heard the back door open and the woman come out. Such adventuresses must be left to give their own signs.

Several minutes passed, during which he continued

working without so much as a glance toward the house. At last footsteps were heard approaching across the grass behind him. He could no longer control himself. He turned around.

Horvath came forward, clacking a pair of enormous clippers with which he had been trimming a hedge.

"She wants you to put your shirt on."

"Why?"

"She got guests coming pretty soon. Some other women. So get it on."

"Did you suggest she keep her own on? You done ask de lady dat?" Tattersall said, smiling with lazy tropical derision. His teeth gleamed.

"Well, get your shirt on, like I say she said. Otherwise she says you might offend the people she's got coming pretty soon."

"Lady Loverly's Chatter."

"What?"

"Nothing."

He put his shirt on, but Horvath finally had to let him go anyway. It wasn't working out. The same crooked little smile wreathed his lips as he took his pay and drifted off up the street again, a free man. He carried his coat flung over his shoulder, hooked on two fingers. The poor jigaboo gave up the flat in which he had been living and moved into a rooming house. As a result, Sherry had some trouble locating his whereabouts when she thought the time had come for another serious talk about where they stood — or rather where they were going — and what should be done. But she finally found him in a hall bedroom near the Pennsylvania Railroad tracks.

He took her out to dinner in a nearby chophouse. He

refused the ten dollar bill with which she insisted on paying for the meal, assuring her that, though he was unemployed at the moment, he had something lined up and would start work the following day. He was going to make a determined effort to better himself. He was going to sell a line of toilet articles door-to-door, and had to wait till he got his shirts back from the laundry before beginning. He could clearly pay for the dinner, and when he laid down the tip he said, "You've heard the expression, 'old money'? Well, just look at that dollar bill." It was so worn and tattered it was held together with a Band-Aid.

Back in his room, they drank beer. He seemed in good spirits. He gave her the single herniated armchair while he himself sprawled sociably out on the bed, stretching his lazy nigger length and gossiping with his engaging drawl. "C'meah," he said, patting the bed.

"No," Sherry said. She set her glass down. "Look, I can't go along with any more of this. I can't take any more. Or rather I don't want to."

She was as neat and crisp as ever, in a tailored blue suit down the front of which she periodically swept a hand, though there was nothing to brush away or tidy up, not a hair or speck of lint.

"I don't understand you any more, if I ever did," she continued. "What these kicks are that you go on, or what I'm supposed to do next. Now this Southern gentleman you've become, or whatever. I can't figure it out, unless you're looking for a character to fit your personality."

"We is all protean figures. Many-faceted, composed of varied and even contradictory elements, any of which can assume command at a given moment. We is like kaleidoscopes shaken into new forms by fresh nudges from a reality dat ain't pow'ful consistent either. Ah is not de effete and decadent intellectual dat y'all once knew. No *suh*. Ah is a new man, wit de primitive vitality and simple integrity dat we all craves. So mah me."

"No. I'm not going to marry you any more, Hank. But I'll tell you what I will do. I'll give you a divorce. We'll compromise. It's the next best thing. Then you can start fresh with somebody else, free and clear with somebody who may understand you better than I do. Or what you're trying to do, or want out of life."

He shook his head. "No. Y'all stick around, heah? If you won't grow old along wit me, den we grow young again, start fresh like kids. Cause a lifetime ain't enough to 'commodate de identities of which we is capable," he said, grinning his persuasive grin at her from the pillow. But his efforts were of no avail. On whatever note he strove to disarm or beguile her, whether he stretched out his lazy nigger length or poured out his simple wop heart, it did no good. She was adamant about bringing their relationship to an end.

At midnight she rose, assuring him that it would all be perfectly amicable, and that she would of course expect nothing from him, but that he would definitely hear from her lawyer. Then she left.

He heard her go down the stairs, get into her car and drive off. He lay silent a moment, and then, as though she were still there and could hear him, he shook his head sadly, and said, "I simply don't know what you want."

ten

TATTERSALL tilted his chair back against the white clapboard front of the rooming house, his heels hooked on the lower spindle. He clasped his hands behind his head, on which a plaid cap was shoved slightly forward, and gazed out at the world from under its visor. He chewed a match with an air of lazy colloquialism. He was known as Handyman Hank in the neighborhood to which he had now come. That he took only enough odd jobs to keep body and soul together represented, as much as it did shiftlessness, a certain renunciation of all vainglory, all acquisitive fume and fret. He was sitting on the front porch.

It was an evening in early autumn. Indian summer lingered, and the hum of reprieved insects filled the air together with the late cries of children at their play. Lace curtains blew softly at the open window beside which he lounged. A few neighbors still watered their patches of front lawn, and the gentle sibilance of their hoses was a steady, pleasant thread in the random weft of night sounds. East Maple was a crowded street of cottages and two-flat houses, on whose porches, in the warm weather, families still gathered, and passersby still paused to chat.

A car somewhat more impressive than most parked along the curb or traversing the street drew to a stop in front of the cottage, and a man and a woman alighted from it who were somewhat better dressed than most to be seen here. Tattersall instantly recognized them, but for the moment he gave no sign. He remained alert but absolutely motionless under the bent peak of the cap, like a lizard. For some reason, what crossed his mind as he saw his wife and Harry Wurlitzer spring from Wurlitzer's Cadillac was a postcard he had once got from a friend vacationing in San Antonio, reading: "The Alamo is now air-conditioned." It was one of those associations that bear no surface relation to the context in which they are evoked, only some kind of subterranean logic.

They were going to try again with him. It was the second time Sherry had brought Wurlitzer along to remonstrate with him, once in the old rooming house by the Pennsylvania tracks, and now here to where she had also managed to trace him. He was accompanying her for one last attempt to bring him to his senses. In doing so he was letting bygones be bygones. He was demonstrating his readiness to be big about the Christmas bonus incident — now in perspective seen as probably the first fissure in what had been taken to be a sound mind. "Is there nothing that means anything to you?" he had asked the first time, as the trains rumbled by. "Tell me, Hank. I'm always curious about this basic thing in a guy. Don't you believe in God?"

"No, and he doesn't believe in me."

Tattersall eyed them from under the cap until they

were well up the steps to the porch. Then he rose and shuffled over, the match wagging as he greeted them with a welcome word. "Well, well, I was just beginning to wonder who I could sit and chew the rag with tonight," he said in his amiable drawl. "And here you are. Mighty nice of you to call."

"Come on home, fellow," Wurlitzer said almost without preamble, laying a hand on Tattersall's shoulder.

"I am home. This is where I live."

Sherry and Wurlitzer rocked on the glider, while Tattersall perched his heels on the porch railing, up to which he had hitched his chair in order to be more sociable. He nodded to neighbors as they passed by on the sidewalk. "Evening, Mrs. Larkin. Evening, Bill. How's the new baby? Still teething, eh? Oh, shucks, don't you fret yourself about that crying. It don't bother us none. You forget all about that now, hear?" When the pair had gone by, he said to his callers, "Nice folks. Like all of them in this neighborhood, including my landlady, Mrs. Yutch. You'll meet her soon."

It was difficult to assess his features in the thickening twilight, but Wurlitzer's had visibly paled. He shot a look around the porch. "Christ, can't we go someplace else and talk? This place gives me the creeps."

"Does it now, Harry? Well, some folks just can't seem to relax and set a spell any more these days, seems like, and that's the truth. Just take things as they come." Tattersall had by now packed a pipe, lighting it with the match struck on his thumbnail. He puffed a few times, savoring the aroma of the smoke drifting away into the warm air. He shoved his cap forward a little farther on his head and grinned his easy-going, sociable grin. "How's Lucy?"

"Terrible!" Wurlitzer said with a sudden twitching motion. "She's just as upset as the rest of us about you, Hank, but she couldn't stand the thought of coming here. She's broken out in a rash. Everywhere!"

"I'm sorry to hear that. I remember how it was always more than she could do to visit friends in the hospital, because it upset her so. You tell her I was asking about her, hear?"

"So I came along with Sherry."

"Like I say, people can't seem to relax any more and, I don't know, just plain enjoy the things that really count. The simple things. The real values. And speaking of values, there's a clearance sale down to the corner drugstore, and there's some remarkable values there, if you need anything in that line. I mean from raincoats to automobile bumpers, cause, like I say, it's a drugstore," he added with a sly chuckle.

He rapped out the pipe against the rail and drew from his hind pocket a harmonica, which he began to play. He blew a soft, sentimental tune, fluttering his hand over the instrument in a way that sent the melody drifting off through the darkness in gently plaintive, pulsing waves. When he finished he wiped the mouth organ on the side of his pants and put it back into his pocket.

Wurlitzer popped to his feet and pulled his double-breasted jacket down over his bulging middle. He seemed to stand at attention, staring straight ahead at the houses across the street, and his voice had an odd, cracked quality as he spoke. "Is there anything we can do? Will you let us recommend a doctor?"

148

"Naw, I don't need any doctor."

"Well, I do!"

"All I got's the occasional sour, and Doc Moreland's syrup more'n takes care of that. Thanks just the same though."

Tattersall removed his heels from the porch rail and climbed to his own feet.

"And now let's go meet Mrs. Yutch."

"Is that the woman who means the world and all to you?" Sherry said.

He led the way into the cottage. Passing through a small vestibule very nearly filled by a hall seat with a back consisting of an oval mirror encircled by iron pegs, on all of which articles of clothing hung, and to one of which he adroitly added his cap, they entered a parlor whose sole occupant was a broad, muscular woman in shorts and halter. Her masses of brown hair were piled in arrangements that suggested an attempt to incorporate a variety of passing fads at once, as well as numerous shades of its basic color. She was in her forties. Her thick bare legs were crossed, and on one knee was propped a composition pad on which she was writing with a pencil stub. She paused from time to time to consult a dictionary. She was chewing her lips in thought as they entered, but when they did she put her materials aside to shake hands. "Ha da do," she said, pumping vigorously. "Pleased to meet you."

When the visitors were seated, she suggested a cold glass of beer, which they all agreed would hit the spot. "Hank, do you want to do the honors? I'm sure there's a half a gallon bottle on the ice. Well now!"

In Tattersall's brief absence from the parlor, the

149

callers had a chance to take it in. Its mistress would certainly have had no way of knowing that its contents — button-leather sofa and chairs, beaded lamps and tables covered with lace doilies — were camp, any more than she could have been expected to know that the pattern of her shorts were derivative of Mondriaan. She sat under a sign reading: POSITIVELY NO SMOKING.

When Tattersall returned with the beer and four tumblers on a tray, Mrs. Yutch was explaining what she had been writing.

"Those damn tongue twisters. You've seen them in the papers?"

"Oh, yes," Sherry said. "I try one in my head occasionally, but I never get very far. They pay five dollars, don't they?"

"Ten. Don't let the bug get a hold of you. I could kill the guy who started it, like you could kill the guy who invented solitaire. But I'm bound and determined to get one accepted. I submitted three, with no luck. Hank here helps me — I don't think!" She threw a magazine at him.

"Mrs. Yutch is really smitten," Tattersall said, finding a chair for himself. "Recite some you've written, Mrs. Yutch. Can you remember any?"

"Ah, nuts," she declined, with humorous self-belittlement. "Well, here's what I've got so far on this one." She took a pull of her beer and licked the foam from her lips. "Wild Willy Walker woke Wilhelmina Wakefield with — That's as far as I've got. You need ten words, and that's only five."

"Isn't it seven?" Sherry asked.

Mrs. Yutch shook her head, gulping again. "Proper names only count for one."

"My name's Wurlitzer," Harry said, edgily. "You're welcome to use it instead of Wakefield. It's more tongue-twisty."

"Gee, thanks. That is a mouthful of peanut butter." Mrs. Yutch briskly erased Wakefield and jotted in the substitution. "But that don't give me no new words. What are some more that begin with W? The bigger the better. Hank here is the one who knows the big words. Come on, Hank, let's have some jawbreakers!"

Tattersall threw out a few suggestions, smiling with amused affection across the room. "Walloping, whithersoever, Wiener schnitzel, woebegone . . ." To which the others added such contributions as "wobble," "waterlogged," and "Wauwatosa." "Water ouzel," said Wurlitzer hoarsely, twisting a handkerchief in his fingers.

Mrs. Yutch periodically interrupted this alliterative spate to go to the foot of a stairway and shout an order up to some child. "Go to sleep now!" she would call, or "I hear you up there, don't think I don't!" Sometimes she would tramp up three or four steps in a threatening manner, always stopping partway. Once she was heard to say, "And keep your hands above the covers. You know what that habit will do. First the insane asylum. Next stop — the graveyard!"

One such sortie was completed, however. She went all the way up, and could be overheard in one of the bedrooms, moving about and talking. Tattersall took this opportunity to tell the others something.

"I don't know quite how to say this," he began. "It

has to do with something between Mrs. Yutch and me that's a little more than the landlady-boarder relationship, if you know what I mean. Mrs. Yutch is a widow. Her husband died a few years ago, leaving her with these five children. Well, now it seems like she's going to have her sixth, if you know what I mean, thanks to yours truly."

Wurlitzer still seemed jumpy. He popped to his feet again and started to pull a package of cigarettes from his pocket, but remembering the sign on the wall hastily shoved it back again. Tattersall's pipe apparently implied that smoking was permitted on the porch. Sherry picked something from her drink with a neat crimson fingernail. The occasion would seem to call for some such rejoinder as, "Why, Henry Sedgewick Tattersall!" but the words did not occur to her.

"It just doesn't seem fair," Tattersall went on. "We know a fellow is responsible for his actions, and is expected to do the right thing for a momentary indiscretion. But to get six at a clip."

"Will you be sucked into supporting the lot?" Sherry asked.

"We'll just have to see what we see."

"You'll marry Mrs. Yutch then?"

"I'll do the right thing, whatever that is. We'll see."

"In any case now there's no point in our trying to patch it up, is there? I'll give you a divorce." Sherry sighed and looked at Wurlitzer; or, more accurately, to him, as to the moderator of a discussion come to an impasse, and which it is his responsibility to revive. He turned and gave some more determined hitches to his clothing.

"Hank, this is a mell of a hess. Of whose making I don't know, and can't stop to figure out." He started to pace, which in the congested interior consisted largely in circumventing articles of furniture. "You're in a bind because of some slide you've been going through, starting how or when or why God only knows, but of which this is the tail end. At least we hope it's the tail end! You're your own unbeatable foe, is the way it's beginning to look to me. But that's neither here nor there. The thing is, Sherry's and my very presence here proves we won't give you up, whatever you're trying to do to yourself. We'll all give you another chance, but you've got to agree to make some effort to pull yourself together. I'll let bygones be bygones, and more. I'll even take you back into the firm, for another crack at that. At, say — well, salary we can talk later. I'll tell you what. You can write speeches for me. I've been in more and more demand, and can't possibly keep up with it myself. I've got three kickoff dinners lined up for this fall alone. I need somebody who can write a good speech for me, and that might be more up your alley than copy. So come pack your things and let us take you at least out of all this. You can do right by this Mrs. Yutch woman, or whatever you want to call her, without staying here."

"No, Harry, thanks just the same. It's good of you to make the offer, but I got to be honest. There's no guarantee I won't take and throw another bonus back at you, come Christmas."

"I won't *give* you a bonus. Now what could be fairer than that? Not that you're apt to find any temptation on that score any more. We've abandoned the tradition — as you can well imagine after that episode. You say it made you all look like a pack of beggars being thrown alms. All I was trying to do was keep a one-happy-family feeling. Maybe they had reason to resent it. I don't know. Life can get so damn screwed up sometimes you begin to wonder if it's any damn use. And I'm a guy who's supposed to have made it."

Tattersall was adamant. His place was here, which, moreover, he advised them to leave before Mrs. Yutch returned, possibly to reopen under that much more awkward circumstances a conversation better terminated. He bundled them out of the house to the car. Before climbing in, Wurlitzer paused and gave him a well-wishing swipe across the arm with his fist. "Keep pitching, fellow."

When Tattersall went back into the house, Mrs. Yutch was once again in her chair, working on the tongue twister.

"You said Mrs. Tattersall. She your wife?"

"Yes."

"Quite a looker. And neat's a pin. What did you ever leave her for?"

"She left me."

"That figures," said Mrs. Yutch, with a burst of good-natured laughter that exploded in turn into an even more voluminous fit of coughing. She was always choking on something, if not her mirth then her food, and sometimes both. She had got out a bag of popcorn in their absence, to have with the beer, and once in the course of the evening Tattersall had to cross the room to thump her on her back when she got a husk caught in her throat. "Thanks," she said with watery eyes. He did this almost without interrupting his reading of the evening paper. He returned to his chair with it.

He was reading a front page story about a gruesome triple murder that had just been committed in a rural area of the state. He told Mrs. Yutch about it. "He killed three members of his family, including a mother-in-law, sawed the bodies into sections with a hacksaw, and stuffed them down a well."

"I hate that sort of thing," Mrs. Yutch said.

"It's a crime," Tattersall agreed, turning a page.

So the evening passed like many another. It was another cozy evening at home. He had met Mrs. Yutch when, ringing her doorbell to solicit work, he had been given some odd jobs to do around the place. They had hit it off instantly. Her hair was in curlers when she had let him in. "The house is a mess," she had explained, of the empty beer cans, the bushel basket of unmended clothes beside which a poorly trained mongrel snoozed, and even the skillet full of cold beans with a spoon in it resting on top of the upright piano. The secret smile had come to Tattersall's lips at the sight of it. He was indefinably braced by it. This was so clearly and unmistakably the destination toward which his footsteps had tended that he would have been a fool not to recognize it. This was It. There was a ROOM TO LET sign in the window, which he told her might now be removed. It had been there so long, behind the fly-blown glass between the soiled curtains, that she had forgotten it. For a moment she didn't know what he was talking about. "Oh, that. I gave up hopes of ever renting the spare room. People go away when they see it. They ain't interested."

"I'll take it," Tattersall said, without asking to see it.

Mrs. Yutch asked three dollars a week for it, and was indifferent about collecting that once she saw what Tattersall could do around the house. She ran a cash register at a check-out counter in a nearby supermarket. She made it clear that the hospitality of her own bed was his for the taking, but he declined. This out of an integrity more intellectual than moral. He had by now come to see the meaning of his life, his mission on this earth, as it were. He was out to prove the purposeless squalor of human existence, but he could not both deplore it and be guilty of it. It would have undermined his position, cost him his case against fate. And his case was more valuable to him now than any amelioration of the lot on which it was based. The right to his hate must be earned, as the right to love must be. Being in any way outrageous would have forfeited him his outrage.

So the story he had told Sherry and Wurlitzer was completely fictitious, a way of compelling them once and for all to write him off. They could now forget him and go their way, leaving him to go his. He was now off everyone's back but his own. Mrs. Yutch had only one child, a halfwit son who was all Tattersall needed to sell him on this house as his terminal abode, if he needed anything. It was the last missing piece in the mosaic, the capstone of the arch. The boy grinned wickedly at him from around a corner when he carried his things up to his room, and Tattersall grinned understandingly back at him.

Tattersall tried his hand at a few tongue twisters himself. "Vile Vernon Vogelsang violently vomited vast —" Stumped for a noun at a crucial juncture, he switched to another initial. "Poor Peter Plunkett puked putridly putrescent portions . . ."

The evening wore pleasantly on. There was many another. Then Mrs. Yutch caused rather a tarnish on their life together by telling him that he should try to make something of himself. He had just noticed that an old movie was playing on television before which he had hoped they might settle down with their beer and peanuts. It was *The Phantom of the Opera*. In proposing it, he had pronounced it "phanthom," the way she did. But instead she insisted on nagging him about the matter she had raised, just like a wife. "You weren't meant to be a handyman," she said.

"I was once known as Handout Hank," he reminded her, of the interval when he had in fact panhandled on the street, wearing a frayed tweed coat, slouch hat, and an ascot that had also seen better days. "So you can say I *have* made something of myself."

"You can make still more. Didn't you say you were once a door-to-door salesman?" She bit off a length of thread with which she was darning some clothes. "You can do it again. Why don't you try to better yourself? Go to night school, or even take a correspondence course in something." She opened vistas of self-improvement, held out the hope of an occupational ladder slowly climbed, and a social one with it, a future in which he might one day reach the better part of town, and then at last even the suburbs, where people not merely lived but resided.

Tattersall was willing to sell door-to-door again provided he could find an item openly and honestly pointless, not snidely so, like the toilet goods and kitchen aids he had once peddled, or the commodities for which he had once tried to write copy. In his canvassing kit had been, for example, a hair curler that "lets your hair breathe," a piece of patent nonsense to which he would not again stoop, as he would not to the combs for cleaning brushes and the brushes for cleaning combs. But something frankly idiotic, possibly even symbolically so, yes, he might consider. He was now testing his own tensile strength as much as he was the folly and fatuity of the world.

One night in a bar to which he had been driven by Mrs. Yutch's calls to greatness, he heard something that made him prick up his ears. Another drinker was talking about having got the wholesale regional agency for cans of fresh air.

"What did you say?" Tattersall asked.

"It's a gag item, a novelty. Conversation pieces, or whatever you want to call them. Lots of people buy them to give away at Christmas, especially to people who live in the cities with all this air pollution. Or when your house is full of cigarette smoke when you're giving a party, you can trot one out then for a laugh. Time to break out the fresh air and take a whiff. Although you'd be surprised, some people take it seriously. I remember once —"

"How much are they?"

"I let you have them for a nickel apiece. You sell them for whatever you want. Lots of guys get as high as half a buck."

"I'll take some," Tattersall said.

So he became again a white-collar salesman, peddling cans of fresh air door-to-door. He liked this work. Sometimes, on good days, he would take Raymond the back-

158

ward boy with him, trailed in turn by the poorly trained dog. He made a fairly good day's pay at it. Things went along like that for several months, with Mrs. Yutch watching with moderate expectancy for the rung this advancement might next yield to, and then suddenly Mrs. Yutch died, leaving him with the boy and the dog. Her manner of passing might have been anticipated (as we always say after such a thing has happened) though scarcely prepared for.

They were throwing a party for some neighbors early the following spring. They all sat in shirtsleeves around a picnic table in the back yard, eating fried chicken and drinking cold beer. Bursts of laughter became bawdier and more boisterous as the hour grew later and the jokes more robust. Midnight found them under the Japanese lanterns swapping stories of the kind to which most all parties come, those of the lower orders perhaps a little sooner. Tattersall had little capacity for "stories," but he set a brisk example in extemporaneous byplay. One story had to do with a present with which a fictional adulterer tried to hoodwink his wife, and it prompted some lively banter among the women on the subject of general male delinquency in not bringing flowers and candy home simply on general principles. A neighbor named Jerry Caxton began to twit another called Al Bohack over his exposed parsimony on this score. "Don't you ever feel the urge to do something just to make Millie feel good?" he asked. "Just to tickle her pink?"

"Tickle her pink what?" Tattersall said, and they all roared.

They threw their heads back and screamed with laughter, some banging their beer cans on the table-boards in sheer delight. Mrs. Yutch, who had been in stitches all evening, now became positively hysterical.

It was so late that the leftover platters of cold chicken had been again brought out for a midnight snack, together with the potato salad and coleslaw. She had been eating a drumstick at the time Tattersall made his joke, and, not surprisingly, choked on a piece of it. The trouble was so habitual with her that no one thought anything of it, until her predicament was seen to be serious. Then they began thumping her on the back — to no avail. Periodically one hears or reads of somebody choking to death in a restaurant, or at home before the amazed eyes of friends or family, but it is never anybody you know, and the occurrences have nothing to do with real life as it is commonly experienced. No one there would believe his senses when Mrs. Yutch simply toppled forward to the ground. She was rushed to a doctor's office three blocks down the street, but it was too late.

Tattersall was left with the mongoloid boy and the mongrel dog, and a free hand to affirm negation as he could.

eleven

FORTUNATELY he could throw himself into his work, which steadily advanced his study of human folly. When Raymond was not along, traipsing without trouble in his wake, he was an ideal companion to come home to, after a day of selling tins of fresh air. The table would be set, ready for the steak Tattersall would broil outside or the beef Stroganoff he would cook inside. The boy was eleven or twelve, but like his kind could easily have been confused with twenty or thirty. He could get the table ready and clear it, he could be trusted to turn the stove off and on, and would fetch what you pointed to, gargling unintelligibly as he waddled over with it. It suited Tattersall's purpose at this juncture to treat him as an equal.

"Joyce used to say that the only true colors are to be found in a grocery store," he chatted as he unpacked the day's shopping. "And he was right. Look at that orange, that peach, those string beans. They quite undermine the assumption that there are three primary colors, don't you think? There are dozens! Fruit and vegetables I find more exhilarating than flowers, for color. More genuinely satisfying."

The idiot washed the provisions at the sink, making mouths and chewing his tongue as he worked, occasionally giving out some guttural, gurgling noise which Tattersall would take up and develop.

"Yes, I quite agree. The present status of Joyce is rather a mixed one. The farther you get into his epic works the more, it seems to me, the more you're confronted with something to be admired rather than enjoyed. You remember Mary Colum's remark after his famous Paris reading from *Finnegans Wake*. 'It's outside literature,' she told Joyce, shaking in her shoes though she was. Incidentally, Hemingway was in that audience. It would be interesting to know what he said, if anything. Well, as I was saying, I enjoy *Finnegans Wake* less than I do *Ulyssess, Ulysses* less than the *Portrait*. So there you have it. I'm not a true Joycean any more than I am a true Jamesian, I fear. I prefer *his* early novels to the Late Great Phase. All that upholstery! And in all those miles of criticism, I don't think there's a line that sums James up better than his aunt's remark. That he chewed more than he bit off."

The vegetables went into a casserole called Chicken *Haute Loire*, which Tattersall baked in a bedpan. He had found one in an upstairs cabinet, never so far put to any purpose, judging from the label he had had to scrape off before sterilizing it in the dishwasher, and it struck him as ideal for culinary purposes, certainly a waste not to use, especially as there was no casserole among the jumble of pots and pans under the kitchen sink. The dish simmered succulently in its juices, and in the white wine later added. With it, he drank the rest of the bottle, a Corton Charlemagne of an unimpeachable year. He grew more expansive at table.

"While I'm not prepared to say of Joyce what is often said of Eliot, namely that he is a good writer but a bad influence, anyone who has ever taught knows the evidence for either charge." He paused to hold his glass up by the stem and study its deep gold contents appreciatively. The idiot ate lustily, bent over his plate and snuffling into the chicken which he picked up with his fingers. Tattersall decided that he loved him. And that they both alike loved the poorly trained dog whom the idiot paused to smile down at, and who, oddly nameless as yet, wheezed and slobbered ruefully as he watched the banqueters from below. "Lazarus," Tattersall said, baptizing him with a dollop of white wine, which the dog thirstily licked from his coat. He tossed him a gobbet of meat. Then he returned to his point.

"Now, that may be universally true of the really original artist, that he becomes a headache in his imitators. He thins out, you see, turns into a cliché. Christ becomes his disciples, the disciples the apostles, the apostles the church, and the church — yicch! Still, getting back to the subject, you can't, you know, expect from talent what you do from genius. Talent — how shall I put it?" He paused again to sip his Burgundy. "Genius gives us a vision, talent merely a view. Something like that. I'm sure you've thought all this out for yourself long ago, so I shan't bore you any longer by laboring the obvious, my dear Raymond."

The boy took out a handkerchief to blow his nose.

"Oh, indubitably. And I agree absolutely that we must

163

always bear that end of it in mind. But to get back to what we were discussing. The paradox here is that genius often learns from talent, as well as the other way around. I'm thinking of the interesting phenomenon of the forerunner. Freud had his Janet, Eliot his Laforgue, and it is supposedly the 'ethereally divided violins' of the *Lohengrin* Prelude, as well as some of Wagner's other aching near-dissonances, that put the bug in Schönberg's bonnet for the twelve-tone scale."

He finished off his wine and rose, stretching. The discussion had put him in the mood for music. He set some Schönberg going on the phonograph. The sound whetted rather than slaked his thirst for discord. With the Schönberg going full blast, he sat down at the piano and played something else, next singing at the top of his voice something altogether different again. The house reverberated with a cacophony that shook the walls. Keeping Schönberg for a background, he pounded out *Little Gray Home in the West* while singing the words of *I'll Be Glad When You're Dead, You Rascal You*. He rose a moment to turn the radio on, getting some rock and roll, then went back to the piano and combined *Jesus Wants Me for a Sunbeam* with *It Ain't No Sin to Take Off Your Skin and Dance Around in Your Bones*, thumping the keys and singing the words with all his might. By now the racket was so deafening that he did not for some time notice that the jangle of the telephone had been added to it. The caller was a neighbor bleating, "Could you turn it down a little? My wife is dying."

The idiot could not be entirely entrusted with the dishwasher, so Tattersall stacked the dishes in the sink for the time being to muck about a bit. Cockroaches on which he could not personally lay hands and against which he neglected to pit an exterminator traversed the kitchen in growing numbers. He would brush them away with a whisk broom, saying to an occasional scuttler, "Gimme a break, will ya!" The centuries brought really little change in what man had to put up with, or what he devised to make the remainder coherent or tolerable. Even speech styles on which the acutely contemporary preened themselves were not all that new, or without precedent. Mod youngsters able to bear that antiquated fuddy-duddy, Carlyle, long enough to read *The French Revolution* would be rewarded with the sentence: "Dandoins stands with folded arms, and what look of indifference and disdainful garrison-air a man can, while the heart is like leaping out of him." Christ, how grotesque things could be, how unexpectedly and in what unlikely quarters one could be getting his hacks!

Tattersall sucked on a bottle of beer as he mucked about. Scraping some leftovers into the dog's dish, he remembered how eagerly it had lapped up the wine. He poured the rest of his beer into the empty water pan. He did so in a playful spirit, but also out of a certain whimsical curiosity. It amused him to see the dog lap it up greedily. He opened another bottle and split it with him. Having drunk his fill, the dog proceeded to wobble and stagger around the house, its stubby legs buckling under it. It stumbled against the furniture and slid about on the linoleum floor. It hiccuped. Tattersall was by that time three sheets to the wind himself. Toward midnight they repaired to their separate sleeping quarters, the dog flopping down on his kitchen bed and Tattersall, fully clothed, on his upstairs.

The next evening, the dog barked insistently, looking up at Tattersall in a manner leaving little doubt about what he was trying to communicate. Tattersall said, "No, no," but the dog followed him around, nipping at his heels. There was no peace until he had opened a can of beer and poured it into the dog's pan. The mutt guzzled it thirstily till it was gone. The next night the same thing happened. The dog refused water. He simply wasn't interested. By the end of the week Tattersall realized he had an alcoholic on his hands.

This completed the menage into which, toward the close of that month, a woman walked who identified herself as a social case worker for the city, come to check on it. Their little paradise was threatened.

twelve

SHE was a slender woman past forty, with brown eyes at which it took some doing to get a good look because of a seeming reluctance to meet your own gaze head-on. She would begin a statement, or a question, with her eyes shut. Only as she approached its conclusion would they flutter violently open, and she would look at you. Their behavior was a little like that of fluorescent lights. Then the process would start all over again. Tattersall had known several people with this mannerism, all women as it happened, and he wondered whether it was in fact more frequent among them than among men, or whether it was merely an accident of his own impression. Emerson had closed his eyes when he smiled, which may have accounted for his benign optimism: he never really saw what he beamed on.

Mrs. Seltzer's habit was, at any rate, not in evidence when she looked around the room. That she took in with a wide stare.

"I'm afraid the house is a mess," Tattersall said, smiling.

Mrs. Seltzer gave the impression of thinking the spectacle deserved rather a stronger word, or one of another order altogether; that this was the product of something other than mere neglect. Soiled dishes and glasses standing everywhere were only the beginning. A drip-dry shirt hung from the chandelier, from one of whose sockets depended also a length of electric cord ending in no visible appliance, but just vanishing under the piano among an assortment of empty bottles. It was like a strand of vine in an untended yard. There was some leftover beef Stroganoff in the bedpan, along with a spoon from which, supposedly, it was extemporaneously eaten cold on impulse by any resident epicures. Half-finished tongue twisters lay everywhere. In one corner the dog was sleeping off a drunk. An electric razor seemed plugged into a can of lard. That was an example of something not the product of neglect, but only of a conscious intelligence. There might have been lurking about the premises someone waiting just to be asked about it, in order to be able to answer, "Oh, I forgot to disconnect it." Unless it was to be accounted for on some other ground, such as free-form improvisation in creative therapy. The chair to which Mrs. Seltzer was eventually waved had first to be cleared of a pile of frayed sheet music. That was dropped on the floor with a thud that disturbed the dog. Putting a hand to his head, as it were, the dog rose and wobbled into the kitchen. Seeing him stagger through the door, Mrs. Seltzer asked, "What is the matter with him?"

"He hasn't been himself lately."

An insistent barking from the kitchen sent Tattersall into it, excusing himself. He took a cold half-gallon bottle of beer from the refrigerator and poured some of it out, murmuring, "Hair of the dog?" When he returned, the caller, fluttering her eyelids, said, "Is that animal drunk?"

"I'm afraid he does hit the bottle."

She had opened a notebook on her lap, and now paused over it, doubtful of her first entry. "Is this of long standing?" she asked at last.

"Oh, no. And he may pull out of it. Of course it's hard to say. Bassetts are notorious bums, you know."

"He's a mutt."

"He's a mutt, but mostly bassett. He'd probably be worse if he was purebred, because you know the reputation they have. That there's a bassett bum hanging around every supermarket. We try to understand."

She had been waggling a pencil inconclusively over the notebook. Now she said, "You say we. Which brings us to my business. Where's Raymond? I'm supposed to check on him, as you probably realize. That's why I'm here. He's not, of course, yours."

"I intend to adopt him."

"Do you think this is a good environment for an idiot?"

"Why don't you ask him?"

"I intend to. But as for adopting anyone, you have to go through channels, of course, and while that's not precisely my end of it, they'll ask you the same questions. Do you think you'd make a good parent?"

"I won't know till I try."

"You mean you don't know whether or not you can talk Polish, you've never tried."

"Not exactly a parallel, would you say? Anyone can grow vegetables. And I rather like talking to plants."

Mrs. Seltzer drew a long breath, by way of transition, and then, with the point of her pencil poised rather more resolutely over the notebook, she said: "We've had to check on him from time to time even when his mother was still alive, because she would put him in a public institution now and again, for varying periods. Not just when she went on vacation, or thought the worry about how he was getting along alone at home interfered with her work, but on general principles. There are always two schools of thought about what to do with children like that. Sometimes it's better for the family not to . . . Well, I mean the martyr policy is often a waste. They don't really care where they are, and they're often happier with other unfortunates around. Though that may not be a word you'd use. Anyway, where is he now?"

"I'll go see."

In Tattersall's brief absence at the back of the house, the woman read one or two of the tongue twisters. She could do so without leaving her chair or even reaching out to pick one up. They were everywhere. Merely by turning her head she read: "Appalled Paul Pawling perished putrescently pickling putrid pickerel parts." And "Dreadful diseases dilapidated drunken Duncan Dunkenfield during diabolically diversified deliriums."

Mrs. Seltzer straightened in her chair as a faint smile came to her lips. She was not going to be put out, put off, or, above all God knew, put on. She would bite her tongue to keep from asking about the electric razor plugged into a can of lard. She knew very well the story about the man who hauled a horse up the stairs and left it in the bathtub, simply to excite inquiry, to which he would give a nonchalant answer explaining nothing. And as for the *pièce de resistance* over there on her left, she could play that as cool as anyone too.

Tattersall returned with the information that the boy had wandered off somewhere in the neighborhood, as he often did, and would drift back in his own good time, if she cared to wait. "I could fix you a bite of lunch," he said. "What are you staring at?"

"Isn't that beef Stroganoff in there?"

"Yes. Why do you ask?"

"Well, I'm curious about one thing, if you don't mind a personal question."

"Not at all. What is it?"

"Why do you fix it with tomato paste? I just use sour cream."

"Matter of personal taste," Tattersall said. "Have you had lunch?"

"Yes, I've eaten, thanks just the same."

"How about a Coke? I'm a little thirsty myself."

"A Coke would be fine."

They sat sipping their soft drinks while she fired her questions at him and he answered. The interview took its inevitably purposeful course, and resolved though she was to remain unperturbed about what she saw, the point was reached when direct queries about it had to be put.

"Just what is this all about?" she said.

"What is what all about?" Tattersall said.

"This." She gestured in all directions. "Is this surrealism in everyday life? Instant despair? Are you a black humorist living it up? Or a do-it-yourself God knows what? Or is it just the put-on to end all put-ons?"

"It's just home," he said.

"Is it the new irreverence?"

"It's just home."

"Why don't you get a good cleaning woman?"

"Can you recommend one?"

"I'll see what I can do. But make sure you straighten the place up before she gets here." Mrs. Seltzer closed the notebook and tucked it into her briefcase. "No Raymond, and I've got to go. Well, I'll call again in a few days. Meanwhile I won't make any report. Please don't trouble. I'll shovel my own way to the door."

She had not intended to look back. But finding he had followed her out onto the front porch, she paused and turned. She was about to say something when he interrupted her. There was a dead bird on the top step, perhaps deposited there by some neighborhood cat. He brushed it into the weeds with his toe. "Nature is a slob," he said. "Have you ever thought that we spend most of our time mopping up after her?"

"Most of us at any rate." She appraised him abruptly again, as best she could through fluttering lids. "You're biting down on an aching tooth, aren't you?" She paused only long enough to see that he was not going to answer. "But if so, whatever it is, I'll play a hunch. Whatever happened, you brought it on yourself. But don't make the mistake of thinking you're too rich for my blood, because you aren't. My most vivid childhood recollection is of my father with his mouth wired shut after a dentist broke his jawbone pulling three impacted teeth. It was wired shut tight, so that all the nourishment he could take in was liquid, through a straw."

"I knew a woman like that once."

"I'm not finished. One day some soup he drank didn't

172

agree with him. He was nauseated, and not with the universe. You can imagine the crisis. Another man in our home town went out one night to a compost heap he had spent ten years building up, immaculately dressed in white tie and tails, and with a bullet from a pistol added himself to it. So I mean it's tough on you romantics. There's always somebody who's gone you one better. You will always be topped. Despair is a losing game."

"Where are you going now?"

"Oh, I think I'll drop in on the Collier brothers. See you later."

She marched down the stairs to a rather worn looking Chevrolet sedan, and he watched her get in and drive off without looking back.

Tattersall now regularly took the idiot boy and the drunken dog with him on his rounds. The boy would trail him, and the dog the boy, at widening intervals as the day wore on. Tattersall himself rarely tired. He swung his suitcase briskly as he strode along. Together with the cans of fresh air, he had taken on one other item. It was a NO PEDDLERS ALLOWED sign, with which he did a lively business, especially in the large apartment houses springing up everywhere. The boy managed to hold his own fairly well, and Tattersall thought the exercise was good for him. It was the dog who had trouble keeping up the pace. He was now a regular lush. He drank like a fish every night, and every morning needed a good belt to pull himself together. He declined faster than the outdoor air and sunshine could build him up. Still, for a time, Tattersall insisted he tag along. Sunny days, that year, again lingered on well into autumn, and Tattersall found them bracing as he walked along under the weeping oaks and maples. He made a decent living — enough for rent, food, clothes, and something left over.

There came a time when the dog could no longer make it. He got so stewed every night that he was good for nothing till noon but sleeping it off. When Tattersall withheld liquor from him, he made Tattersall's life miserable, barking and yapping and nipping at his legs till given another drink. Or he would go upstairs and pull the bedcovers off of him. All this posed a problem, serious when the dog was home alone in a locked house. Tattersall solved it by installing something he often saw on his rounds. It was one of those "dog doors" which are fitted into the lower half of a house door, through which small animals can push their way in and out at will without the door itself being opened. The kind he inserted in the kitchen door was a panel of triangular plastic wedges converging to a point like the slices of a pie, which could be pushed open either way from the center, after which it closed automatically. Tattersall spent the best part of a week shoving the dog back and forth through it in an effort to make him understand what it was all about, for his faculties had become dulled by drink. "Will you get *in* there, for Christ's sake! Now get *out*, can't you!"

One Saturday morning a large crate arrived from Sherry. It contained what she thought might fairly be considered his half of their wedding presents. She had written him asking what he would like to have, and he had replied telling her to keep everything. That had not satisfied her, and she had taken it upon herself to divide things up as equitably as she could. He received some assorted silver, including flatware, an electric clock, a cocktail shaker, and several exquisite Venetian glasses sent over from a European relative of his. There was a lace tablecloth from a Boston aunt. And everything they had brought back from their summer abroad when he had been a street singer.

Tattersall cooked a rousing dinner for a beautifully set table. It was ham hocks and sauerkraut, a long-time favorite. Into his Venetian goblet he poured some properly chilled rosé, into the idiot's a soft drink called Slurp. Great dripping clumps of sauerkraut were heaped on the Wedgwood plates with carved silver tongs, also used to drop ice cubes into their tinkling tumblers.

"Fine crystal is one of the world's joys," Tattersall mused. He snicked the rim of his wineglass with a fingernail to make it give off a delicate musical ring. "And to think it all began in the sand beside the sea. Have you wondered who that first man was, centuries ago, who by accident noticed what fire did to those tiny glittering flakes along the shore? The man who created glass."

He paused to pour another dollop of beer into the Steuben bowl at which the dog guzzled.

"Anything so subtly reminiscent of ice is an odd end-product of fire, isn't it. But then it's all part of the quintessential paradox of existence itself. I see ceramics is one of the subjects in the course of lectures at the library this winter. We must get season tickets. Someone else is speaking on Chopin. Chopin has always seemed to me a kind of audible crystal. What is it, Raymond?"

The boy was pointing to the window, gargling vehemently as he did so. Tattersall looked in time to see a face withdrawn from it. He ran outside, but by the time he got there the intruder had vanished. There wasn't a sign of life anywhere, only the rustle of trees and the play of their shadows around the streetlamp.

He shrugged and went back to the house. "Nobody there," he said. They returned to their meal. But he had scarcely sat down when the front doorbell rang. It was Mrs. Seltzer.

"I was just going by," she said, "and thought I'd drop in. I'm supposed to keep looking you over without warning. I hope you don't mind."

"Not at all. We're just having dinner. Won't you join us?" he said. "If you've already eaten, you might like a glass of wine, or some coffee later. I've baked a chocolate soufflé."

"What in?"

"In the oven, naturally. Come here."

He beckoned her on into the kitchen, where, with the aid of two hotpads, he drew from the oven a red Dansk casserole.

"Some treasures I've just inherited. From myself," he added, with an odd laugh. "Look at this coffeepot. Have you ever seen more beautifully carved silver, or a more graceful teak handle? But give me your coat, and then come sit down. How does that verse of Edna Millay's go? There shall be plates a-plenty, and mugs to melt the chill, of all the gray-eyed people who happen up the hill."

Tattersall nudged a third chair up to the table, at which Mrs. Seltzer was already admiring the lace cloth, and poured out another glass of rosé. After splashing some more Slurp into Raymond's glass he took his seat.

Mrs. Seltzer glanced down at the bowl the dog had been drinking out of.

"Isn't that Steuben?"

"I wouldn't be surprised."

"Some people sure know how to live. I couldn't eat another thing, thanks, just the wine. Ham hocks. You like them? They're a special taste. I had an uncle who was insane about them."

"God gives us ham hocks for our bodies, hollyhocks for our souls."

"Yes, I know. Cheers."

He tempted Mrs. Seltzer with a little sauerkraut, which he had fixed with fragments of lean bacon and slices of crisp water chestnuts. She was lavish in her praise of it, and asked for the recipe. All this while the phonograph had been going, and though it was playing low and in another room, Tattersall now found it to be interfering with the conversation, and he went to turn it off.

"Works a lot better since it's been fixed, doesn't it?" he said to the boy when he came back. "Even Delius sounds better." Mrs. Seltzer quickly emptied her glass, which Tattersall as nimbly refilled. "We normally find Delius a little treacly," he explained to her as he did so, "but not this piece. A rather interesting man, by all accounts. For all his plaintiveness and sweetness he was apparently a forbidding man. One of the great detesters, in Nietzsche's phrase. I suppose all misanthropes have that soft streak in them . . ."

Mrs. Seltzer found her tongue on the third glass.

"Misanthropes all hate themselves," she said, addressing herself to the boy also, in an evident determination to show that two could play at this game. "We think of the world what we think of ourselves. The question about a beef is always how legitimate is it. I had a teacher who was a Frost nut, and he used to quote Frost on the distinction between griefs and grievances. Griefs shut up — these are my words now. Grievances — now I can't even remember what he said. Oh, well." She sighed and lowered her head into her hand. Then she immediately raised it again and said, "No, let me put it my way then. Grievances are less worthy, though they're what generally make themselves heard. I think the truer it is that Everything Stinks the less one should call it to others' attention. Quiet is requested for the benefit of other patients. These people — they can't forgive God for not existing. I'm sure you've known people like that," she continued to the boy, who was smiling down at the dog, who sat begging beside the table. "We all do. They gorge themselves on Nothing. They can't get enough of Nothing. They can't suck enough out of that Existentialist tit. They cozy up to it till they're glutted, they're drooling, it's running down their chin. It's the old Dusty Answer deal. But this Someone they can't forgive for not existing, neither can they stop going on to him, or it. Don't try to divert me with beauty, they say. Don't try to buy me off with spring flowers, or young May moons, or falling snow. I want to stay mad."

She held out her glass to be refilled, and after Tattersall had emptied what remained of the bottle into it, she resumed.

"There are two ways of doing it. Two possible attitudes to take, you see. Some rub it out. That's suicide. The other type want to do the opposite. They want to rub it in. They want to live as long as possible, to rub all of it in they can. They know it'll be rubbed into them in the end, as it is into everybody, but they do want to get in as much rubbing in as they can while the rubbing in is good. I know somebody like that, and I think you do too. His tack is simple. His program. He is self-destructive, up to a point. He does want to stick around, though he knows what you're stuck with as long as you do. He wants to eat his cake and have it too. He will commit as much suicide as possible without killing himself."

Mrs. Seltzer had apparently finished. She sat back and looked at her wine, though without holding it aloft by the stem. It simply sat on the table. Tattersall pushed his chair back to get the soufflé. When he returned from the kitchen with it, she was still staring at her wineglass, and he imagined that her eyes were moist, though it was hard to tell because of her idiosyncrasy. She had been talking to the boy, but much more softly and in an altogether different tone. She put her hand over his as she said: "So all in all you will probably find it a lot better there again, the way you did before. You remember. In the Home, where there is so much more company, and so many other children your age to play with, and help each other, and all. You'll have lots more fun there. Truly you will."

Tattersall set the casserole on a trivet and dished up three helpings of the steaming chocolate. He poured thick cream over it from a cut-glass pitcher and passed it around.

Mrs. Seltzer gave a murmur of appreciation even before she had swallowed her first spoonful. "My God, this is terrific," she said. "It's absolutely wonderful." Tattersall saw that the tears were in fact rolling down her cheeks.

Thirteen

WINTER took the city by surprise. It arrived suddenly one November afternoon, following a spell of fine weather.

It had been an average day for Tattersall, with its spot of color here and there such as sometimes made his daily rounds mildly memorable. A jolly woman weighing at least three hundred pounds had once bought everything he had in his suitcase to distribute as favors for a party she was throwing. That morning, an old woman so gnarled with rheumatism she could hardly get to the door had listened to his sales spiel, then, holding a can doubtfully in her bony fingers, had hesitated a moment. "How do I know the air in here is fresh?" she said. "I'll stake my professional reputation on it," Tattersall said. She finally bought one, creaking off and returning with a bag from which she dug a fifty-cent piece. Pocketing the coin, Tattersall shook his head at the awfulness of life as he descended the stairs. Pity was important to him now. He had wanted to knock the old lady down as a means of eliciting it. A stray mutt had next followed him for several blocks, perhaps with a view to adopting him. As he often had with his own dog, Tattersall rambled reminiscently on to it as it traipsed at his heels, recalling the days of his greatness and the feats that had checkered them. ". . . so I says to de Pope, listen, wise ass . . ." At length the dog left him, turning up a side street. Tattersall was reduced to talking to himself, a thing which he did not mind except that, in the role of listener, his attention often wandered. There were times when he didn't hear a word he said.

The gray of the sky abruptly darkened, and then it began to snow. Thick wet flakes silently, dreamily descended upon boughs that had not quite yet shed the gold of their leaves. By evening the world was white. As he always did with the first snowfall, he remembered the poem of that name from everyone's childhood. "The snow had begun in the gloaming, and busily all the night . . ."

Each of us has a single, special memory, cherished as our most beautiful, the key to our past; or if not that, at least the embodiment of all we yearn to unlock. Not the earliest recollection soiled with explanation by the psychologists, but the memory of some particular bliss heartbreaking to recall, safe from contradiction, which is perhaps the memory of purity itself. This is no doubt why snow is always evocative of childhood. Tattersall's great sweet memory was not an event, it was this poem. He remembered having to recite it before the class, and of doing so, but what he treasured was not the recollection of success, but the verses themselves and what they communicated. The fluttering flakes seemed like an enormous shuttling loom from which the whole tapestry of childhood was rewoven: the hope and fear of school, the poetry of the hours, the secrecy of dreams, all suspended in some eternal playtime. The silence deep and white, the rails softened to swansdown, the sheds new-roofed with Carrara, from which came chanticleer's muffled crow, all this was once again evoked by the magical product of skies that would seem incapable of shedding anything but soot.

After dinner he drew on his overshoes, bundled himself into a sweater, and went for a walk. He made the dog come along. He thought the invigorating air as well as the exercise would do him good. Indeed the dog did find it exhilarating at first, frisking about in the snow, but soon the excitement wore off, and he trotted reluctantly at Tattersall's heels the rest of the hike. Tattersall was surprised to see how much more thickly the snow was falling than when he had come in out of it, and how much colder it was. After half a mile or so he began to think about the warm house himself, and he turned back, to find how biting the wind was now that he had it in his face instead of at his back. It stung his cheeks and eyes, and blew in sharp gusts around his feet and even up his trouser legs. He held a corner of his muffler to his mouth, and puffed along. Nearly four inches had fallen by now. It was turning into a blizzard. There was nobody else abroad. Most of the few cars out were foundering or stalled. He glanced enviously at house windows, their golden glow veiled in swirling white. He was glad to get home.

When he did, it was to find the front door locked. He had forgotten to take a key, or had assumed Raymond would let him in. There was no response, however, to the bell, or when he banged on the door. "He's watching television," Tattersall said to the dog. "Let's go around the back way."

That locked door was thumped with no better luck. He pounded it with both fists, calling the boy's name. Nothing happened. He peered into the kitchen window. The house was fully lighted, but there was no sign of activity. He could hear nothing. Not that the television would be audible there, since the set was upstairs.

He went down the stairs into the yard. There was a light on in the room where the television set was, and Tattersall made some snowballs and threw them at the window. They brought no face to it. "Damn," he said, and tramped back up the stairs to the porch again. The kitchen window was latched, and he was about to break it and climb in when he thought of something else. He thought of the dog door, and it gave him an inspiration.

"You go in and bark at him," he said to the dog, who for some reason had not yet taken advantage of the access available to him, preferring to follow Tattersall on his mysterious activities. "You know — like Lassie. Woof, woof! Wrrroof! Upstairs. Tell him something is wrong, wroof, wroof! Then down again. Bring him here. Show them how smart you are. Get Raymond." He supplemented these instructons with a vigorous illustrative pantomime. "Go!" he concluded, and started the dog through the door with a push.

Nothing happened after that either. Tattersall could hear its claws on the kitchen linoleum as it trotted toward its food pan. After snuffling at that for a few moments it went to its accustomed warm corner and flopped down to sleep. Angry, out there in the cold, Tattersall said, "God damn it all!" and, getting down on all fours himself, he unwound his bulky muffler and thrust his head through the aperture to have a look.

He had a clear view of the kitchen, the lower half at any rate, and could satisfy himself that things were precisely as he suspected. The animal was sprawled out in his cozy corner, already fast asleep.

"You're a great help. Raymond! Raymond!"

Here Tattersall could resume his shouts to better advantage. His head at least was in the house. So he bellowed at the top of his voice. There was still no response. The house was silent. That meant Raymond wasn't looking at the television. He was asleep. And he slept the sleep of the dead. Only the most prolonged and violent shaking could possibly awaken him. Shouts, never. Certainly not from this distance. All these thoughts ran through Tattersall's mind while a far more chilling realization came over him. He couldn't get his head out again.

The dog door was in a sense a kind of circular shutter. The triangular wedges converging, sliced-pie-wise, at the center were of a brown plastic, similar to artificial leather, their wide ends attached to the circumference of the aperture on hinges which permitted them to swing in or out with equal ease. But the whole was so constructed that it had to be pushed all the way before it could be reversed. Tattersall naturally could not complete the process. It stopped where his shoulders met the frame. His head could only thrust the door in halfway, where it locked in an inconclusive position around his neck.

He wished now that he had not removed his muffler, though it would probably have done him no good in the long run. Already the wedges, which were reenforced with steel ribs, were beginning to cut his neck, so that he had not only to remain still for fear of garroting himself, but even to stop shouting. Therefore his calls for help were infrequent. Little confidence was to be put in them in any case since they went unheard here and in the houses next door, and, certainly, in the streets. Once he dimly heard somebody putting a car in a garage, and he set up a last tumult, fading at last into silence.

That was nearly an hour later. The snow had been falling steadily, and the wind rising. Cold gusts were blowing up the stairs and even around the porch. He could sense the snow drifting behind him. By morning it would certainly have covered him over, wrapping him close in its woolen coat.

He was soon no longer cold, then actually rather warm, pleasantly numbed. A giddy feeling came over him, and he began to laugh, as he had the time he'd gotten high on marijuana. He imagined the spectacle he would offer those fortunate enough to be chosen by fate to come upon him. The sight would be unique in human annals, that much was sure. There would never have been anything quite like it. There never would be again.

He began to imagine that he heard voices. Was he growing delirious? The fear crossed his mind that help might come in time. Then he laughed again. Of course, he might have known — it was the Doppelgänger. Come one last time, come for a parting shot.

"Well, your end is in sight, Tattersall," he said. "I think we can safely say that."

"And so, thank God, is yours," Tattersall answered with a gentle, grateful sigh, and remembering, as he did so, that death by freezing was not by any means the worst of fates.

He had only one regret. It was too bad Lucy Stiles had not meant any more to him than she did. She had never meant anything at all to him. Nothing, really, at all.

2
Witch's Milk

one

WHEN Tillie Shilepsky first laid eyes on her husband-to-be she thought, "No. Uh-uh. He's out." One's school-girl fancies of course ran to dark, deferential strangers who accosted you in foreign lands to warn you against the local drinking water and then, Homburg in hand, asked whether you believed in fate. Such dreams are soon liquidated, but fate was at least not going to deal her a bloke with a cigarette on one ear who called everyone Frisbee. When he lit the cigarette it would probably be with a kitchen match struck on a thumbnail. There would almost certainly be that. "No, I'm sorry. He's out. Thanks just the same though."

The hostess responsible for this misguided piece of blind dating stood at her side, beaming on her catch. She was Gertrude Wilson, an old friend who was hardly one's speed herself. "He's called Pete Seltzer."

"I'll bet."

Tillie meant that the name was so right it had the ring of an adroitly timed thrust. That was the joke, not that a woman so obtuse at matchmaking was likely to get it. Standing shoulder to shoulder in the blue smoke, amid the tinkle of highballs flourished in evening gestures, they watched the Seltzer knock out a couple of girls sitting on the floor at his feet. He was amusing them with double talk, a craft in which he was apparently quite skilled. The party was by now well on the boil.

"The reason I haven't gotten married at the age of thirty is for fear of becoming a real person," he was explaining. "To that in itself I have no objection. But the day-to-day togetherness can finally mucilaginate the smuffockles, if you know what I mean. Till it's impossible to extropert each other's thropplestance."

"Come and meet him." Gertrude took Tillie by the hand and towed her through the crowd.

It was the first time Tillie had ever heard anyone talk double talk in real life. Entertainers doing it had usually amused her, or at least fascinated her with the art as such, which calls for the most minutely calculated effects, the most perfectly timed deflations. Nonsense is such a difficult art! A mere handful of men have achieved it, while the centuries are stocked with Homers and Mozarts. An intellectual escort with whom she had once listened to some double talk in a night club had analyzed the laughter it provoked as "the pleasurable collapse of meaning." One shook helplessly at having the epistemological rug pulled out from under one, at being dropped through a hatch into the logical void.

"Why isn't he hauled over to meet me?" Tillie wondered. By the time they reached him he was smoking the cigarette. So she had missed the manner in which fire had been set to it. Well, perhaps another time.

"Oh, hi." The Seltzer type rose from the sofa, also moving aside after the introduction to make room for

Tillie on it. The routine was thereupon instantly resumed, the two girls being by no means ready to let it drop. Tillie took them in with almost as much interest as she paid the Seltzer, struck by the amazing similarity between them without their in the least resembling one another physically. They seemed blonde and brunette, thin and plump, tall and short versions of the same low-threshold risibility. Wet-eyed, they took turns egging the Seltzer on.

"What kind of work do you do, Pete?"

"Motivational research. We send canvassers out to discover what the public threeks. What they're looking for in an after-shaving mint or an automatic contaminator. We're very selective about our clients. We only take people who come to us."

"What are some other products?"

"We've just completed a survey for a dietetic shampoo, and are now helping launch a reversible mayonnaise."

The term rolling on the floor would not exaggerate the response of the two girls. Pete Seltzer, however, seemed more aware of his date sitting silently beside him, with her arms folded on her chest.

"What do you think?" he asked.

"I disagree with what you say, but I'll defend to the death your right to say it," Tillie answered.

"Well said. A girl who deserves every thermonsenpoos."

They were all presently engulfed in the general conversation, into an unfeatured role in which the Seltzer, somewhat to Tillie's surprise, seemed perfectly content to sink. He had no interest in hogging the floor, as

Gertrude's interior decorator, Jimmy Twitchell, now did, adroitly steering the talk among matters of gossip in which he was wickedly versed. Pete Seltzer had no wish to cut a figure, or, apparently, to be the life of the party. He had no opinions about the human scene. He was more interested in personal relations, as Tillie concluded from the steadily solidifying pressure of his elbow against hers. Even the fractured girls took a brisker part in the political debate by which the initiative was at last wrested from Jimmy Twitchell.

"What do you think about the present administration?" Tillie at last asked Pete Seltzer, point-blank.

"I think they're doing their best to bolster the economy and reassure the country by fiduciating the morsnorfles without negromifying the status quo."

Either Olympian detachment or abysmal ignorance was on exhibit here, it was too early to tell which. A zealous member of the Americans for Democratic Action had come armed with a petition, which Tillie favored but refused to sign here because bringing it to a party had been rude, but to which the Seltzer had courteously affixed his signature without reading the contents. "Do you always keep your arms folded?" he asked as he reached past her for her empty glass, in order to refill it. She bristled, then sensed that no stricture was intended: he grinned at her in a sort of loose, lupine way, at the same time flicking blue eyes across her person. He didn't expect an answer, but, plucking up his glass along with hers, rose and headed for the bar. It was then she saw that he was lame.

By the time he returned, worming and sidling eccentrically through the steaming congestion, the discussion had shifted to the beatniks, as they were then called.

"What do you think of them?" Tillie catechized.

"I don't know any." He leaned toward her with an easy familiarity, as though he felt he had known her for years, and with the slipshod grin reported out of the side of his mouth an encounter at the bar with Jimmy Twitchell. Jimmy was being terribly acid about the political pugilist who had brung the petition, not for that reason, but for wrenching the floor from Jimmy precisely when he was going so well about the London season. The A.D.A. organizer's grasp of the international scene was by no means all he thought. "He doesn't even know who's at Cannes this year," Jimmy had said.

"That rich?" Pete said, poking her with his elbow.

"Who's our ambassador to France?" Tillie tersely asked, persevering in her quiz. She had a right to know precisely what she had been paired off with.

"Wait, that's not all," said Sneaky Pete, his duckbill nose seeming to broaden with his smile. "He not only did this place, you understand," rolling an eye along the dapper walls, "he's a damn good dress designer too, one of the best. So he's a two-time loser. But — this'll kill you — he sniffed and said, 'What's that cologne you're wearing?' To me. And I said, 'Only some shaving lotion I picked up in a drugstore, and I'm not wearing it, for Christ's sakes, I've just got it on!' We don't hit it off at all well," he concluded rather smugly.

Tillie of course wondered whether any of her questions had been in the least answered by this certainly very slippery character; but another mystery soon supplanted that: how, since he had not asked, had he

193

known she drank Scotch, and that she took water instead of soda, and how much? Had he gulped off her dregs on the way to see? These wonders yielded to others still. Toward midnight he leaned in her direction again and said: "Shall we go?"

"I have a car. Thanks just the same though."

"But I don't."

Bygone ambitions to be an actress had caused Tillie Shilepsky to practice in private the double take, the almost imperceptible head twitch of which only the most skilled craftsmen are capable in its refined form. The art lies in not being too obvious — otherwise it is just mugging. The emotion is almost telegraphed rather than registered. She did such a take now, apparently quite successfully, for the Seltzer himself gave no sign that he had noticed anything. He was gathering himself up to go. "I'm your escort after all," he said.

"You mean you want me to drop you."

"No, no. I'll take you home. I'm sure I can get a cab from there."

The term unmitigated gall sprang to mind as she rose in response to his example, and said her goodbyes with him. She felt Gertrude's speculative smile follow their departure, like something burning a hole in the back of her coat. Playing God was not the healthiest of signs in a woman; a regulatory interest in other people's lives is never far from the urge to meddle in them, nor that ever wholly divorced from the taste for disaster. It was no accident that the most zealous matchmaker Tillie knew, namely Gertrude Wilson, was also the worst gossip. She's talking to Jimmy Twitchell about us right now, Tillie thought as she reached the dark October street.

"Turn the clocks back tonight," said Pete, clumping alongside her toward the parked Chevrolet. "Giving us all an extra hour of insomnia."

"That's right."

He saw her settled behind the wheel, then hopped briskly around to the other side, as though afraid she might spurt off without him. Soon they were tooling along toward her place. "You needn't have troubled," she said, sensing the irony to be wasted. She thought she saw a way of turning her martyrdom to account, though.

Like many another woman, Tillie had been trying for years to learn Gertrude's age. She now felt that putting up with Gertrude's romantic selection in such stout fashion earned her the right to any information he might have on the score. So after a few circling preliminaries intended to be innocuous, such as how long the Seltzer had known her, etc., she asked negligently, "Have you any idea how old Gertrude is?" He threw out his hands with a comic grunt indicating the universal hopelessness of such a quest. "I don't even think Burt knows," he said, meaning Gertrude's husband.

He spoke with a vague mumble so nearly indistinguishable, almost like some more double talk, that it was half a block before Tillie had deciphered it. Meanwhile he mumbled some more in the same fashion, so that she finally turned to see what the matter was. She thought at first he had a cigarette in his mouth, but closer scrutiny revealed a sickroom thermometer to be jutting upward out of the corner of his mouth.

"Aren't you well?"

"I woke up this morning with a touch of something," he said, removing it. "Headachy, and a kind of upset in

the propinquity." She asked him drily whether he realized that was an actual word with a specific meaning, at
the same time glancing out her window to make it clear
that she had little or no interest in the reply. "But I was
determined to keep this date," he said. "Something told
me." He tried to read the thermometer in the fitful light
from streetlamps they were passing at increasing speeds,
turning it this way and that. Finally he held it down in
the glow of the dash. "No fever. I can come in."

Then all her efforts to discourage him were nothing
more than the time-honored technique for hooking a
husband. Indifference, playing hard to get, all that business, were devices to which she had certainly never
hitherto stooped, but they apparently paid off. For in the
short walk from the garage to her place he hobbled
adhesively along beside her, sometimes slipping a bit
into her wake. One leg was just a tiny bit shorter than
the other, was the thing, and Pete Seltzer amused her
now by showing how he would have looked normal by
walking with the good one in the gutter. That evened off
the difference. Her heart went out to him ("He doesn't
ask for sympathy") then was abruptly recalled, like a Yo-
Yo on a string ("That's how he gets it"). He sauntered
along in this fashion for a good part of the block, till an
approaching car sent him back to her side on the sidewalk. There he continued to patter along like a stray dog
that had decided to adopt her.

Waving a fresh highball, his free arm along the back
of an otherwise unoccupied sofa, Tillie watching from an
opposing chair, he talked about himself, his past, his
family, slaking what would be a natural thirst for all the
poop obtainable on a newcomer. His father had been a

196

spiffy gink, enhancing a reputation as a man about town, rather than otherwise, by a succession of business failures. One had been a public gymnasium, or health club, from which a member was hurried with a heart attack a week after the Grand Opening, following a workout on the parallel bars. The stricken man's family had sued, not successfully but with a publicity that put an end to the health club.

"Where is Seltzer *père* now?"

"Who?"

"Your father. Is he still alive?"

"Practically. He's in a nursing home not far from here. I visit him every Saturday evening. This time I think I'll go in the afternoon because I've got tickets to a dance that night. Would you like to go? It's a benefit for my father's burial society."

"I think I'm busy then."

"The customer eventually died."

"Oh, all right."

He was a surprisingly good dancer. His walking gait suggested the eccentric principle of the camshaft, with its regularly irregular rhythm. Dancing utilized that much more the motive strength inherent in it, as of something thrown into higher gear. He pumped them both across the floor with bursts of sure mechanical power. Tillie had trouble keeping up with him, as did the orchestra, which tended to lag a beat or two behind the pace he set. She was grateful for the intermissions, though the crowds were so dense there was no place to sit and they stood facing one another beside potted palms. It was a huge ballroom hung with a single colossal chandelier heavy with menacing reminders of *The Phantom of the*

Opera. The Something-or-other room of a local hotel. They drew on cigarettes, ignited, as it happily developed, from a silver lighter Pete Seltzer carried, and not by a kitchen match struck on the thumbnail, much less swiped across the seat of the pants. He wore a rented tuxedo which he said he was going to sublet to a friend of the same shape and size who needed it the following night for a shindig being thrown here by the Ukrainian Sick Benefit Society. He shook his head with an expressionless snort, whether deploring man's afflicted condition, or his venality in subcontracting suits of clothing not his own, was not made clear. He critically studied the cigarette given him with the remark that he preferred cigars, as did his father, but that they had for some time been unable to obtain the clear Havanas which were all they liked. He seemed puzzled by this difficulty. Tillie therefore now said, gazing at him above folded arms:

"That's because we no longer trade with Cuba."

"Oh?" He spoke as one interested in current events, eager to learn more. So she continued:

"For a while, I was afraid I might not be able to get my own favorite brand of tea, lapsang souchong, for the same reason. Because it comes from Red China, with whom we no longer trade either. But of course England does, and we import it from her. I don't see why we allow in tea from there and not tobacco from Canada, but anyway there it is. Mainland China is now completely in the hands of the Communists. Chiang Kai-shek only has Formosa."

"Ah, I see."

She had dropped her cigarette into the sandpot, and

now he did his, and escorted her back onto the dance floor. There, as he drove her around the ballroom at breakneck speeds, he whispered into the pink shell of her ear, "How would you like to go bowling next Saturday?"

"Mustn't you see your father?"

"He's not having any visitors. I doubt whether he'll pull through."

"Oh, well, in that case . . ."

She was hot and wretched, convinced that things would get worse before they got better. She was both galled by the persistence with which he kept dating her, and gratified at the early hour in each evening at which he procured himself another. It showed an endearing uncertainty, and tended to indicate that she was needed. The realization filled a rather sharp necessity of her own.

These were her scrambled thoughts each time she plodded up the steps to her apartment behind him. He always preceded her, as though instinctively sensing she was one of those women who preferred this fine inversion of courtesy to being themselves trailed up a stairway. Such subtle filaments were always turning up in his nature, making it difficult to end this as she would have liked. He had more redeeming features than any man she knew — but should a man need that many! He bowled insufferably well too, his gimp in this case putting an extra thrust into his delivery at just the right terminal moment. He gave her pointers about her own, explaining that to hit the front pin head-on always resulted in a split, or railroad, while an impact slightly on one side or other of it gave you a better pin-mix. She continued aiming straight for the center, banking on a certain inaccuracy to get the ball slightly to the right or left.

It was that night over hamburgers that he criticized her on a scale, and with a candor, to which no man would resort who was not seriously interested in you. Such, at least, was the thinking with which she saved face for both of them — bailed both of them out of this rather nasty little dilemma.

"Want to know something about yourself? Don't wear a girdle," he said. "I mean give the whollies a chance. I mean you haven't got that much that you need to go around with it in a sling, tightening in the natural curves and flattening out the wherewithal. Let it breathe. Same thing up here. Give the mercy-me's a chance. *Here,*" he persisted when she looked away with an injured *hauteur,* silently eating. "Mezzanine. Ribbons, laces, notions. So give the Jaspers notions. You know what? You're the kind of woman who could go without a bra altogether, let alone always folding your arms on top of it, like an Indian. With sweaters and even the right dress. Let the merchandise gallop a little."

He's got to go, she told herself as she tramped up the stairs angrily behind him. He knows nothing about the new emerging African nations — he thinks Cameroons are some kind of cookie — the ghetto problems, or what a megalopolis is. He seems to think *that's* some kind of prehistoric animal. That the country was about to become three or four of them, one of which would spread from Boston down to Washington and be known as Boswash, was wholly lost on him. With each succeeding such topic that sprang to mind she trod the stairs that much more indignantly, her numb legs notwithstanding.

She remembered her mother saying how awful her father was. Mrs. Shilepsky said she sometimes crossed the street to avoid him, or popped into a closet till he had passed her in the hall. Tillie didn't want to get into that. No, she would break it off. Tonight.

"How old are you?"

The question stung her like a whip. Regret for her lost youth was so keen in Tillie's unmarried case that to be asked her age was a threat of which she stood in actual physical fear. That was how she understood Gertrude as fiercely as she did. Her recoil was literally a reflex: her nerves jumped before her brain comprehended the words that had made them do so, as pain makes us withdraw our hand from a stove without the intervention of thought. A shock went through her, a blast of hot air, of cold wind.

"Thuh — thirty-two," she said, compounding her sensation by catching herself in a Gertrude lie. Tillie had turned thirty-three, but so recently that the falsehood might be forgiven; it would have been accurate a week ago. I'm three years older than this Pete Seltzer, she told herself through gritted teeth.

The incident made her fear the telephone wouldn't ring as, had it not occurred, she might have begun to hope it wouldn't. Instead of making a date that night, he kissed her goodnight at the door with only the promise that he would give her a jangle. A week passed without his doing so. By Wednesday of the following week she was frantic. Then the phone rang.

"Care to chop some more wood tonight? I think this is the best night for a lane there. Not a league night."

"Why, swell. But don't bother to come all the way over here to pick me up. I'll come by and honk."

That was the night she dressed as he had suggested. But it was for only one reason, and that not to give the whollies a chance, or certainly to let the merchandise gallop a little, or whatever: it was to put Pete Seltzer to a very crucial test, one that entailed, for her, the very criterion of sensibility. Would he crudely comment, or would he have the grace not to?

He passed the test with flying colors. There was only the merest murmur of extra pleasure at what his loitering palm found under her coat when he kissed her goodnight at the door. "Dear Diary," she mentally noted in the imaginary journal she kept, "he is incapable of the gaucherie of remarking that he saw I had taken his advice."

So against his jazzy raffishness and political immaturity (he signed any petition thrust at him without reading it, on the ground that anyone stellar enough to pound pavements and ring doorbells deserved your admiration per se) must be balanced this innate delicacy of which she had now so many tenuous but none the less palpable proofs. He was a bad Jasper from one point of view, but what foraging male wasn't, from that? Only the gray, proctoring presence of her mother with whom she lived kept him from "trying anything" there. The question was only when he would suggest they go "up to his place"— par for the course today.

But what was he really like all told? she asked herself again as, from the curtain of her third-story window, she watched him pump along home by way of the corner bus stop. She remembered something her mother used to say, in the humor of the spiffy-gink days of Pete's father, now, at last, departed. "Men are like streetcars. If you miss one, there'll be another along pretty soon," Mrs. Shilepsky would tell Tillie. And Tillie now answered aloud, as though Hollywood cameras were grinding behind her, "Yes, but they don't run after midnight." She waited a moment, imbibing the pity of the night streets, till Pete had swung aboard the last bus and vanished, before dropping the upheld curtain and turning to bed.

So having been forced into giving him a hearing, she began to see that he had possibilities. He was something like an old barn standing in an open field, ignored by the hurrying passerby but irresistible to the discerning eye, its foundation found on scrutiny to be firm and its beams sound, and, for the rest, crying out to be remodeled.

"Why don't you get your hair cut, Pete?" It was after all her turn.

He looked woundedly away across the restaurant, as the sheep before his shearers is dumb.

"All I mean is, I don't think long hair is right for you, Pete. It's still thick, and that wiry kind I think looks better short. I don't mean crew cut, but what's the term? *En brosse.* I think that would be right for you."

She did not comment after he had made his long overdue trip to the barber, but noted to herself how cruelly young the high-clipper jobs made men look. Then it seemed a pity he hadn't something better to go with the result than the frayed sport coat in which he kept turning up. So she accompanied him to a men's store where they picked out a gray herringbone suit as well as a standard navy blue blazer. That gave her the courage to bring up the subject of his teeth. They were in visible need of repairs thanks in part to a habit of sucking lozenges in order to keep his mouth wholesome in the grapplethrocks.

"How often do you see your dentist, Pete?"

"My dentist died some years ago."

"Aw, I'm sorry. I was looking for one myself."

The hint was taken, and he wound up having his teeth not only filled but capped, which gave his smile a rather villainous air, at least until you got accustomed to it.

Instinct told her that now he was going to pop the question. All the signs pointed to it. She knew it was coming one night in a French restaurant, after a lot of good food and wine. He cleared his throat as he picked up the coins from a saucer, leaving a pair of bills for the waiter.

"How would you like to come up to my place for a spot of heavy breathing?" he asked.

"All right," she said, gathering up her bag and gloves.

After all, if she was going to reform him, she would have to start mending her ways.

two

"THIS sort of thing does go on," she assured him as they mounted a flight of stairs even dingier than her own. She had told him before that she didn't find the neighborhood in which he lived very appetizing. To which he had replied, "It's the safest neighborhood in town. It's protected by the Mafia." His flat was over a Chinese restaurant, which Pete said had his favorite waiter in the world. Every time he spilled a plate of food or a bowl of soup all over you, he viewed the resulting havoc with Oriental resignation.

Then she was sitting in an overstuffed chair of russet brown, as nearly as could be judged in the light shed from a distant lamp, for the living room, at least, was a large one. Some kind of small doll-like trinket dangled from the lamp's tasseled pull, one feminine touch undoubtedly left behind by a forerunner. There was an upright piano against the opposite wall, while in another corner sat another short, rather frightened girl wearing Tillie's fun-fur coat of sheared rabbit, smiling tautly back at her from an oval mirror.

Pete took her coat, leaving her in her red wool dress.

She felt as though she were being stripped for surgery, not, as it happened, altogether inappropriately. "I'll whip us up a little anti-freeze," he said, vanishing into what by inference would be the kitchen. She didn't want to see it, right away. Out of the tail of her eye she caught a glimpse of an open bedroom with an unmade bed.

She rose to make a tour of this room, examining one by one a wealth of snapshots surely illustrating a sentimental turn of mind? There were some people picnicking in a field, a woman waving in bright sunlight from an open roadster with wooden spokes in the wheels, a fat boy humorously hugging the pillar of a white porch-rail on which he sat. Then she came upon a fleshy man in middle age, buttoned into a Chesterfield and holding a Homburg. His thick, not yet graying hair was short and brushed back, a cane was hooked on one arm, and Tillie could fairly smell the 4711 cologne she herself so loved, scent, label and all. The diamond eyes, though probably as blue as Pete's, looked vaguely Irish rather than Teutonic. She was holding the picture, stroking its small gilt frame and its glass cover with her thumb when Pete returned with their highballs.

"Your father?"

"Yes. Cheers."

Leaning back on the sofa with an arm characteristically spread along its back, he told her a story he'd just read in the medical section of a news magazine. A young woman nearly seven feet tall had had sections of bone removed from both legs — six inches in all. The operation was a success, making her a woman of at least reasonably normal height. The surgeons crowed. But they had forgotten one thing. When the woman got up out of bed, her arms hung down to her knees.

"That's some story to tell a girl on her bridal night," Tillie said. She set her glass down and put her ten fingers into her hair, in that tidying gesture with which women seem also about to claw themselves. She was really ready to grab her coat and run when Pete said, "Doctors have said they could fix my hoof, but what the hell," so she stayed.

Walking to the piano, for he was going to entertain her, he saw that she was reading a large novelty-shop button lying on a table beside her. "I make friends easily. Strangers take a little time," it said. "An out-of-town client gave that to me," he explained. "Do you realized I had to wear the damned thing all through lunch?" He dropped it into a wastebasket and continued on to the piano.

He gave the stool a ceremonial twirl and, without further preliminary, hurled himself violently into *Twelfth Street Rag*. She had never heard anything performed at such breakneck speed. Hunched in shirtsleeves over the yellowing keys, he pounded them with a velocity and a ferocity whose object seemed to be that of seeing how fast he could get through the piece. One chorus finished, he would negotiate the systematically stumbling, offbeat interpolation familiar to such low classics, and then instantly fling himself into another, as though determined he could clip a fraction of a second off his record, like a track athlete training for the fifty-yard dash. Also his two hands gave the impression of racing each other to the finish, somehow always winding up in a draw, as you did with Pete on the dance floor,

and, happily, both did with the orchestra. The piano itself was more than a little out of tune — she was certainly seeing life — and that enhanced the "raw" effect
prized in the honky-tonk and cathouse pianists on whom
he obviously modeled himself.

As abruptly as it had begun the squall of syncopation
stopped, and with a last flourish of a hand he rose,
turning around with a modest smile.

"That's terrific, Pete." The adjective seemed for once
right. "Do you play anything but ragtime?"

He gave a vague mumbling shrug intended to be
modest, and the next thing she knew he was gone and
there was water drumming into a bathtub somewhere.
It was then, in his absence, her coat hanging in a closet
from which it could be easily snatched, that the Dark
Stranger reappeared to her in another of the cautionary
visions to which she was subject.

He was that romantic personification of one's school-
girl dreams, visualized as approaching across the lobby of
a European hotel to warn you against the local drinking
water, as a pretext for next asking whether you believed
in fate. He now stood at a gate overhung with eglantine,
or some other old-world flower such as poets used to
weave into their verses, a sad frown on his face as he
gesticulated warnings to her. Raving, deploring, he
called to her, but she could hear nothing, as he existed
only in a picture with the sound track dead, or, still
worse, a silent film with nothing but the splatter of
piano music against it. His clothes were new, but old-
fashioned: a gray frock coat, rich dark cravat with high
collar, and the Homburg, clutched at breast level like a
steering wheel. The figure had taken root in her mind

when she was traveling abroad with her mother long ago, and was modeled on some of the men she had actually seen promenading in the streets of some of the smaller European towns from one to another of which she was whisked in her mother's half of some kind of experiment her parents were conducting, called separate vacations. She was still not old enough to be a virgin at the time, but would, as she understood the term, become one. The phantom began definitely to haunt her at Oberammergau, where they paused to take in the Passion Play, which had sounded enticing enough. He had flickered and floated in and out of her thoughts these twenty years since, that one who after discreetly accosting you in the lobby asked your mother's permission to "pay his respects" and then to take you to tea. She would have had to be at least twenty for that to seem feasible, and that was how the principals in the drama had proliferated into four. There was the girl of thirteen standing on tiptoe to peer into the tea shop to see herself at twenty sitting inside with the Dark Stranger, and now her thirty-three-year-old self watching all of that. It was intensely cinematic in flavor, and now it was all "wipe dissolved" except for one corner of the screen where the Dark Stranger remained, rocking his head in his hands, at the gate overhung with eglantine.

"You never turned up, you know," Tillie told him hurriedly, "and now here comes Pete Seltzer, so if you'll excuse me." And with an eyeblink *he* was wipe dissolved.

Pete could be heard tearing the bed apart and re-making it with fresh linen. She finished off her highball, like a thirsty child gulping down a glass of milk. When he came to fetch her, she saw from his gleaming jowls that he had shaved into the bargain, and was sure that the bathtub had been scoured as well, in preparation for her. "I'll go bathe now," she said, but he checked her with a hand on her elbow, quixotically murmuring that not all flowers needed watering, as he steered her into the bedroom.

Shivering on the cold floor, as her last silks dropped like flags lowered in surrender, she told herself that ignorance was correctable, but innate delicacy such as his could never be taught. He was a gentleman to his fingertips — those now breaking the bread of her body. He worshiped on his knees, Pete, stroking her smooth sides and babbling skillfully as he sought the garden where the whollies grew. She broke and ran away from him, into the bed.

"Do you like Joyce?" she asked through chattering teeth.

"Joyce who?" he asked, popping in beside her.

"Well, your interest in language."

It was clear to Pete how much tutoring she herself needed. After caressing her persuasively for a bit, he took her hand in his and guided it gently to what he called "the hardened sinner." It was after he had spent himself that he realized how she was shivering, and became once more tender. "Why, what have we here. There, there." He gathered her close into his arms, and was so solicitous that before she knew it he had appeased himself again. It was, all in all, though, not as bad as she had feared. Tillie had been overprepared for the Bridal Night by a mother given to the warning, "It's something every woman has to go through." And if Tillie had taken rather the inherited attitude of being stripped for surgery, she could now enjoy the sense of the operation's having proved a success.

She was a little dismayed by Pete's quick recovery. He was evidently not one to loiter with soft endearments in what the sex manuals called the Afterglow. He returned unclothed to the kitchen to whip them up a little jetsonflots. That was all right. The plate of largely unidentifiable odds and ends he had dug out of the icebox were brought to her, and, she lying in the bed with the sheet to her chin and he sitting on it side-saddle, they washed their snacks down with cold beer. Then he waddled away into the living room, where through the open door she could watch him again sitting at the piano with his back to her, playing *Twelfth Street Rag* at, if anything, even dizzier speeds than before. He finished with the flourish, faced her with a concert-hall bow, and came back to her applause. The hardened sinner drooped with contrition now, halfway to his knees. She no longer felt sorry for him; he just seemed to have three legs of unequal length, instead of two. "Isn't that more than you need?" He gave the vague prudential grunt with which men try to acknowledge a compliment without looking too utterly like an ass, and removed the plate of midnight debris from her chest and set it aside on a table. It was amazing how quickly you became sophisticated. Our dear Tillie, once so up-tight, yes, fairly creaking with inhibitions, was now liberated, wide open to sex and its vested humors. Able to enjoy Pete's story about a country doctor he swore he had known, who went around lecturing to youth groups on the evils of masturbation, advising any boy who practiced it to get a firm grip on himself. Tillie recalled the newspaper headline: "Bishop withdraws at birth control conference." Pete said it was people who didn't know what they were saying who spread the real sunshine. They were worth a hundred of your malicious wits.

Tillie closed her eyes, and now, smoothing the sheet to either side of her like a contented convalescent, had a very sweet sensation indeed.

She had a *déjà vu*. That is normally a phenomenon so characteristic only of the very young that to have one after thirty is rare. She had not had one in years. The moment was like recovering her girlhood, rather than losing it. Thus her delight at having absolutely known, as Pete turned away with the plate, that he was going to say: "Look, I don't want to feel guilty about something. But are my suspicions correct?"

"Well, I like to think of a line from Hart Crane. The 'Powhatan's Daughter' section of *The Bridge*, you know. 'And she is virgin to the last of men.'"

"He the one who goes ape with the ink?"

"Yes. You've read him then?"

"I doubt whether you could call it that. Something I prolly saw in a paperback I picked up in an airport."

"I suppose *Beowulf* is more your speed."

"No, I haven't read him either."

"Silly, it's the name of the poem, not the poet."

"Who wrote it?"

"We don't know."

"Then nobody's one up. But I want you to know how grateful I feel, hell, that's not the word, well, yes, why not — grateful, and a little guilty," he said and lowered his eyes in shame, to hide his smug expression, prolly.

Well, Diary, he's not one of your dried-up intellectuals, always with their nose in a book — hah! not him — always analyzing everything to a fare-thee-well, she would mentally scribble while she buffed her nails or rinsed out a pair of hose. He doesn't anatomize and define everything till there's no fun left at all in it, including double talk. *He* doesn't know that's a series of pleasurable unexpected epistemological suspensions. Why should he? He lost twenty clams on the election, in which he thus had more interest than I had thought . . . But getting back to the fun, he doesn't destroy it by vivisecting it, he *is* fun. After a movie we had a sandwich at one of those Prexy joints that have the slogan, "The Hamburger with a college education." "Mine's a dropout," mutters he, lifting the bun from an underdone patty. Adjacent diners in stitches.

She continued to sleep with him to prove that she wasn't promiscuous, as a single fling would have done. He was often short of funds those days, thanks, he said, to his saving so much a week toward a car of his own. Tillie was working at the time in a producer's office, and sometimes took him out to dinner when he was broke. Once she insisted on their trying the Chinese restaurant, where he found all the wall mirrors unnerving. He said he never looked into mirrors, or had his picture taken if he could help it, "out of vanity." She assured him that he was handsomer than he looked, just as Bartók's music is better than it sounds, tapping him on the nose with a clean spoon as she did so. "Why do you have a glass hanging in your living room then?" she asked him playfully. He replied that it was an heirloom brought from the old country, which his mother made him promise to keep and treasure always. "That was before she died," he said. Then he sighed and glanced at the ceiling. "Well, shall we go up to my place?"

Another *déjà vu!*

That was the night she saw a hairpin on the floor as she was drawing a stocking up. She didn't use them. She picked it up and confronted him with it. "You have a cleaning woman come in, don't you?"

"Yes, once a week."

"Tell her to tidy herself up. Not to shed her hairpins all over the place."

"Right."

They sipped brandies as they gossiped, she in Pete's robe and Pete in the raw. Gertrude and Burt Wilson were moving across the river into a New Jersey suburb where Jimmy Twitchell had a small country place. He had found theirs for them, and would undoubtedly "do" it for them — or for Gertrude, since Burt took no interest in his surroundings. Tillie and Pete laughed as they pictured him slumped in front of the television set while Gertrude and Jimmy twittered over fabrics and colors. Pete yawned, showing a single gleam of gold far back in his mouth. "Burt's no intellectual," he said. Then he rose and went over to the piano, where he played *Twelfth Street Rag.*

"Would —?" Tillie began when she thought he had finished, but it was only a pause between choruses. It took two or three more such attempts before she was at last able to say: "Would you like to meet my mother?"

"I already have."

"Oh, you've been introduced to her, and you've heard her shuffling around in the back room while we try to neck, but that's not really meeting her. I mean come to dinner. She's crazy about ragtime. You're just a buff, but it's her past. Well then, how's Friday?"

Mrs. Shilepsky, a thin gray woman in a lilac dress of shot silk, pointed out, with a finger like an autumn twig, the merits of the tablecloth off of which they were eating the beef Strogonoff she and Tillie had fixed. It was an ancestral damask into which figures of the twelve disciples were embroidered, each of which Mrs. Shilepsky indicated by name as she rose and made a circuit of the table. Pete lifted his plate to discover Judas Iscariot underneath it. The cloth had been exhumed from a trunk for the occasion. "A trunk, Pete, not a drawer! So little do people care about these things any more." Pete was relieved that it was the cloth that smelled of mothballs and not Mrs. Shilepsky, that is, her dress, though perhaps both did. Long before a complete orbit had regained for Mrs. Shilepsky her own seat at the head of the table, she had given off talking about the disciples and begun to mourn her husband's indifference to familial treasures and the continuity they embodied. He had run away, nowhere to be seen these twenty years: he had made the separate vacations permanent. "I'd leave him in a minute if I could locate him!" Mrs. Shilepsky cried as she circled along behind Pete. He ran a finger under his shirt collar, like a bad actor illustrating discomfiture. But after a few glasses of wine he loosened up, and then Tillie made her first request.

"Talk some double talk for Mother, Pete."

"Oh, I don't think so," he said. "People don't understand that your thoughts are just as hersensnerth as theirs, even though you may not abiquine them with the same perambisnath."

"Well, don't, then," Mrs. Shilepsky said, patting him on the hand as a guest who was not going to be forced to do anything he didn't want to do. She turned her head to look into the kitchen before rising to clear the plates and fetch the dessert, a strawberry mousse whose virtues she extolled well before they had begun to eat it. "Tillie made this herself. Young brides these days don't care about cooking. They'd just as soon feed their man something dumped out of a can, like a dog." She enacted a graphic pantomine of someone slapping an overturned tin with the heel of the hand, in order to release its contents, assumed to be adhering to the sides. It was obvious where Tillie had got her dramatic ability. "Well, you won't find this one afraid to pitch in, I can tell you that," she said, pointing the finger straight at Tillie as though accusing her of something like probity or diligence or something else hopelessly out of fashion.

After the mousse, which was all it had been cracked up to be, Tillie clapped her hands gaily, as though they were all having more fun than might at first blush appear, and said, "Now Pete's going to play the piano. Won't you play something for us, Pete? Anything."

Pete played *Twelfth Street Rag*, ripping it off at a rate possibly never before equaled except by members of the Philharmonic seeing how fast they could get through *The Flight of the Bumblebee*. Mrs. Shilepsky sat on the sofa spanking her palms together to the rhythm of it, rocking her head from side to side as she exclaimed, "I always liked swing." When he had finished a couple of choruses he was prevailed on to do another and then still another, in lieu of anything else in the way of encores. Then Mrs. Shilepsky rose to excuse herself, but Pete insisted she stay a while. He had begun to find her interesting, if not downright amazing.

That left only the question of his improvidence still unsettled — but not for long. He greeted Tillie one evening with the news that he had been kicked upstairs. No longer need he spend his days in the streets, buttonholing strangers in order to quiz them, clipboard and pencil at the ready. Now he had an office job as a supervisor, collating and organizing the data gathered by others. The promotion included a raise, and he was already spending the money. He had his eye on a new Buick, or, if that was too expensive for his pocketbook, at least a new Chevrolet. "I wonder how much a convertible would cost me," he said.

"That depends on what they'll allow us on mine," Tillie answered, levelly.

She resented being taken for granted. But romantic avowal was not Pete Seltzer's speed, and certainly the tableau of a ceremonial proposal on bended knee was more than could reasonably be expected in this case — or any, for that matter. This was a more casual era, whatever the Dark Stranger of her Oberammergau dreams might think, raving and despairing at the garden gate, there in the upper-right-hand corner of her fancy. How casual was driven home to her by the manner in which such elements now fairly regarded as having ripened between these literal lovers were, at last, brought to harvest.

Mrs. Shilepsky spent a weekend with her sister in Ohio. Tillie invited Pete into her bed that Saturday night. Sunday morning she fixed them a late breakfast, over which they dallied beween the sheets. After clearing their trays away, she took a shower, and then came back into the bedroom for her robe. Seeing Pete lying there, a cigarette in his hand, with an air of lolling content- ment, she said something not intended as a wisecrack at all, which, however, the instant it was out, struck her as quite a funny commentary on what could certainly be called the new era. She later claimed it as a witticism.

"The honeymoon's over," she said, throwing a pillow at his head. "Time to get married."

three

TILLIE did not invite the Wilsons to the wedding reception because it was kept purposely small, mostly just a few relatives, and for a number of other more incidental reasons, but mainly because of the poor judgment Gertrude had shown as a matchmaker.

Pairing two such utterly dissimilar people as Tillie and Pete could only be the product of the most brilliantly acute and incisive perception or downright obtuseness, and Gertrude Wilson was not the former. She was a notoriously indiscriminate meddler who liked playing God, and who did not mind playing with fire in order to do so provided others ran the risk of being burned. Tillie had elected to run that risk on her own, with her eyes open, and no escape hatches. Pairing her and Pete Seltzer had been dumb, *given the matchmaker's lack of access to, and therefore total ignorance of, the subtle, subterranean elements that finally made the union possible despite its surface absurdity.* Perhaps every marriage involves close harmony, but a chord is not produced by bringing two hands blindly down upon the keyboard to see what we shall see, as Gertrude was always irresponsibly doing. If one was produced by chance in this case — if one of Huxley's apes had thumped out *Point Counter Point* again — it was no thanks to Gertrude. No. On the basis of the facts available at the time, the blind date was a booboo. The emerging results had no bearing on the matter. Life abounds in instructive parallels, but one from the world of baseball would suffice.

A manager tells a batter to bunt. The batter swings instead and hits a home run, winning the game — and is fined a hundred dollars. The manager is quite right in taking that punitive measure. Given the assessable facts at the time — who's pitching, on second, up next — taking a cut at the ball was dumb. So was doubling her off with Pete Seltzer, given the above facts. The odds had been wildly against anything coming of it (as they are against filling an inside straight in a poker game). The fact that you do fill it, or do happen to smack the apple out of the park, does not alter your stupidity in having banked on it. Besides, owing her husband to a woman with so little grasp of the human merchandise galled Tillie. She was fining Gertrude a hundred dollars.

Pete's favorite literature, as it turned out, was outmoded sex advice. He combed the secondhand bookstores for old-fashioned marriage manuals, the cornier the better; the gems they yielded were, of course, more priceless the farther back in time you went. In his collection were treasures rarer than those landmarks of the unintentionally laughable, *What a Young Man Ought to Know* and *What a Young Woman Ought to Know*. In a musty jumble shop he had found a handbook called *Preparing for Marriage*, which had a chapter dealing with how a bride should behave on her honeymoon, parts of which he read aloud to Tillie on theirs — the real one. He had packed it in his bag to amuse her with. They were pounding through the night on the Canadian Pacific railroad, homeward bound after a week at Lake Louise. He lay in the upper berth of their bedroom while she did her nails in the lower.

"Listen to this," Pete said, reading a passage on the subject of the wedding night. " 'Having, by disrobing, unveiled to her man that supreme work of the Creator, a Woman, let her permit herself to be gathered into his arms, and, having done so, kiss him full on the mouth. Then let her engage in some dallying byplay, such as teasing him with the fib that her wedding ring is lost, and asking him to look for it. Let her hide it in that other treasure, the ultimate flower that he seeks, nestled betwixt her thighs, and slowly, coyly lead him on with clues and subtle hints, blushing sweetly all the while —' No, I'm serious. I mean it. I'm not making this up. Here, look for yourself." He hung down like a bat from the upper, pointing to the passage in the book.

Tillie believed it. "Where should she hide it?" she teased, smiling at her inverted lord. "What in, Pete?"

She had read somewhere that many passionate men, even bawdy ones, are squeamish about the words physically repressed people often throw around unblushingly. This was rather true of Pete, odd as it seemed with the newfangledness implied in his amusement with the old. He said that the English vocabulary for sex was hopeless, very nearly all down the line. There were only the coarse words on the one hand, and, on the other, the bookish ones, hardly less embarrassing. There was nothing in between, nothing really and honestly usable for two people. But he not only talked about it; he did something about it. He applied himself to filling this need by revamping the entire erotic vocabulary.

For every organ or act for which a foul or a stilted word was the only existing alternative, he tried to think of a suitable one, from the phonetic and other standpoints. He kept a notebook of his creations, tirelessly changing, resubstituting, polishing and perfecting, till his scholarship yielded at last a finished dictionary, and they had a whole new glossary for "thrunkling," as the act was now called. The word was deliberately devised to convey implications of muffled intimate uproar, of drunken bedded ecstasies, and so much more. It packed a host of related concepts such as throbbing, rumpling, tumbling, grunting, humping, pumping, and Christ knew what all. Even spelunking, with its Freudian overtones of darkly penetrated mammalian caverns, was embedded in it (though not always with the speaker's awareness, of course, and possibly not even Pete's, except on a subliminal level which was the important one). Poe had not put more painstaking and systematic thought into what combination of syllables would best communicate melancholy, before deciding on Ulalume for that.

When the lexicon was finished, he showed it to her with an air of long, exhausted inquiry, like one showing you a thesis that must be his life's work. She read it through with nods and murmurs of approval. "Very good," she said. "Some of these are marvelous. So expressive. Onomatopoeic."

"Vut?"

"They combine sense with sound. I see what you mean now about the old words being absolutely no good for general use. Either dirty or medical. This language two people could talk."

"Well, then, let's talk it. We can begin tonight."

"Aren't you too tired?"

"No."

Now it was Tillie's turn to demur. She begged off by explaining that she had no objection to the revolution as such, but talking sex was not her speed in any case, if he remembered, the way it seemed to be his. She did not want to hurt his feelings or belittle his masterwork, certainly to be a poop, but she was not by temperament given to verbalizing what she was doing, as, she knew in all fairness, some people were. Since she never used the old words either, no offense need be taken at her not moaning their equivalents while engaged in — or, as was more often the case, submitting to — what they stood for.

"But you go right ahead," she told him. "Make yourself at home in me, on me, or anything else. I've emphasized this before. I think everyone should be happy in his own way."

And he was. He wallowed in his twofold freedom, physical and linguistic. Extolling her soft white yummels, he would bury his face in them, sometimes as though trying to achieve death by suffocation. Or he would lip their little pink phelps as his hand strayed independently downward, across her dimpled woburn to her thrombush, into which he sank at last with many a grateful cry in praise of it. He tended to engage in unbroken staccato exclamations about what he had done, was doing, and would do, in the end crouching over her in a manner that put her uncontrollably in mind, not so much of a philologist, as of a jockey flailing his mount up

223

the homestretch. She sometimes got up in the morning with her whollies black and blue. He was equally conscientious in the more tender and quiet moments, which she said were movements marked *lento*, an anatomical term with which he said he was not familiar. He tutored her in the most exquisite caresses. With her long red talons, he loved to have her, not quite stroke, nor yet exactly scratch, but ever so gently to scroke, his quonkles.

"Swell?" he said when she threatened to fall asleep in the midst of these labors, giving her a poke. She mumbled agreement, shifting aside to ease the pressure of his hand under her splaything.

Faced with the charge that this was nothing more or less than jabberwocky, he defied you to cite a word that wasn't. All language was simply jabberwocky that had become familiar. The proof? The speed with which any word could be reduced to absurdity by repetition. Pick 'a word — pool, spindle, chicken, Tuscaloosa, anything — say it over to yourself a few times, and the meaning will drain out of it faster than water out of a bucket in which a hole has been shot. Bucket, hole, shot . . . all ludicrous — and *strange* if you stare at them hard enough on the printed page. Keep it up and you will feel meaning running like sawdust out of yourself.

Tillie nodded as she knitted boots . . . boots . . . boots for her expected child. "That's right," she said. "In a moment you're holding your empty sides, a mere semantic rag flapping in the cognitive void."

"*Vut?* So in other words, all we talk is gibberish. That's what's so fascinating about watching two guys talk in a foreign language. In one way the advantage is theirs, or so they think, because you don't know what the hell they're saying, but in another way it's you who are one up on them, because you can see that in the long run it's all so much systematic hissing and gasping and gurgling."

"And gesticulating. In other words, you're an Existentialist."

"How the hell do I know? What do they stand for?"

"They don't 'stand for' anything. They just believe man makes out as best he can in a meaningless universe."

"The universe. I've got more to worry about than that," Pete said, and wandered off to the kitchen for some beer.

He stayed there long enough to scour a broiling pan, a kind of chore he did not mind since he didn't want her to break her nails any more than she did. She smiled gratefully as she listened, thanking heaven for what it had sent her. When he returned with two glasses of beer, he made sure there were coasters to set them down on, and then when he removed his shirt, it being warm, he first asked her permission. Experiencing the warm maternal feeling she had had for him almost from the first, she took in the Boy Scout look about him, again accentuated by a haircut; the way he licked his lips after gulping from his glass; the careful manner in which he set it down on the coaster.

"You have an awful lot of moles, Pete," she joshed.

"And the swans have all gone."

So Tillie awoke from a dream of love to find herself married to a model husband. This was music with which she certainly wanted to taunt Gertrude a little. She wanted her to know what a diamond-in-the-rough she

225

had given her, in case she had thought it merely a polished stone. Or the last streetcar, or the last available lug of a life preserver thrown to a woman past thirty. But opportunity remained lacking because Gertrude failed to return Tillie's telephone calls, left with the maid. It devolved on Jimmy Twitchell to tattle, helpfully of course, that Gertrude was miffed over not having been invited to the reception. He was tickled only too pink to be able to discharge these painful duties, and when Tillie telephoned him as a last resort to pick his brains about it, he invited himself to tea in order to discuss it in the depth required.

Thank God Pete was out when Jimmy wafted through the doorway in a tight tweed coat with side vents, carrying a porkpie hat and lemon-yellow gloves, trailing some expensive scent. Tillie remembered Pete's outrage at being asked by Jimmy what cologne he was "wearing," the night of the blind date. Jimmy marched on into the living room, his black little eyes flicking every which way on the lookout for "horrors." He was evidently not disappointed.

"What an interesting place," he said. "Where did you ever find it?"

This was fag stuff, but nobody minded, as they didn't the malice behind it, because he was so amusing. He drove men out of their minds, but the women loved him, a common enough paradox. He carried the pollen of gossip everywhere, breeding and crossbreeding half-truths and untruths with the facts, hatching and crosshatching the mutual resentments, fears, jealousies and social spites of women he outdid at their own game. He plied his trade with the skill of a court eunuch. He was a liar and a thief, creating scandal where there was none, and keeping his conversational quiver stocked with witticisms stolen from everywhere. Women relished his mischief making, though they knew that an hour after they had been its beneficiaries they would be its butts. An insane snoop, he had insisted on calling partly to see how Tillie lived. It was instantly obvious that he was slumming. She had expected such a reaction to the way her apartment was "done," and had tried to redeem herself a little by plucking Franck's D Minor off the phonograph just before his arrival and replacing it with something a little less de trop — Sibelius. She shut that off a few minutes after she had taken his hat and gloves.

"Don't turn it off on my account, darling," he said. He was the only man who had ever called her darling, and she rather liked it.

"We can talk better. It's Sibelius's Second. Do you like it?"

"I always thought it was marred by a poor score." He flicked his beady eyes at her in wicked expectation.

Now that the music had ended she could hear his shoes squeaking as he walked about the room, still taking things in. Incredibly natty as he was, his feet always struck you as somehow the neatest thing about him, very tiny and beautifully shod, with what seemed shoes a size too small, as though he wanted to make them appear even daintier than they were. As he strolled around, it seemed the feet themselves, rather than the Oxfords in which they were encased, that were uttering little cries of protest, like pining cats.

"Gertrude *is* in a snit, you know," he said.

"I don't see why. The reception was private."

"Ah, yes, like a funeral service. Well, I'll take that back to her, or perish in the attempt. That it was only for relatives."

"I wish you would, Jimmy." It was a slight falsehood, since there had been a few "intimate friends," but since Gertrude would never realize the category did not include her, as hers would not have included Tillie were the roles reversed, it seemed relatively justified, even called for in the interest of composing ruffled spirits.

"Shall do," Jimmy said, sitting down to the tea. He flapped a napkin out on his knee. "The main thing is that Gertrude now knows you know she's ignoring you. So that's been tidied up. Now we can go on from there. Do show me the silver pitcher with which she said she heaped coals of fire on your head."

Tillie fetched the wedding gift, and while Jimmy admired it she drew out a few more grains of gossip about Gertrude, an attempt which found him nothing loth.

"Oh, she's up to the ears in her pet charity again. The Mental Health Ball, you know. She had her picture in the local paper as usual, sitting in her morning room in a stunning suit, 'addressing' invitations that all the poor drones, you know, have already addressed. It's all a mare's nest, darling, of course. You might get yourself clear out of the doghouse by sending a check as Patrons for the Ball. I think it's a hundred dollars."

So that was that. He finished his tea and was off and away, hurrying through the doorway on meowing feet.

Tillie sent the check, though they couldn't afford it, and though the Ball was in Gertrude's suburb, not the city, where the Seltzers still lived. She sent it directly to

Gertrude, who had, of course, to acknowledge it. She had the grace to do so by phone. They made a date for lunch the following Wednesday, when Gertrude was coming to town to shop anyway.

By now there was another virtue to report in the case of Pete. The apartment building in which Mrs. Shilepsky had continued to live was torn down, and while she looked for another flat she moved in with them. The arrangement was only temporary, of course, but Pete's good-humored efforts to make her feel at home were commendable by any standards.

"Imagine a guy who likes his mother-in-law," Tillie said across the luncheon table.

Gertrude did not take this at all well. She seemed, in fact, to freeze up for a few moments. This struck Tillie as an odd reaction to the grades one's protégé is earning, and, puzzled, she decided that another consultation with Jimmy Twitchell was indicated. She called him on the phone to report what had happened, and it made his day.

"You've put your foot in it this time, darling," he told her. "The subject of mothers-in-law is a sore spot with the Wilsons. Gertrude won't have Burt's mother's toes under her table for one minute, even though they'll get her money — the old woman's only sitting on half a million dollars — while your — what's his name? Pete? While Pete welcomes into the family bosom a mother-in-law without a sou. No wonder Gertrude's mad. She thought you were rubbing it in. There are fewer burdens in life harder to bear than the irritation of a good example," he said, not bothering to credit Mark Twain with the aphorism. "What else did you talk about?" he asked, hopefully.

Tillie had not meant to air the conversation with which she had subsequently tried to mend the uncomprehended damage. Now suddenly Jimmy, treacherous as he could be in these matters, struck her with a flash as a possible ally in sailing social waters she clearly could not navigate on her own. No harm could be done by trying to enlist him, certainly. And the moment on the telephone offered an unexpected chance to show Pete off in quarters where he was, surely, held in the lowest possible esteem.

"Well, I tried to change the subject, but we did seem to stay on the subject of husbands, and in the course of something or other, I forget what, I repeated something Pete said that I thought rather amusing. He calls himself a sonofabitch manqué. He wouldn't *mind* a little adultery, but he'll never make the grade. Not the type." Gertrude would appreciate that it was the "after" Pete talking, the one exposed to Tillie's influence, not the "before" of the blind first date. The silk purse, not the sow's ear. To Jimmy she merely said, "Don't you think that's rather cute? A sonofabitch manqué?"

There was a brief pause at the other end. Then Jimmy said: "You never miss, do you? With all Burt's bed hopping — all right, anyway the slap-and-tickle he's famous for at parties — how did you expect *that* to go down? Darling, you need an editor."

That much Tillie had realized at the moment. She knew she'd put her foot in it as soon as the words were out. She also knew how you didn't need an enemy if you had Gertrude for a friend. In her panic therefore she had seized on every possible means of placating her. By instinct she knew that one thing a woman dearly loves is a compromising confidence from another. Before she knew it she was chattering about how instantly she and Pete Seltzer had hit it off, whatever doubts Gertrude herself might have secretly harbored.

". . . and so at last I said, 'O.K., old boy, the honeymoon's over. Time to get married.' "

Tillie had looked across the restaurant in blank disbelief at what she had just heard. *How much had she had to drink?* "Give me another," she told the waiter hurriedly. "Gertrude?"

Gertrude shook her head sweetly, her eyes shut. She had Tillie in her pocket. She had been fed a plump canary indeed, and could sit back and lick the feathers off her whiskers.

Aghast as she was that she had as much as told Gertrude that she and Pete had slept together before they were married, she at the same time wondered why she cared. People took it for granted these days — that was the whole point of the wisecrack. It was a commentary on the times. The truth of the matter was simply that Tillie by temperament shrank from having anything that intimate known about herself, especially by a woman like Gertrude who could be counted on to spread her secret in turn. She would retail it instantly to Jimmy Twitchell, who would scatter it to the four winds. Seeing at what price she had bought back her drop in the woman's graces, she immediately reversed herself and tried to recover some of the forfeited self-esteem.

"But getting back to Mother, she'll stay with us at least until she finds an apartment she can afford. Which may be a long time, because, of course, she doesn't have a dime," Tillie added with a touch of pride. "But getting back to Pete, it's really touching the way he befriends her. And kind of funny too. He never leaves the woman's side."

"That shouldn't be hard in four rooms."

They both laughed heartily at that as they opened their menus to order. It was high time they had something to eat.

Evenings at the Seltzers' continued to be everything Gertrude might have cause to resent, could she but be vouchsafed an actual glimpse of them. Mrs. Shilepsky kept recommending Pete to Tillie. "You won't find them coming any better than that one," she would say, pointing at him and sometimes tapping him with a finger. "More all wool and a yard wide." Pete would sit wearing his good-boy smile, looking younger than ever in the high short haircuts that he got with regular frequency now that he realized what they did for you. He would not hear of Mrs. Shilepsky banishing herself to her bedroom after the evening meal, but insisted that she consider this her home as much as theirs. It was an order. Tillie shook her head, unable to believe her luck, as her knitting needles clicked. Pete would work on his library, composed, in the nature of things, of volumes ready to fall apart, some first editions though he didn't know it till they were pointed out to him. He would mend the spines with a special glue another bibliophile had told him about, patch torn pages with Scotch tape. Mrs. Shilepsky often joined in with needlework, cozily relating harrowing incidents from her own marriage, whose hell and high water were pleasant to recall now amid the peaches and cream of this one.

"Shilepsky would fly into rages," she said. "He would throw every dish in the house, one by one, quiet, deliberate like. Oh, never at me. Just at the wall. He would take a cup and — children, listen — wind up before throwing it, just like a pitcher. That terrible? He would be crazy mad. It would be the cold deliberate way he'd do it, so worse than hot words or flying off the handle. Well, I kept my temper. I would sit there calmly in the chair watching, and broadcast it."

"Broadcast it?" said Pete softly.

Mrs. Shilepsky nodded, shifting a clove in her mouth.

"Like an announcer in the baseball park. 'Here comes the windup,' I'd say, 'the pitch, *and* it's another piece of second-best china smashed to smithereens against the wall. But this Shilepsky on the mound there isn't second-best. No siree Bob. He's in good form today, never better.' Till he was crazy mad. Oh, he was a mean devil. Tillie'll tell you that. But there were the good times," she added, and would amuse them with stories to prove it, or by cracking jokes illustrative of the household, or, more particularly, the era.

Mrs. Shilepsky's jokes were things you had only your sense of humor to see you through. They were mostly vintage anecdotes about public figures of a more robust time, such as William Jennings Bryan who, speaking to a bunch of Iowa farmers from a manure spreader while stumping for the presidency, said, "Ladies and gentlemen, this is the first time I've ever addressed an audience from a Republican platform." Mrs. Shilepsky herself finally dug Pete's double talk, possibly because it was after all not so far in spirit from the spiffy ginks and fancy gazebos of her own day who would tell you their epizootic was sagatiating, when you asked them how they were.

She usually did retire early. Then after a while Pete would stretch and say to Tillie, "Well, shall we put the ears on the kid tonight?"

The reason why Pete clung to his mother-in-law was a long time in dawning on Tillie, but at last it did.

He didn't know what to call her. Therefore he moved heaven and earth not to have to call her anything. "Mother" he apparently couldn't swing, as many husbands can't. "Mrs. Shilepsky" was the reverse, too formal. "Mother Shilepsky" was out. He wasn't going to sound like a nun in a convent. The mother-in-law's first name is often a way out for self-conscious husbands, but he could not bend his tongue into the shapes necessary to say "Blossom," or "Bloss," as her few remaining friends sometimes called her. So it went. If absolutely forced to a direct salutation, it would be "Say" or "Why, er" or even "Hey." He was at his wits' end, on pins and needles against the threat of having some day, under some circumstance, to call the length of the house, or even of the room, to get her attention, and thus address her by some name or other. Meanwhile, if he had something to say to her when she was elsewhere, he would go where she was and then, after a convincing interval in her vicinity, begin, "Look," or "Oh, by the way." That was why he was always at the woman's side, why the two were "so close," or "absolutely inseparable," as Tillie sometimes put it in bragging about him to her friends.

When it dawned on her that he was simply going to

fantastic lengths to avoid or postpone that critical moment when he would be absolutely forced to a direct vocative, she decided to have some sport with him. She chose her moment carefully. She was in the bathtub and he was pulling his shaving gear from the medicine chest.

"Oh, look, would you do me a favor?" she said. "Ask Mother whether Gertrude telephoned today while I was at the hairdresser's."

"I'm in my shorts."

"You don't have to go to her. Just call down."

"Call *down?* Where is she?"

"In the back yard. Just slip on your robe and yell off the porch."

"Can't you?"

"I'm in the tub."

"Can't it wait till you get out? I've got lather all over me," Pete said, briskly plying his shaving brush to make this true.

"No, it's important, and I may forget it." Closing her eyes and trying to keep a straight face, she said, "My God, all you have to do is holler down over the banister. She's right there in her usual chair."

Pete set his brush down, clearing his throat nervously. He was evidently under great strain. He got his bathrobe from the hook behind the door, put it on, and started slowly off in his slippers. It was clear that he was suffering. This was It — the moment preordained and not to be evaded.

Tillie lay very still in the tub, listening. Pete could be heard miserably clearing his throat again as he scuffed through the nearby kitchen and out onto the porch. The door was open, it being summertime, and she could hear him through the screen door. That twanged shut behind him. Now he was crossing the porch, now standing at the rail, looking down at where Mrs. Shilepsky sat sunning herself, three floors below. There was a long pause. Then Tillie heard, shrill and piercing, the whistle Pete could so adroitly produce by putting two fingers into his mouth. It stood them in such good stead when summoning taxis in the rain. It must have served him well now. She could imagine her mother twisting about in her Adirondack chair to squint inquiringly upward, as well as hear Pete calling down, perhaps between cupped hands, "Did Gertrude Wilson telephone today? No? Thanks. That's all."

He had outwitted her. But she would trap him yet, Tillie thought, lathering a leg.

She never did. The problem was solved for poor Pete as it has been for so many countless husbands before him, simply by their becoming fathers. By mid-autumn he was off the hook. He could call Mrs. Shilepsky "Grandma."

four

TILLIE made sure Gertrude Wilson was one of the first to know she was expecting, and when the child was born, a boy, Gertrude sent along a handsome silver runcible spoon with his name, Charles, engraved on it in a flowing script. Their relationship entered on a period of relative felicity. Gertrude assured her that no one could raise a child in the city, and that she would keep an eye peeled for a house for the Seltzers in her neck of New Jersey. Perhaps in part because she had no children of her own, she displayed here the same proprietorial force with which she did her matchmaking, and with every remembrance that the Seltzers couldn't afford to buy, yet at least, but would have to rent.

When Charlie was turning two she stumbled on just the thing. A five-room Colonial which could only be rented because it belonged to an estate over which the heirs were wrangling at a rate that guaranteed its unsalability for years. The Seltzers drove out to look at it one Sunday afternoon, paid the agent two months' rent on the spot, and moved in six weeks later, after subletting their apartment.

Their first visitor was Jimmy Twitchell, or Tillie's was, as Jimmy called one weekday morning when Pete was in the city. He brought a cut-leaf philodendron for a house present. He assured her, as he strolled among disemboweled packing crates on meowing feet, that this suburb was becoming terribly chic. "The plumbers won't make house calls any longer," he jabbered, darting her the expectant glance. Tillie laughed all right, being too exhausted not to, though the jest had a familiar ring. Had she heard it on some television variety hour? No matter. Jimmy openly declared himself to be a cultural Robin Hood, stealing from the witty to give to the dull. Pete, who returned the Twitchell distaste with interest "up to as high as ten percent," had a rather blunter way of putting it. "He steals jokes and then files the serial numbers off them and gives them a fresh paint job, so nobody will recognize them," he said. So it might have been electricians who no longer made house calls, out Connecticut way, in the routine Tillie could therefore now not place. Why couldn't Jimmy stand Pete? Gertrude had an explanation. Jimmy was one of the farthest-out of human specialties — fags who can't stand men. What's left after that? Jimmy, little dreaming how he was getting his own back, said Gertrude "looked like a Lesbian with doubts about her masculinity." Thus Tillie found herself in a crossfire in which she could hardly hope to engage, but no matter: it *was* a chic address, in a set by which she could hope to remain forever dazzled. Pete didn't bat in that league either, but as if she cared! He was the salt of the earth. Let the Jimmy Twitchells be its pepper, mustard and vinegar.

Mrs. Shilepsky would come out from her new city

apartment for stays of two or three days, sometimes a week, liberating the Seltzers for the interval by acting as sitter. Once when she was on deck, Tillie spent the day in town shopping, and after a late lunch thought she'd surprise Pete by dropping in on him at his office.

Though it was a quarter to three, he still hadn't returned from lunch himself. She waited in the outer office till three, when a certain self-consciousness between her and the typing receptionist near whom she sat drove her into the ladies' room to primp for a hasty departure. She wanted to catch a train leaving in twenty minutes anyway.

As she emerged, she caught sight of Pete at the far end of the corridor, saying goodbye to a girl in a red checked coat. Tillie stopped short, half in and half out of the washroom, her hand holding the door open. There was an exchange of murmurs and low laughter between them, and a sense of dallying, reluctant leave-taking. Then the girl, a tall blonde, put a hand to Pete's brow to see whether he had any fever. A sudden pause in the surrounding office clatter made their words momentarily distinguishable. He felt warm, the girl laughingly said, but whether he had any temperature was hard to tell because her own hand was cold. "I'll be all right," he said. Their actual departure for respective offices was lost on Tillie, who, with the odd but instinctive guilt sense of the sexual witness, turned and fled back into the washroom. There she stayed for a few more minutes before making her furtive escape from the building, running with her head down into the welcome street.

Her guilt had quite worn off by evening. She was waiting for Pete when he arrived home at the usual time, holding a drink in her hand and a cigarette in the other with an air of ominous composure. Mrs. Shilepsky was in the nursery with Charlie. Pete seemed in good spirits.

"Sorry I missed you today," he said. "You should call beforehand so I'll know. Miss Templeton said you were in town shopping, which I hope means you haven't fixed anything. Because I thought we might take your mother out to dinner. If we can get a sitter. She deserves it after this hitch."

He wore the disarming smile that from now on would automatically arouse her defenses.

"She'd like to go to the church bingo," Tillie said, wondering just how far you had to, or could, graduate satire for anyone as unscrupulously wholesome as this. She now remembered his saying, of a male miscreant they had been discussing — it might have been Burt Wilson — that *he* would not cast the first stone. "I don't sit in judgment," he said. This was Pete Seltzer being charitable. He was an early Christian.

"Well, all right," he said. "Let's do that then."

"Go to the church bingo?"

"Yes."

"It may snow."

"Lies, all lies!"

Having divested himself of hat, coat and briefcase, he kissed her, large-minded about the cheek only presented to him. He walked to the liquor cabinet, after a knightly check of her own glass that was really something to behold.

"I left around three. I saw you come in," she said, nudging them an inch closer to the abyss. Her own war of nerves was too much for her, and she quickly added, "Or I think I did. I wasn't sure."

That put the burden of honesty squarely up to him, by offering him also the opportunity for deception. She wasn't at all sure she didn't want that.

"Then why the hell didn't you speak up?" he said, turning his head but leaving his back to her.

She decided she preferred doubt, and to recover it, said, "I was down in the street by that time, half a block away at the corner, looking for a cab. I couldn't be certain it was you."

"Who could mistake a gimpy?" He laughed, again asking for no sympathy.

She rejected that game now, but did safeguard the chance, for him, at the hankypanky that would obscure from her too harsh a truth, a smoke screen that for some wild reason they might both need. It was not so much a matter of letting sleeping dogs lie as keeping a mad one out. There was after all a child in a nearby room.

He turned around and came back, a drink in his hand and a smile on his face.

"How did you like the package?"

"The what?"

"The girl I was with. Didn't you get a look at her? That's the one I was telling you about the other night. Or did I?"

"Oh, the new girl. I believe you said something about her. You're breaking her in as a canvasser or something."

"Yes. We're buttonholing men in the street these days to see whether they like their shaving lather warm or not. Did you know they've developed one that turns warm on your fingertips? Skoal."

"Skoal. Do you still have to go out? I thought you were definitely in the office."

"Oh, you have to keep your hand in at the field level if you want to supervise right. Besides, you get saddle sores in that damn swivel chair all day. And you don't get them like Miss Lund all the time."

"Did you take her to lunch, Pete?"

"You bet your sweet bundle I did. And don't think your correspondent wouldn't like to parlay that into a little hard breathing. But you know me. The old louse manqué. Not to first base. Aren't you ashamed, such a schlep for a husband. I suppose it reflects on you, but . . . Well, so. What else was by you? Were the walls perpendicular today?"

"Oh, I'm fine — except for this premonition of disaster."

"Don't tell me it's extrasensory perception time in Dixie again. Every twenty-eight days like clockwork. Let me take you out of all this. Look, let's get out the Belly Baedekers and see if they write up that French restaurant over on Route 22."

It was a term he used for eating guides, of which they had several, since they both liked good food. When she had the blight, Pete would lead her about the bedroom in imitations of those classical paintings depicting Adam and Eve being banished from Paradise. It was how he literally took the Curse, as something laid on them. His arm around her waist, he would roll his stricken eyes as he led her through the imaginary gate, smiting his breast and uttering wails of despair at heaven, or throwing backward glances of hopeless regret at the Garden from which they were exiled by the angel with the flaming sword. She laughed at his horseplay again tonight, after they returned from dinner and a movie, just the two of them, but said that she could nevertheless still not shed the sense of uneasiness that had come over her. She had vague fears about the future, or a fear, which she could not define.

"Nonsense," he said, "everything's going to be ragasocky." His personal variant of such predecessors as scrumptious and kopacetik.

Well, it was nothing of the kind. Miss Lund telephoned one day to introduce herself as "someone you don't know, but know of," and to ask whether Mrs. Seltzer cared to sit down like two civilized people and talk the whole thing over.

"I can't," Tillie said.

"Why not?"

"I can't sit down like two civilized people, since I'm only one, but I often sit down with another, if I can find one."

"Well, swell. It's about Peter of course."

"Who?"

"Peter. Your husband."

She was so used to thinking of him as Pete that for a second she honestly hadn't realized whom the girl was talking about. There is something of a gulf between Peter and Pete, so wide they could hardly be interchangeable names for any man consummately either the one or the other, and Pete was so hopelessly, so unvarnishedly Pete that hearing him called Peter for the first time in her life almost made her laugh in the girl's face. She had asked Pete whether the Lund wasn't kind of dumb, and he had answered, "Not from the neck down." That wasn't a very Peterish thing to say.

"I know he's told you about me — I insisted that he do or break it off, as I don't like deception and won't have any part of it — and so I thought the only intelligent thing would be to have a drink together and lay our cards on the table."

They made a date to meet for drinks the following Saturday, in a bar a few miles from where Tillie lived. The girl would be only too happy to make the half-hour's trip out from the city. Tillie's one proviso was that Pete be told absolutely nothing about this.

Miss Lund was waiting for her in a booth. She bore out Tillie's original fleeting impression in the office passage, that she was in her mid-twenties. She had the demolishing combination of blonde hair and brown eyes. She looked at once fragile and indestructible because, though she talked glibly about her innermost thoughts, or pretended to, not even her surface could be touched. She seemed to have been sprayed with some invisible protective film, like silicone.

"My husband," Tillie said when they had sized one another up. "What on earth do you see in him?"

Miss Lund began a willing enough enumeration of Pete's credits: that he was amusing, good-natured, generous, kind, a blast in his way, and — hinting at how far the affair had progressed — a pistol.

"A what?" Tillie said. She had heard perfectly well, but the word made the girl momentarily absurd, and she wanted it repeated.

"A pistol."

244

"Do you have an apartment in New York, Miss Lund?"

"Yes. Not far from the office, marfact."

Through Tillie's dismay ran a counter-thrill of hope that this was the adversity about which the premonitions had persisted; that this was all the blow to be dealt her, and not such a fatal one at that; one, indeed, curiously softened by a mitigation she could not deny her vanity had secretly seized on the instant she saw Miss Lund plain. She, Tillie, had not had to settle for somebody for whom she was, in turn, the last streetcar. Far from it! Here before her was living proof — far more living than the feminine touches noted in Pete's apartment on her first visits there — of what he could attract. She was almost proud of him. Bastard manqué indeed! Mentally she told Gertrude Wilson to put *this* in her pipe and smoke it.

Under the elation of a few more drinks, she extrapolated this triumph of Pete's into a future of now thoroughly conceivable successors who would confirm the evidence that she had hooked a ladies' man. Not all as young and pretty as Miss Lund, perhaps, but toothsome conquests nonetheless, trophies who would not disgrace her. Holding her chin up and straight out, so as to minify the throat wrinkles (which she knew to be the correct word, and not minimize, which meant the reverse, to underestimate), sitting erect in this fashion, she told this girl exactly what she was up against: to wit, her probable failure to domesticate our nonesuch any more than Tillie had. "Pete simply can't be housebroken," she said, with a touch of loftiness. The first qualification to

245

be looked for in any second Mrs. Seltzer would be her capacity for putting up with precisely such threats as this encounter of a third. She was certainly bragging about her prize now. "Are you and he engaged?" she asked, carelessly. Her performance was beautiful. The girl gaped.

"How could we be engaged? He's married, isn't he?"

"I suppose."

Tillie shrugged like a woman of the world, from whom pointers might well be taken by anyone seriously interested in essaying the role she was wearily enough ready to abdicate.

"I don't want to be cruel, my dear, but if all of us got together to talk things over who've something to talk over, we'd have to rent a hall. You're only one of half a dozen or more — to my knowledge, of course," she added with a tight smile not intended to be needlessly caustic.

Miss Lund let herself slump to the table in a semi-comic pantomime of flabbergastation. "Blumph!" she said. A sense of sorority had developed between them, far above the mere mutual tolerance to which she had looked forward as the best possible fruit of this meeting. When she learned that they shared a grievance rather than an issue, nothing would do but that Mrs. Seltzer join her in some hard analysis of the cause.

"What do you suppose is Peter's trouble?"

"Well, he's not attractive to the other sex, you see, and so he must make up for it by having so many of them," Tillie said. "Or feels he has to."

Burlesque was not in the least detected. The girl

nodded as she studied the dregs of her whiskey sour astutely. She was evidently somewhat educated at least. "Men who are pistols," she said, frowning, as though picking her way carefully through an extremely labyrinthine thought, "are that because they feel a need to be. They're afraid that at bottom they aren't, and so have to prove to themselves over and over again that they are."

"Are what?" One more time.

"Pistols."

Tillie had long ago wearied of popular psychology (a fifty-year-old neighbor greeting with outflung arms all the women coming to see his wife laid out at the local undertaker's was by consensus said to be in shock), and at this point she decided to wind the interview up. She told Miss Lund that she, too, was civilized (how Grandma Shilepsky would have torn her hair out at that!), and that she relied on the girl's intelligence and good taste to decide for herself whether or not she would continue to see "Peter" in the city, for long lunches or short, or in the putative overtime lately become a frequent thing. Then she gathered up her bag and gloves.

"Wait."

Miss Lund had a curiosity Mrs. Seltzer would understand and forgive.

"Did you know what he was like before you married him?"

"Certainly."

"Then why did you marry him and why do you want to stay married to him?"

"Because he's a pistol," she flung amiably down over her shoulder, and walked out of the tavern, remembering, as she did so, that she had good legs. Several women had told her so.

Driving the five miles home, she felt like the heroine in a Pirandello play for whom a character is one thing while, to another, he is something else altogether, and so on, the conflicting versions between them offering some cumulative sense of the fluidity of human nature and the relativity of truth. She wondered whether Miss Lund's beautiful blonde truth could ever become hers by an incantatory repetition of "Peter," so new to her vocabulary. She remembered how on her first hearing that he was called Pete the name had had the ring of a *mot juste*. Would he become Peter if she treated him as though he were, shedding at last, by life's unresting sea, the grosser shell of Pete? There was a play about *that* too, of somewhat more primitive grain than Pirandello's, called *The Passing of the Third Floor Back*. An infinitely understanding Christ-like central protagonist makes people what they might be simply by pretending that they are. Thus the dishonest landlady becomes honest, the painted lady modest, and so on, till some improvement in the overall human lot is discernible by the time the curtain falls on act three. Tillie now a little desperately but also hypnotically repeated "Peter, Peter" all the way home, trying to resist its more grotesque implications and holding firmly in focus the sensitive and faithful gentleman evoked by the name, and trying not to laugh throughout the incantation. That was important too. "Peter," she whispered one last time as she coasted into the garage and shut the motor off.

The strains of *Twelfth Street Rag* greeted her as she

entered the house. Peter (Oh, my God) was playing it
for Charlie, who sat nearby in his playpen, banging a
metal toy against the bars of his prison, if not in time to
the music, then at least with a rollicking sense of its zest.
He jiggled up and down, like a rider on horseback, and
saliva ran down his chin as he grinned, his lower front
teeth showing, like two grains of rice. She changed her
incantation. "He's a good father, he's a good father," she
repeated to herself, then and in the months, even the
years, to come.

For what Tillie had told Miss Lund proved clairvoy-
ant. Fresh traces of infidelity continued to arrive,
whether direct or indirect. He came home late, or he
stayed in town overnight. What was the motivation of
his light o' loves? Did he elicit in them the maternal
instinct admittedly aroused in her so early on? Or were
they simply the female half of that irreducible fraction
of mankind not geared to monogamy, whose radar was
always out for the signals given off by their untamable
counterparts — the glance solicited and held, the smile
caught like a moth on the wing and subtly detained,
the touch tried and returned?

Tillie's own maternal instinct had, in any case, by now
evaporated. Who could mother such a child?

five

LIFE, though it was henceforth to deal Tillie her share of dark clouds, copiously rewarded her search for silver linings. It saw that she suffered no want of bright sides. Was Pete unable to pass up anything in skirts? Neither did his devotion to her ever sway or flag. Had she to be satisfied with double talk, and never so much as when he spoke the King's English? There was still more between them than in many of the "meaningful dialogues" supposedly going on all around them, which often rose to pitches unknown to them. He never raised his voice to her. He never uttered a harsh word. He hadn't, as her mother put it, a malicious bone in his body. He was the kindest man she knew. He ridiculed everything — and nobody. And was he, finally, a child? It made him the perfect playmate for Charlie's early years. And — the blackest cloud or the most silver of linings — it was in time made manifest that the boy would have no other. He would only have a childhood.

At nine he fell ill with something for which certain laboratory tests seemed, at last, best. When Dr. Willett called to say he had the results, and would be by to report them, Tillie knew what they were. A happier out-come could have been given over the phone. This, then, was the hour for which she had known all along that she was being groomed by premonition. A malevolence was cruising in the child's bloodstream. A year of life re-mained to him at most, no more, probably less. He would never need a father. A playmate was enough.

When the doctor had dealt his blow, he bent to kiss Tillie on the cheek, almost ceremoniously, as brides are kissed, then as ceremoniously turned and shook hands with Pete, who saw him to the door. It was a lesson in form, a reminder that the suffering at hand and the grief to come were private matters, not for public con-sumption.

Tillie sat staring at the living room floor, tracing idioti-cally the convolutions in the carpet pattern, listening to the low exchange of voices in the driveway and then the doctor's car driving off, wondering when the fantasy into which she had been sucked would disperse. The hospital would call to say that an error had been discovered in the laboratory technician's report, that the diagnosis was mistaken. She would momentarily awaken in her own bed to find this was all a dream. But it remained a dream from which she did not awaken. Pete came back in as far as the living room doorway, and stood there. What was generated, now, was a weird sense of embarrassment. There was no other word for it. Not turning to look at him directly, she could see him stoop to smooth a rug, and then straighten up again. He put his hands in his hind pockets and cleared his throat. "Well."

Two people cannot share grief. She was to formulate that later to herself, but she discovered it then without making the actual notation. Doomed to go on performing the motions of reality in a phantom world, they were phantoms to one another, curiously stripped of all recognizable characteristics and negotiable qualities. They had been picked up and deposited in some country where their currency was foreign and their language alien. It was a kingdom as mythical as Graustark.

Upstairs Prince Charlie lay transfigured. You would not dare to touch him now, he was that holy. He was a phantom too. Because of the sacred obligation of deception laid upon her, she could no longer embrace him as she might wish, for fear of giving the truth away. He must never know, or be let suspect. Thus a secrecy like that of her pregnancy again closed around her. She would bear his death as she had his birth — alone with him. She would see him out of this life as she had seen him into it. From this Pete must already sense a subtle exclusion.

She could feel a ring tighten and close around her, insubstantial as mist yet hard as steel. The ghostly unreality grew, swelled the house, threatened soundlessly to shatter the windows and burst the walls. She would not have been surprised to see an angel sweep in, to make her some kind of formal Annunciation, or to ignore her and instead touch the boy with his burning coal. She and Pete were locked in an Absurdity as complete as could be imagined. The constraint between them was as palpable as if they had quarreled. They avoided one another's eyes, as if chagrined. She never compared notes with Pete about it, but her sensation upon hearing the outrage which she must digest was shame — the impotent infuriated shame of victims whom swindlers have wiped out. The whole thing was a scandal.

But of course the immediate problem was not of communicating between themselves, but with Charlie. A face had to be put on matters, a technique of deception scrupulously adhered to. She began domestically scolding Pete. "When are you ever going to take down those storm windows and put up the screens?" she said. "Or practice your piano. Go on, let's hear how you're coming along with your new piece."

Pete had been trying to expand his repertoire, as far as that was possible in the ragtime tradition within which he was rather rigidly locked, and within further limits of having to play by ear. He had learned *Kitten on the Keys* and *Nola*, and was at present working on *Chattanooga Choo Choo*. She motioned for him to sit down at the piano in order to effect a casual, business-as-usual atmosphere, and it was to the strains of *Chattanooga Choo Choo*, somewhat raggedly picked out behind her, that she mounted the stairs, pulling herself up slowly by the banister. She still had no idea what she was going to say. What would her first words as Niobe be?

Charlie was sitting propped up on two pillows, trying to work a puzzle. It was the two entangled nails of which the object is to pull them apart. He sighed as she entered and threw the puzzle across the room. Now he put his hands together and looked over at her with an inquiring expression. He cleared his throat but said nothing.

"Well, how would you like some boiled thripples with almagoody sauce for lunch?" she said. "I always think they're good this time of year."

"What did the doctor say?"

"He says your blood is homogenized or something, from that attack of flu. You need building up is the main thing, because you really are run-down. If you must know it's something called post-influenzal debility. Sounds like something Pete made up. But the thing is, he gave me a prescription for some medicine that's going to pick you up like a shot, now that we know what it is. You'll be out of that bed inside of a week, and we can begin thinking about that trip."

"When is Pete's vacation?"

"Couple of weeks." It hadn't been decided yet, but she picked the time at which the doctor had assured her the first remission — of whatever duration — might be expected from the medication prescribed.

The music below ended in a sudden crash, as though the player had brought his two fists violently down on the keyboard. The sound reverberated through the house, in echoes of jangled strings. Tillie swiftly closed the door and came back in and sat down on the bed.

"Look," she said, lowering her voice, "how would you like to take some kind of music lessons? That sound you just heard will show you how frustrated grownups get when they can't play an instrument the way they'd like. I guarantee you that if you don't learn to play something you'll have the same regret, like I have about the violin. Oh, how I wish my parents had made me keep at it when I was young. That's the time to. Why don't we ask Mrs. Ditwielder if she can give you piano lessons? You've got rhythm in your system, and you know where you got it."

Its source was also that of the thick yellow hair through which Charlie scratched his head, as of the inherited grin with which he now regarded her from the pillow. "You mean I could play in a cathouse like Pete always wanted to?"

"What's a cathouse?"

"A joint like a saloon or something where they stay up all night and raise hell."

"Playing all those jazz instruments that made caterwauling noises. Like a cat. That's where the term comes from. But if that's the ambition a father inspires in his son, it's plain who needs the discipline." She opened the door again and called down in her "schoolmarm" tone, "Peter. Peter! Will you step into the principal's office please."

The comedy, she saw, had only begun. Charlie was kept safe in a world of nonsense. No harm could come to him there. Never had a boy's father more completely waived the paternal role for a fraternal one. They were quite literally playmates. Tillie had indeed two boys to deal with. They collaborated on pranks, some on her, the most ambitious a complex and prolonged trick on a next-door neighbor named Mr. Tucker.

Tucker had an obsession common among American motorists, the mileage they get out of their cars. Pete did not think much of practical jokes as a general rule, but Charlie did, and he joined in to keep him amused. Tucker, in any case, with his solemnly kept purchase records and speedometer notations, asked for it. The car in question was a Volkswagen, a second car which he kept outside on the driveway. Pete and Charlie stole across the yard under cover of night, dragging a can of gasoline, and secretly refueled it. A few nights later they repeated the transfusion, then again, adding now a gallon, now two. The result was that Mr. Tucker glowed with a pride of ownership rarely before experienced. He went around boasting of getting forty, fifty, and even up to sixty miles a gallon.

"Maybe there's something wrong with it," Pete said with a straight face when Mr. Tucker buttonholed him to extol the car's merits.

When this had gone on for several weeks, he and Charlie suddenly reversed the procedure. Up the hill separating the two properties they now crept with a bucket and a length of rubber hose, and began siphoning gasoline *out* of the tank. The abrupt drop in the car's performance now had Mr. Tucker going around in utter bafflement and confusion, scratching his head over charts over which he had once gloated, checking and rechecking his figures and also the fuel gauge, spreading, among garage folk, a wake of bewilderment second only to his own. Mechanics spent long periods with their heads under the hood, only to pull them out again, shaking them. Filling station attendants were challenged as to the accuracy of their pumps; brands of gasoline were switched, as well as octane strengths — all to no avail.

The Seltzers heard all about it one Sunday afternoon when the Tuckers had them in for drinks. Pete looked down at the figures in Mr. Tucker's hand, shaking his own head as he drew on the pipe he had taken up and murmuring "Hm's" of consternation. Charlie sat turned on the sofa, looking out of the window with his fist in his mouth. Strolling back to his own chair, Pete reminded them of the almost human perversity of which machinery was capable, quoting someone's phrase about "the total depravity of inanimate objects."

256

"We've got an electric percolator that brews absolutely marvelous coffee one morning," he said, "and the next morning it tastes like snoxmethyl."

Or gasoline, Tillie thought to herself, remembering Pete sliding home to her down the hill, still spitting out the mouthful you had to suck through the hose to get it started, Charlie clutching the paraphernalia and choking with hysterics. Pete showed the wear and tear of the dedicated craftsman, someone bent on doing something really fine of its kind. His kisses smelled of petrol. When the joke had gone on long enough, and they all decided to call it off, Tillie thought Mr. Tucker should be left with some hint of explanation.

"Maybe somebody's been monkeying with your fuel tank," she said, by now feeling sorry for him, and even for the Volkswagen people, in whose side he had become a famous thorn. He would turn up there alternately beaming with pleasure and fuming with indignation — a Dissatisfied Customer if they ever saw one, possibly even on his way to becoming one of those cranks, also in the American grain, who ride around with signs on their cars publicly declaring them to be lemons and where they had been bought. It would be ironic if importers of a foreign make ran foul of one, though poetically appropriate as a pitfall of the native market.

"What do you mean?" Mr. Tucker asked.

"As a joke. Putting it in and taking it out. I mean the spread between twenty-two miles and sixty to the gallon is just too much, Mr. Tucker."

"A joke! I wouldn't think that was very funny. That wouldn't be my idea of humor, or Milly's here either," said Mr. Tucker, who always spoke for both himself and his wife.

Their month's vacation, hastily arranged when it was certain that the remission was a solid one, was spent crossing the country in a new car of their own. The trip was all horseplay. In one restaurant, Pete summoned the headwaiter to complain that there was a sardine in his food. He posed as a gourmet, dropping hints that he was not just any *Feinschmecker*, but represented a Belly Baedeker with power of life and death over such establishments. In a motel, they pretended to be plainclothesmen in pursuit of wanted convicts, in another, on the lam themselves.

Tillie joined in the sport, at least as a smiling witness, but, once home again in the house they were not long to share, she gave way. She walked in the garden in the cool of the evening, awaiting the coming of the Lord. There had been a sudden summer shower, leaving everything a fresh and brilliant green. The smell of honeysuckle haunted the air. Birds fluted in the dripping trees. A pair of lovers walked by along the road, hand in hand. She looked up at the sky, and, parting her hands in the gentlest of protests, said, "This is *my* beloved son, in whom I am well pleased." A thin moon cleared the darkening trees. She wandered in circles, passing under a bedroom window through which drifted the sound of Pete reading to the boy, then an exchange of low, conspiratorial laughter. They were cooking something up.

Suddenly she gave in to a burst of rage. She cursed and blasphemed, reviling the name of God and all the members of the Trinity individually. She heaped abuse upon the mother of Christ, in a stream of language so obscene that she later recoiled in horror from the memory of it. Grief for a child is enough; mourning for one still alive will strain the fabric of sanity.

She was destined to give way to these convulsions periodically, however regularly they alternated with contrition, or at least amazement. She would prepare for them, plan them, anticipating some break in her household chores that would give her an hour free with the Scotch bottle, and the resulting purgative. What Pete did to get it out of his system, if anything, she never knew. They bore their trouble separately. It was never discussed. He let her weep alone at night, having found that best. Once when he found her sobbing in bed he lay down and slipped an arm around her, but some similarity to the first rough overtures of love touched a resentful chord, and she moved away. Is comfort impossible because we refuse it, or do we refuse it because it is vain?

The night came, as come it must, when the reassembled fragments of his manhood required their natural appeasement, and he did turn to her in the wakeful dark. The feel of his hand on her breast turned her to stone. When he tried, with a delicately graduated insistence, to draw her around, she said, "How can you think of that?" Pete crept downstairs to the recreation room where the television set was. He often drugged himself stupid till early morning there, watching old movies. He soaked himself in them, as people soak themselves in drink. Sometimes he went to bed early and then got up around midnight for the late shows, stealing back again at two and three o'clock, doped by the ham emotions and prohibited sentiments that are still bottled and bootlegged in the early films. He became an authority on camp, that pernickety little frill of taste that bored and irritated her. It was his companionship with Charlie that remained the one sustaining feature of their life together.

That Charlie was Pete Seltzer all over again — or would have become so had he been let — was almost comically obvious. He looked, acted, thought like Pete. He had the same large, rather loose-jointed frame, the same long legs and arms that Pete had allowed to grow soft and flabby (except for the bursts of exercise inspired by a new attachment). He had the same bright blue eyes and the same wide mouth combined in the same rather shifty expression, though how much of that was heredity and how much imitation was a question, as it always is in familial resemblances. Pete was certainly his hero, and he a willing disciple. He laughed like a fool over all of Pete's jokes. The recent thundershower had been the only relief in a drought now in its second year, and people were losing lawns, shrubs and valuable old trees right and left. Wells were going dry by the dozen. "Into each life some rain must fall," Pete said philosophically, and they both guffawed like oafs, though it was doubtful whether Charlie really got the point. He laughed because his parents did, though his mother shook her head as she did so. He took all his cues from Pete. Left momentarily alone in the front office of a nursery where they had gone to buy a Christmas tree, Pete swiped a batch of invoice blanks he saw lying on the counter, and on these they typed out whopping bills for plants and landscaping service, in stitches as they imagined friends and neighbors, to whom they sent them, opening them and getting the nursery on the phone to raise hell and ask what this was all about. Gertrude and Burt Wilson were mailed a bill of eleven hundred dollars for the construction of a retaining wall. The "mistakes" were undoubtedly rectified, but identical statements went out the first of the next month, marked "Overdue" and "If remittance is not recieved within ten days we shall turn this over to a collection agency."

They invented nonsense products, like Pete's reversible mayonnaise — things like collapsible popcorn, dehydrated water and what not. Charlie sought Pete's approval more in matters relating to the antic world they now all inhabited than for school grades, for Charlie was an indifferent student at best. They let him do his homework in the living room, while they read and drank. He would sit at a table wearing some crazy headpiece or other garment remaining from the day's play, as boys will, or with beer cans still clamped to his shoes. Once he sat with his feet hanging into an empty bushel basket. He would inevitably look up from the lessons that bored him, and offer a contribution to the swelling store of "end" products. "Hey, Pete, how about fireproof pickles? Pete?" Knowing what was up, his teachers gave him straight A's and B's.

Tillie thought him rather like the boy leading the horse in the Picasso painting, not because there was that much physical resemblance, but because the boy in the picture was an idealization without sentiment or fakery — he was no Blue Boy — and, perhaps equally, because he was there to be relished in his nakedness, as she had so often relished Charlie. She could remember the feel of him when she had bathed him as a baby, laughing as he tried to wriggle from her slippery grasp. He had more true zest than Pete, more quicksilver, more fire — what the doctor called a kinetic child. He sprang from bed every morning with an erection you could hang your hat on, eager for the day, washing and brushing without being told, neatly tucking into his briefcase the school-books he did little justice to otherwise. His room was neat, all his treasures in their accustomed places, though taken down almost nightly for perusal. One of her most piercing memories would always be the night, toward the end of his remission, when she found him lying on his stomach on his bed, after his bath, poring over all his Scout patches and camp certificates and school citations. These had included a Physical Fitness Award. She could summon it up any time she wanted to skewer her heart, but for the most part she preferred to remember Charlie as he was before the suffering that defaced him: the naked lad leading the horse; the sweet, hard, still un-opened bud of childhood; oh, my brave, bright, still seed-less boy.

He left them in the dead of winter. Snow was drifting down outside the hospital window where they sat beside his bed. Pete walked out, his shoulders hunched and his hands in his pockets, but she stayed to the end, like a sentry at his post, sparing herself nothing. No ghost would haunt her, bearing the prints of his needles, to say, "Could you not watch with me one hour?" She watched the last quivering breath drawn and then yielded up, the spirit with it. She stayed on even then, bending to kiss his cheek, to smooth back the hair from the battered face. She held him in her arms once yet before smoothing his pillow to lay him back. She was making the bed when a nurse came in and led her away, an arm around her shoulder. As though she needed support! She was perfectly in control of herself. Her heart was a hoard of unspoken curses. They would keep. She went calmly and efficiently through the red tape required by the hospital, before taking leave of it for her world of phantoms.

She drove as they made their way home through whirls of thinning snow. It was early afternoon. Pete sat slumped in his seat, looking out the window. To a casual observer he would have seemed listless. Their voices, when they spoke to one another, were flat, reflecting little more of emotion than its exhaustion; at most, the inevitable relief at suffering ended. The grief itself was an old story. Death had, if anything, put an end to that too.

It was only when they got home and had to discuss some kind of service with the local Congregationalist minister that they came to life. They had only attended his church twice, when Tillie's mother was visiting them, but he didn't seem to mind. He was willing not only to officiate, but to do anything they wished. He was fully prepared to intermingle his more or less standard readings from Scripture with poems of a secular nature, for people of a less believing turn of mind than his own. The verses from Edna St. Vincent Millay and Wallace Stevens which Tillie handed him somewhat strained this liberality, but he did not balk. He incorporated into his service also the prayer by Robert Louis Stevenson of which she was fond, because it appeared in a notebook that was a keepsake from her schooldays, and pressed on the good man as an example of the petitions that might validly be uttered by people who didn't really think anyone was listening.

"Purge out of every heart the lurking grudge," it ran. "Give us courage and gaiety and the quiet mind. Spare us to our friends, soften us to our enemies. Bless us, if it may be, in all our innocent endeavours. If it may not be, give us the strength to encounter that which is to come, that we may be brave in peril, constant in tribulation, temperate in wrath, and in all changes of fortune, and down to the gates of death, loyal and loving one to another."

After that they filed quietly out, the thirty or forty of them, climbed into their cars, and, behind a motorcycle escort furnished by the town police, took Prince Charlie to his rest among the whispering pines at Evergreen.

six

TILLIE Seltzer had ordered a reluctant and somewhat bewildered minister to pray for gaiety and the quiet mind at her son's funeral, simply because the words graced her favorite prayer. Yet when she saw the boy's father managing slowly to recover that ideal, she felt her heart harden.

Friends in time had coaxed them out to a party. She knew "periods of mourning" were a thing of the past, and often hypocritical enough formalities, but the evening was a trial. She found herself mentally talking to Charlie while trying to hold up her end of actual conversations. "Darling, the tree deserts the leaf, not the leaf the tree, I know, I know. But I'm here with you. A scar forms, they say, and the leaf is abandoned, left to flutter to the earth, and to winter. But I'll never abandon you. I'm with you always. This means nothing to me." She felt sorry for those who were stuck with her, and really tried to pull herself together and weave her thread into the evening's fabric. Pete seemed to have no trouble doing so, especially after getting himself knit up with a redheaded woman in a corner, with whom at one point she overheard him exchanging a joke. The president of Anaconda Copper heard about Tijuana Brass and wanted to take it over. Why resist life's remorseless resumptions, or begrudge another's living as he must? Why doubt Pete was feeling the same pain as hers, since she presented the same exterior as his?

What went through his mind as he slipped into bed beside her that night? He saw that she was crying, and retreated. She was certainly far less to be wooed than comforted. Putting forth the claims of the flesh seemed to her that much more forgetful; making love the final betrayal of Charlie. She flinched at the thought, steeled herself against it, as against another kind of defloration. It would be letting the dead bury their dead, at last and in truth, something against which her whole being rebelled. But neither could one forever deny her husband.

Her dialogues with Pete were full of the futile "Why's?" of parental sorrow. "Do you think there's any point to the whole thing?" she would say, knowing she was boring everyone, almost bored herself. She hardly expected answers from Pete, knowing the absurdity of trying to make a philosopher of him. But he knew she was shopping for comfort, and did his best to deliver the merchandise.

"Of course there's point. Look all around you, the patterns," he said. "It's the words we try to do the thinking with that gum the thinking up. Would you think whether life had any meaning if it wasn't for the word meaning? It would never occur to anybody. So try to forget it. Think of other words. Any words. Make some up."

"Then you're an Existentialist," she said, as though

accusing him of intelligence heretofore kept concealed from her.

"Ah, I think it's the name of an insurance company."

"Promise me?" She smiled like a child, trying to recover some of their lost playfulness, even as she batted tearful eyes.

"Cross my heart."

"Will I see Charlie again?"

"Of course you will. There's a lot of new evidence about that. That the societies for psychical research and all are getting. You never know. We don't know anything. I was reading the other day where astronomers have discovered some strange blue particles in the Milky Way they didn't know were there. So cheer up."

He yawned over his breakfast coffee, snapping his mouth shut with a groggy shake of his head.

"I mean if nothing is certain, then everything is possible," he went on. "The whole universe is mysteries to be unlocked, if we can swing it, and I think we can. *It's* like a great heartbeat, is the latest thinking on that. It expands and contracts at intervals of eighty-two billion years. Isn't that terrific? So buck up. What the hell."

He went to get his shoes out of the refrigerator. They were a new pair slightly too large, and he thought chilling them overnight made them fit a little more snugly.

"I expect I'll be home late again tonight," he said, bending over to tie them. "Some reports suddenly to rush through to some poop in South Jesus, Idaho, or somewhere. If we don't get them to the firm by Friday, our names will be Rosenstern and Guildencrantz."

"Stay in town all night if you want," she said, looking

at her fun-house reflection in the coffee pot. "I mean I don't mind." She poured herself some more coffee. "Even if you've got somebody. You've got to live, I know. I've no right to starve you just because I've lost my appetite."

"You can't eat a thing?" he said gently, holding up his coat and using the other hand as a whisk broom to brush it with. "Well, not that it's my night to howl, or anything, but it might be best to stay in rather than take the milk train. That wakes you up too."

He stayed in three or four times, and then came home one night to say he'd heard of a two-room apartment they could sublet from an office colleague bound for a temporary post abroad. "I think you should get out of here and into town more again. We'll see some shows. Or just shop. But get out of here."

They took it, and she joined him a few times. But as she lay in bed listening to the traffic in the streets she was haunted by the thought of her empty house, no one in it at all now, none there to hear the laughter and the footsteps echoing through it that she could, or the child's voice crying to be remembered. Pete would find her weeping silently into her pillow, but there was nothing he could do. His hand on her shoulder meant nothing, save as a touch subtly threatening a caress, a caress an overture. Grief was indivisible. It could not be shared. She had nothing to say. Fairly, she did not complain when he returned late even to that bed. She never asked for an explanation. She went back to the country, leaving him his pied-à-terre.

It was when she was finally alone, not just alone in the house, but alone, that she discovered the ability of grief to accommodate gaiety, or at least to alternate with it, a contradiction that distinguishes it from depression. Merely gloomy people don't laugh, but sorrowing ones can, and often do. Depression is not an emotion, grief is, and one that can sting all the rest into new life. Tillie would drink to numb her mind a little, then suddenly find her spirits rising as she resumed the conversation with Charlie, often with her favorite symphonies going full-blast on the phonograph.

"The first time I laid eyes on your father I knew he was something," she told him aloud as she went about her chores, "but what, remained to be seen. He's probably a bastard with a heart of gold, may be as good a way of putting it as any. You remember what I said about the way he ridicules everything, and nobody. Here's another case in point. One evening when Reverend Pangborn called on Grandma when she was sick, you may remember it, we sat in the parlor where we could overhear the conversation between them in the bedroom. They were talking about the mice we had, and after a few minutes it penetrated us that Grandma was saying something that could only mean she thought mice were baby rats. I can still see the look that came into Pete's eye as he put the newspaper down. It meant that he hoped it was so. And it was. We talked about it. But amused as he was, he didn't laugh at *her*. He simply relished another of the absurdities in which life happily abounds, and of which it may in fact be made. To be enjoyed. He sort of pans the river of life for such nuggets. He would tell them on himself too. There was this secretary he had who called him Pete. Then suddenly after a couple of lunches she began calling him Mr. Seltzer. He said, 'But you used to call me Pete.' And she said, 'That was before I got to know you.' "

It would be wrong to say she was depressed at such times. Her spirit was never more in flight. She would turn off the phonograph, lock up the house and set out for dinner in some restaurant where she could sit alone in a corner and watch the others as she nursed a drink and dawdled over her food. She was particularly aware of the tone set by any family party. Parents bored or impatient with their children made her want to go over and shake them by the shoulders, and ask them how long they thought they had together. She could imagine what she'd say. "We're all on loan to one another, you know, the whole thing can be foreclosed without a moment's notice." Yet once when she saw a family happy with an idiot in its midst, her feelings suddenly reversed themselves — she wanted to rebuke their seemingly mindless oblivion to the outrage perpetrated upon them. But when she walked out she gave the poor thing a smile and a pat on the head, receiving a smile from the parents in return. What a mysterious gift was life in any form, even that lashed by loss into new intensities. When, however, she heard sentimentalists talking about "the precious gift of life" she wanted to say, "This life is no gift. It is a purchase, paid for as we go, at prices often scandalous." Perhaps her dissatisfaction with the banality of the words drove her thoughts back out of the Yea column into the Nay. She usually found herself better at saying Nay: "Don't try to buy me off with spring flowers, or falling snow, or young May moons. I want to stay mad."

It was Gertrude Wilson who got her out of the dumps and the clouds between which she knew she rather precariously alternated, and back onto something like solid ground. She did so by reinvolving her in the petty nuisances of everyday life. Good old Gertrude! There are things for which the cares that infest the day are better than nights filled with music.

She phoned to invite Tillie to lunch, after a long silence during which she had been vaguely reported as "away somewhere." Even as Tillie caught sight of her across the restaurant she knew she'd had her face lifted. She certainly looked under forty now, though suspected to be past fifty. "How much?" Tillie wondered again, with a spasm of envy. No one knew. No one had ever been able to get to the bottom of Gertrude's age. No catch questions, such as are craftily framed to make you spill the beans inadvertently, or extract the truth by indirection, ever tripped her up. She could smell a mile off those queries about the first President you voted for, or whether you were in school when so-and-so taught English there, or such-and-such a song was popular, and parried them with the most incredible ease and the nimblest footwork. She was a match for any woman Tillie knew, and Tillie had overheard and participated in some catty discussions on the subject. "I'm younger but I look older. Certainly now, God knows," she thought.

It would in the circumstance have been indiscreet to comment too extravagantly on Gertrude's appearance, so as she joined her at their table she merely remarked how well she looked, then, as if she didn't know, asked: "What's new?"

"That's what I want to ask you," Gertrude said. The point remained suspended until they had been brought drinks, when, frowning into hers, she said: "I'm sorry about you and Pete. What gives?"

Gertrude still favored her throat by not turning her head on it any more than necessary, thus stretching it into new lines to succeed these temporarily deleted, but twisting her whole body instead. You couldn't say she was posing every minute, exactly, but you were always conscious of her awareness of being looked at, so strongly so that the question arose in your mind whether she mightn't cease to exist when not seen, like the cows in philosophy class. That Tillie was a thief catching a thief hardly softened her censure in these matters. She made other envious notations, concerning particularly the baby-blonde Gertrude had had her cropped hair colored, and how gently it collaborated with her gray-blue eyes. And what a sweetly inquiring gaze the eyes could manage for a woman who wanted only the dirt. In her resentment Tillie gave her more dirt than the facts themselves at the moment would have borne out.

"We'll probably get a divorce," she said.

No such thing had been decided on between her and Pete, or even seriously aired, but the old urge to penalize Gertrude had been too much.

"Yes, I know," Gertrude replied. "Or rather assumed."

This gave Tillie something of a turn, but she struggled successfully to suppress any sign of it. Indeed, she suddenly saw how she might recover the offensive.

"Then it'll come as no surprise to you what I'm going to ask," she said, acting instantly on the inspiration that seized her. "I was hoping you'd agree to testify at the trial. That we're incompatible."

Gertrude was, however, herself not so easily thrown,

much less put to rout. Either missing the irony or concealing its effect on her, she as smoothly answered, "Oh, I sensed it about you and Pete from the first. That you wouldn't hit it off. Not from the first, I shouldn't say, but I knew you weren't each other's speed one night when I saw you together at a party, shortly after you were married. Something between you made me sense there was sand in your gears."

The arrogance of the bitch, Tillie thought. I've a good mind to call it off. And after a few weeks of brooding on the superciliousness to which, she now saw, she'd been subjected over the years, the foil she'd been in another of those friendships with which Gertrude surrounded herself, lesser social lights over whom she could queen it, she did call it off. In her own mind, that is, where alone the project was afoot. Pete himself knew of no divorce plans, and there was as much reason to wait with them as to broach them now. He had no one he wanted to marry, judging from what she could gather in the course of their few telephone conversations. He talked mostly about the office, where everything was appaquimpy — the Frisbees climbing all over each other's backs to get to the top in what was evidently a current shakeup. He seemed apprehensive, and her anxiety for him revived the habit she had developed during Charlie's illness, that of eking out everything she could to his credit. His word game had been wonderful for them. All three of them would play it together. They would imagine themselves to be the first family, commissioned by the Almighty the great task of nomenclature. There were no names for anything yet, in Paradise. What would they call those things with spreading boughs? The creatures twittering among them? The beasts whose skins they wore and whose haunches they gnawed as they squatted around the first of human fires, in the semantic dawn? Their yard became full of quormels and sleeths and whappinstances, all flumping through the sweem, or manganating in the queeglestocks. She remembered all this as she wandered through the house one night rummaging among drawers and pausing before the pictures on the walls. There was a Roman coin he had given Charlie, bearing the date 339 B.C. — a novelty shop gag. Tacked up over a bureau were some other of the absurdities they had collected, like newspaper photographs with the wrong captions. One specified the foreman of a lumber yard accepting a retirement watch, under a melee of basketball players. There was a snapshot of Pete, wearing a striped blazer perilously close in spirit to those in which comedians blowing saxaphones derisively evoke the twenties.

"I'm not going through with the divorce," she told Gertrude when next they met.

There was certainly no chance of claiming prior divination in this case! Not that Gertrude wanted to. She had something else on her mind. Before getting to it, however, she professed admiration for Tillie's charity in postponing action to which she had every right, and on grounds more stringent far than mere incompatibility. "You could get it on adultery, you know," she said.

That made Tillie leap conclusively to Pete's defense, going so far as to use words of Pete's that had, at the time, struck her as sanctimonious to say the least.

"You can't judge a man's sexual conduct apart from the rest of him," she said. "We all have different make-ups and different needs. There are adulterers who are often good husbands and fathers, and mates loyal unto death who kill each other daily."

Tillie tried to look Gertrude squarely in the eye as she said this but couldn't, as Gertrude slid her glance away, curiously resembling, for the moment, Sneaky Pete himself. It did not occur to Tillie till later that she had whitewashed both their husbands. Rather evasively, then, she changed the subject herself, or rather shifted it onto less uncomfortable ground. She recalled what Pete had said about sex in marriage, at the outset of theirs. It was like a medicine. Three times a day for the first week, then once a day for another week, then once every three or four days until the condition has cleared up.

"That's not what I wanted to talk to you about," Gertrude said. "Now you may not like this, but I speak as a friend and won't pull any punches. Some of us are getting a little worried about you. Hate me for it, but you can't go on living like this. Shut up in that house by yourself, shut off from everybody and everything. I know what you've been through, but you can't crawl into a hole and pull the hole in after you. It's a form of self-indulgence," she added, with an air of complexity.

"How do you mean?"

"I mean the world's full of the misery you got a healthy chunk of, so why not go out and try to alleviate a little of it. You've tasted it. Fine, so fight it."

"How?"

"I'm taking on the Mental Health Ball again this year.

You've given us money before. We could use your help now, as a volunteer."

"What would you like me to do, Gertrude?"

"Anything. Head the raffle committee. At midnight we're going to raffle off a trip to — an all-expense-paid trip to — guess where?"

Tillie knew. But she had "fined" Gertrude enough, she felt, and honestly hadn't the heart to deprive her of the pleasure of "springing" this.

"Where?"

"Monaco."

Tillie whistled, raising her eyebrows. Beginning to enjoy her own performance, she next asked Gertrude how she had ever swung it, though she knew that too.

"Jimmy Twitchell knows Princess Grace, and he's gotten her to agree to receive the winning couple at the castle, after a flight on TWA, also donated. It's going to be the best Mental Health Ball we've ever had, and I'd love it if you'd serve as head of the raffle committee."

"I'd love to, but I'll need some, you know, briefing. What do I do?"

"Build a pyramid. You at the top as committee chairman, sub-delegating absolutely everything. I'll give you a list of potential willing workers. I'll have Jimmy Twitchell give you a ring and fill you in on the whole Monaco business, so you'll know what you're asking your henchmen to ask people to plunk down twenty bucks a ticket for. We're making it high so we can limit it to two hundred and fifty tickets, which will give us an almost clear profit of five thousand dollars just on the raffle alone. And, Tillie, I'm glad to see you back in circulation again."

"Working with Jimmy ought to be fun in itself."

"Yes, but a word to the wise. Be careful of him. He's a bitch, and that's bad in a man."

It was a point well taken. Gertrude was herself in Jimmy's bad books at the moment, having had somebody else recently redo her house for her. "Just for a change," she said, but that did not placate Jimmy. He was all Gertrude, and terribly acid about it, when he bustled into Tillie's house for tea again. Princess Grace could wait.

"Getting somebody new for a change is one thing, but Cato Spellman!" he said. "I told her, 'Well, darling, if you want to rough it.' He made a mess of the Jamberson place, as you probably know, that I had to pull him out of. He asked me to, it was that bad. He had used, of all things, chartreuse and red in the drawing room. One at one end, and the other at the other. Do you know how I got him out of it?"

"No. How did you?" Tillie asked, feeling glad to be back in circulation again herself.

"Mocha." He let this sink in a moment. "You wouldn't believe it, but it somehow brought them together. A big. Long. Solid *thing* of mocha. A settee running practically the length of the room. Somehow it brought them in balance. Of course Cato never forgave me. He hasn't spoken to me since. Not that I mind. He's so full of booze, poor thing, he doesn't do much any more but grow redder in the nose himself. Every time I see him I want to say, 'Won't you guide my sleigh tonight?' Well, we shall see what he does for poor Gertrude. How old is she, by the way?"

277

"I have no idea. How can we find out?" she laughed.

He was really awful, bringing out the worst in everybody, but, Tillie again reminded herself, of more value to the community than most men — certainly than most of the husbands of the women he spent his time with. None of them ever raised a finger for any of the charities to which he gave his time unstintingly. He never refused a request, whether it was to "do" a hall being used for a benefit, or to mince up Main Street scrounging ads out of local merchants for the souvenir program, or donations to be raffled off. He emceed countless fashion shows for worthy causes, having also his background as a clothes designer. True, it was all good business, he adored the limelight, and shared the insatiable thirst of his kind for bashes and whingdings, but even after subtracting all that for cynicism, Jimmy Twitchell remained a pillar of the community. Most husbands were worthless to it.

"There are ways," he said now, to answer her question. "You may have noticed that the ages of all drivers in traffic violations or accidents, however slight, are given in local newspaper accounts. Even those of the innocent. Area wives, as the horrid *Blade* calls you, are constantly being unmasked in this fashion. I never miss their Traffic Column. Women parading as thirty-five are suddenly revealed to be forty-eight. So if there's somebody you want to get the goods on, just ram her in the fender somewhere about town, or as she's pulling out of her driveway, nothing much, just enough for a police report, and wham! Her age is out in the next edition. Of course the price is giving your own. But enough of this idle chatter. To the business at hand."

Jimmy explained just what had been agreed on be-

278

tween himself and the Princess in his most recent telephone call, one of several he'd made at his own expense. "She's been worn to a frazzle by these charities, but I've done her a couple of favors over there, and told her she owed me one." The arch glitter came to his eye. "Call it Grace under pressure."

Tillie laughed, reaching for her teacup. "Will she receive the winning couple for lunch, is that the arrangement?"

"Yes, and then a tour of the castle." Jimmy stiffened in his chair, as though racked by a shudder. "I'm sure the same thing went through your mind. The creatures that might win? It's a chance any charity takes in a case like this — not knowing but what a pair of goons might represent them. Well, we won't think about that."

He drew a small black notebook from his pocket and flipped through it.

"Now, you'll need eight or ten good strong ladies of the parish to get those tickets distributed *and kept after.* The italics are mine, darling, because it's absolutely essential that workers be pushed or they won't sell anything. You'll get eight or nine tickets back out of books of ten. Gertrude suggests Molly Webster for your second in command, but I think she should be in charge of tables for the ball instead of Laura Colton. Laura's a dear soul but lacking completely in the tact necessary for anything so touchy as tables."

"Do people really care that much about the tables they're put at?"

Jimmy leaned intimately across the one at which they sat, an almost pitying smile on his lips. "Darling, our job is not to decide whether the human race should survive, only to see to it that it does. I. Have seen. Two women. Pull each other's hair out over precisely this. It was at the Epilepsy do."

"Tell me about it," Tillie said, curling up in her chair for one of Jimmy's stories.

"Well, it was a few days after Christmas, which was wrong in itself because by then people have had so much of their families they're at the end of their tether. But anyhoo, the chairman of the whole shebang saw that the table chairman had put her at table number two, below the salt from all the 'honorary' people at the head table, none of whom had done a lick of work for the ball but whose names are important and doll up the stationery. You know those pictures of Gertrude addressing invitations the grinds have already addressed? Well, what did shebang chairman do when she got a load of the setup but pick up all the place cards and proceed to switch them. This was twenty minutes before the Grand Procession," Jimmy said with some satisfaction. "Then table chairman saw what had been wrought, and started to switch tables. Shebang chairman no like, and tried to stop her. And first thing you knew there was a tug of war going on between them, each trying to pull a table in another direction. All this grunting and heaving while calling each other all the names under the sun, because there were a lot of old scores being settled, a long feud. Finally one blurted out something that was too much for the other, who thereupon went for her. I mean literally. It was a cat fight such as you've never seen. They had to be pulled apart and driven home."

"That's hard to believe," Tillie said, though believing it completely. One of her most vivid childhood memories was of two girls clawing each other to bits in the school-yard.

"It's true. I saw it. It doesn't happen often," Jimmy added, with a touch of wistfulness, "but it happens. And of course it's always there underneath, is what I'm trying to say. The lava's there, and so the volcano *can* erupt."

Tillie shook her head. "But to be so petty over some-thing that's supposed to be a humanitarian cause."

"It's charity that suffereth long and is kind, darling, not charities. You never saw the like of them for bring-ing out the worst in petty jealousies and egotisms. These benefit balls are in their very nature social functions, and a woman instinctively puts her best foot forward, even if it's only to trip another one up. Would you believe that on a garden tour for Birth Defects one hostess said she wouldn't throw her place open again because of what another said about her herbaceous borders?"

"Who was it?"

"Oh, well. Mrs. Lamont. Past whom nothing can be put, as you know. So be careful. I guess I keep telling you that because you're such an innocent."

"Nonsense. I'm just as much of a bitch as the next."

"Matinees we say witch, darling." He paused to con-sult his notes again. "Ah, one more thing."

Jimmy took time out to finish his cake and then his tea. She noticed his eyes watching her with what seemed a special interest as he drank off what remained in his cup. He set the cup down, dabbed at his mouth with his napkin, and resumed.

"Now this is important. Every lottery must be regis-tered with the police. It's a state law. It's gambling, after all, and must be strictly regulated. Now listen very carefully, because if this procedure isn't followed to the letter, you can't hold the raffle no matter how many tickets have been sold. Two of you must go down to the police station and fill out certain forms, and in a very few days, because there's a time limit. You fill out forms, swearing to this and that and the other. Who's in charge, where the drawing will be and when, et cetera, et cetera. You'll have to identify yourselves, of course, with all that that implies. That includes giving your age."

"Well, it won't bother me none," Tillie laughed, striving to make it true. "I'm forty-five."

"Yes, I know. Why should you care, since you don't look it."

"No, I know. I look forty-four. Who told you?"

"Oh, I don't know. Gertrude may have mentioned it in an unguarded moment. I may have said, in an unguarded moment of my own, that I thought you a fine figure of a woman, and asked the natural question."

No woman who fancies she has a good figure likes to hear she's a fine figure of a woman. The two aren't the same at all. Tillie let that pass, being grateful in any case for the smaller favor. "Then I should take somebody to the police station with me who doesn't give a damn either."

"Or somebody you want to get the goods on."

He spoke with such convincing indifference that one unfamiliar with him would have thought he couldn't have cared less about the subject, at least at that moment. Tillie, however, sat staring pensively out the window for some time after he had gone.

Jimmy Twitchell in the role of Iago was something she had not visualized before. Sensing his conspiracy now, she said, "No," aloud. She would not be the instrument of his vengeance. But she forgave herself for imagining, with a sly smile, the scene that might result were she to ask an unsuspecting Gertrude to accompany her to the police station to register the lottery. Did she know the trap it was? To find out, and to measure the scope of her decency, she telephoned to chat about it.

"Look, would you come along with me if I can't get anybody else?" she asked. "It has to be two officers of the organization, or at least committee members, I gather."

"If you can't get anybody else, sure, I don't mind."

So at last she had Gertrude in the palm of her hand. But she would not close it. No. She'd ask dear beat-up old Laura Colton. Everyone knew she was sixty-five, and poor Laura no longer cared.

Two days before the deadline set for the registration of the raffle, Jimmy telephoned. His tone was very solicitous, even sympathetic.

"Hello, Tillie. Jimmy here. Look, it's nothing really. It's just that I heard you've been terribly upset by what Gertrude has been saying. You mustn't mind her really, she means no harm. And of course you mustn't *discuss* your private affairs with anyone so freely."

"Gertrude — ?"

"The nonsense she's been spreading about your marriage going on the rocks because you spent it trying to make an intellectual out of Pete. Isn't that his name?" He laughed encouragingly. "You really mustn't pay any attention to her. She has talent, but she needs an editor. And look. If you haven't an escort for the ball, maybe you'd care to go with me. I dance rather well, you know."

283

"That would be nice, Jimmy. Sure, I'd love to. Thanks."

"Done and done."

She had no more than hung up than she called Gertrude, to say she would take her up on her offer to join her at the police station. Laura Colton was a bit under the weather.

Gertrude looked very spruce in a blue suit of nubbed tweed and a matching pillbox hat. Prudent makeup had erased even the few lines remaining from the recent facial. She had clearly expected a newspaper photographer, and she was not disappointed. He snapped them entering headquarters, and then they went in. Tillie looked her age and more, she knew, thanks to a nagging conscience and a poor night's sleep. It was too late now, though. They lined up at the tribunal.

"Organization?" the bored desk sergeant asked, pulling a form toward him and reaching for a pen.

"Mental Health," Gertrude said.

"Prize?"

"An all-expense trip to Monaco, and a day's hospitality with Her Serene Highness, Princess Grace. The round-trip fares for the winning couple are contributed by TWA."

"Total monetary value?"

The women exchanged shrugs.

"Approximately then. I just have to put something down here."

"Maybe a thousand dollars."

"Price per ticket?"

"Twenty dollars. We're selling two hundred and fifty tickets."

Having noted this data on the sheet, the sergeant said: "Now I must ask for personal identification, beginning with fingerprinting. I usually say," he added with a faint grin, "that this can be done in private. Separately? If you know what I mean."

Gertrude, not sensing disaster, smiled and said, "That won't be necessary."

She had a moment of gratification when, after rolling her fingertips on the ink pad and pressing them on the document, the officer said, "Hm. You could lead a life of crime. No ridges, that they need for identification. Very smooth skin. Now I've got to ask you to swear to all this identification with the necessary vital statistics."

Tillie glanced wildly at the door, but it was too late.

"Your name?"

"Mrs. Burt Wilson."

"Address?"

"Two ten Chestnut Drive."

"Age?"

The shocked hush that followed was like the silence that succeeds a detonation the source and nature of which are not quite comprehended by those stunned by it. Even Tillie was dazed. Then Gertrude seemed to pitch forward, clutching at the edge of the desk that interrupted her fall. She was white as a sheet.

"Fuh — fuh — fuh —"

"Take your time," the sergeant said. "We get this all the time, but it can't be helped. You want to try again to state your age?"

"Fuh — fluh — flug —"

It was no good. Gertrude seemed to be strangling, or drowning. Her voice, normally high-pitched, now trailed upward into a pitiful squeal. Then her grip on the desk-edge relaxed, and she dropped to the floor in a heap.

The sergeant bustled around from behind the desk, at the same time calling for help into an adjacent room, perhaps a lounge, judging from the sound of a television set issuing from it. Another officer appeared, and together they carried Gertrude to a bench and laid her on it.

"She's dead," said the second cop. "I always knew this would happen."

The sergeant was not so pessimistic, or at least not as melodramatic. "She's just in shock," he said. "She went into shock." He began to slap Gertrude's cheeks with both hands, not hard, but briskly. The other cop dashed a paper cup of cold water in her face. Finally her eyes fluttered open, and she asked weakly, "Where am I?"

"In hell, I guess," said the sergeant, already beginning to recover some of his boredom. He rose from the kneeling position in which he had been conducting his ministrations. "You'll be all right. Giver her some water to drink, and send in a substitute. Or a couple of them. Because I think you'll have to see her home, lady," he added to Tillie.

The two women left after a few minutes, walking stiffly side by side toward Tillie's car, in which they had come. It was parked about a block away.

"You did this deliberately," Gertrude said, through clenched teeth. "You planned it deliberately."

"I'll never forgive you for that."

"Go right ahead. But it's true. You're a bitch."

They passed somebody they knew, or at least Tillie knew, and she nodded in greeting. Then they resumed their dialogue.

"Who's a bitch?"

"You."

"Prove it."

"I don't have to prove it. Everybody knows it. It's like two times two are four. You don't have to prove it, everyone knows it. You're a bitch."

"I won't have that."

They had reached a white cottage in the gravel driveway of which smoldered a small heap of autumn leaves, momentarily untended. Beside it lay a bamboo rake and a garden hose, left running against the fire's possibly getting out of hand, for a faint breeze was blowing. A puff of wind blew smoke into their faces, causing them both to pause, coughing, there on the sidewalk. When it cleared, Tillie saw that Gertrude's face had lost its pallor, and a dangerous flush suffused her cheeks. "Well, have it or not, you are," Gertrude said. Then suddenly she swung her pocketbook by the strap and smacked Tillie square on the jaw with the flat of it. Tillie drew back her arm and did the same.

What followed was an exchange of blows, curiously dreamlike in the regularity of their alternations, like the stylized, almost ceremonial retaliations of comics that critics of low humor call reciprocal destruction. It was especially odd since they were both by now Crazy Women. Gertrude bent to pick up the bamboo rake to beat Tillie with, then dropped it in favor of a better idea. She seized the hose and trained it straight on her adversary, playing it across her and up and down till she

287

was drenched from head to foot. Both pocketbooks lay on the sidewalk.

"No wonder your husband left you, you dried up old hag," Gertrude said, catching Tillie full in the face with the stream of water. She adjusted the nozzle to give it greater force. Tillie brought both arms up to fend off the jet, a thrashing motion which she suddenly converted into a counter-attack. Lunging forward through the spray, she caught hold of the nozzle, by the motivation intrinsic to the nightmare in which they were enfolded, and wrested it from Gertrude's grasp with a violence that sent them both pitching to the ground. Tillie recovered her balance first, at least enough to rise to her knees, and in this position proceeded to turn the tables and douse Gertrude. They were now both sopping wet. Their hair was plastered to their heads. With Gertrude still down, Tillie managed to climb to her feet. Which was a mistake, because Gertrude got to her own knees and tackled Tillie about the legs, bringing her down like a football player. The two were wrestling in the puddles, pulling each other's hair and clawing at each other's mud-spattered faces, when a whistle sounded and two cops came galloping up the street and pulled them apart.

Neither woman ever got to the ball. Tillie entered a local sanatarium, while Gertrude was flown for a much-needed rest to an institution in the Bahamas.

seven

TILLIE sat looking out of her window. The sanatarium grounds were pleasantly landscaped, and from her second-story room she had a view of a lawn graced by spruce and balsam, the grass still green in autumn, rolling gently toward the road. Her hands lay motionless in her lap, one palm upturned. She sighed quietly as she followed the passage of a car into the distance.

She turned a little in her chair. Over her shoulder she could see her valise, standing empty on the floor of an open closet. Everything had been removed from it, including some sedatives secreted in a zippered pocket. Now it would be some time before she could start another collection, since a nurse stood by to see that she swallowed the single capsule allotted her every night.

The door was opened after a deferential rap, and Dr. Raymond entered, a short handsome man of forty, dressed in loose tweeds. He smiled as though he had come to invite her on a tramp through the nearby woods. Instead he sat down for his usual chat.

"I gather for one thing you've crawled into a kind of shell," he said.

"My mother used to collect them," Tillie answered listlessly. He smiled by way of attesting as humorous what had merely been a — was that what they called a *klang* association. She had recently read about word salads, and thought that she should perhaps try to supply some of them, to assure the kind doctors that she was nutty enough to be here and deserved all this attention. Possibly Dr. Raymond had divined her thoughts, for he assured her that he had not come to ply his trade.

"I'm not going to talk therapy jargon with you, because I don't think you need it," he said.

"I'm not up to it."

"Not up to what?"

"Therapy."

When he laughed in open appreciation of that joke, she gave a wan smile of gratitude in return.

"That's right," he said. "You may have seen the cartoon about the doctor telling a half-stripped male patient, a Sad Sack, that they would have to get him into shape for a checkup. We'll have to build you up for that, all right. But seriously, I think that when you leave, which should be soon, you should make an effort to mix with people more. Find a job maybe, get into community activities, anything. Throw yourself into some charity."

"All right, I will."

"That's the stuff. We ourselves need support of that kind to keep going. The town's lucky to have this place, you know."

"I know it very well. I'll remember what you said about volunteer work. It's a thought for the day that'll help see me through it."

She was bundled into her coat and driven off with a dozen other women for compulsory volleyball. It was held in the gymnasium of the local Y. After an hour of it they were put back into the pickup truck, counted, and driven back to the sanatarium. Following lunch, on a tray in her room, Tillie got out her notebook and did some work on a prayer she was drafting, in the manner of Robert Louis Stevenson's.

"Give us courage for our fears," she wrote, then sat chewing her pencil for a long time, watching the squirrels at their acrobatics in the maples gold with death. Suddenly she bent over her notebook and wrote out rapidly: "Give us courage for our fears, the wisdom to survive our follies, and charity to bind up the wounds we inflict on one another." She closed the notebook and set it aside with a smile of satisfaction.

Just then there was another rap on the door, and a nurse thrust her head in.

"You have a visitor, Mrs. Seltzer."

Jimmy Twitchell took two steps over the threshold, stopped, opened his mouth in a gasp of recognition, as though surprised to find her here, and came forward with his arms out. He held a bouquet of flowers in one hand and a box of candy in the other. The flowers were yellow chrysanthemums, one of which adorned the lapel of his snug blue pinstripe suit.

Tillie's spirits immediately rose. She suddenly realized how much she had to tell him, including the compulsory volleyball, which alone would make his day. She enjoyed the glance he threw about the room, for there was everything here he could have wished. The gaze of discriminating despair lingered especially on the green walls.

"Must they throw pistachio at you at this hour of the day?" he said. "Couldn't they wait till evening?" Then he embraced her, smothering her in a scent the flowers themselves would certainly lack. "And I suppose there's no way of making those draperies shut up? My dear girl, I'm going to get you out of all this if it takes a letter to Washington."

She told about the compulsory volleyball as she tore open the box of candy, five pounds of Perugino chocolates in which she foraged hungrily, for she had hardly touched her lunch. "This is magnificent, Jimmy," she said with her mouth full. "Have one."

"I shall want several. Leave the box open there and let's sit down on these chairs, if you can call them that. From what mortician were they rented? There. Darling, you look like death warmed over. What exactly happened? But before we get to that, let me tell you a story about candy to cheer you up."

Jimmy popped a cream into his mouth and composed himself on his chair, sitting quite erect.

"I once flew to Chicago to visit an old aunt of mine. She was nearly ninety then, and has since been torn down. But she was still there at the time, and knowing her passion for sweets I took her a box of Rosemaries, which I bought before going out to the airport. Well, as we approached Chicago we were told in the dearest little announcement that the landing gear wouldn't go down. You know? We were instructed in the positions to assume for a crash landing. We were to sit on the floor, facing the sides of the plane, our heads between our knees. We were not to peek. Well, my dear, several people prayed, but all I could think of was that box of

Rosemarie chocolates going to waste, *probably*, and why not enjoy them in my possibly last moments. So I tore the box open and began stuffing them into my mouth one after another, gobbling them down as fast as I could. It was a kind of orgy. Tillie, I ate. The whole. Box."

Tillie was doubled over in her chair. "And what happened? Did the plane land all right?"

"Apparently," he answered drily. "But I nearly died of indigestion, I spent nearly an hour in the men's bog, upchucking."

That preliminary tidbit delivered, Jimmy paused and looked at Tillie reproachfully.

"Well, darling, this is going to give Mental Health a black eye," he said.

"I've got two."

"Whatever in God's name happened?"

"You know very well," Tillie said, contritely. "The shock proved too much for her. I honestly never dreamed it would be all that bad. Honestly. I swear to God."

"Well, you might have guessed." He pouted reprovingly, turning his head to look at her askance. "You *are* a breed."

"And it was all for nothing. Because she never got it out. She just turned deathly pale and choked and gasped. I'm so sorry." Tillie shook her head as the tears rolled down her cheeks. "She lost her voice, the way you do in a terrible fright? Till we got outside. Then pow!" She shook her head again, as though momentarily dazed by even the memory of the blows rained on her. "I never did find out how old she is."

"She's fifty-three," Jimmy answered matter-of-factly.

"How do you know?"

"I read it in the Traffic Column. You know, that I told you about in the *Blade?* As I say, I never miss it. The day before she and Burt took off for Grand Bahama, poor Gertrude failed to yield right of way as she was pulling out of the shopping center. Lucky for her she's gone now, and will never see it, poor thing."

So much for that. Jimmy had already lost interest in the subject. On to other things.

"We've got to get you sprung." He glanced around again with his expression of exquisite distaste. "Do they say how long you'll be in here?"

"At least till after the ball. I'll see to that myself. I could never go now."

Jimmy seemed genuinely disappointed. "Damn, I was looking forward to it. Well, maybe I can take Oceana Bailey. She's agreed to be raffle chairman, so you'll have to turn over all your records to her. You must give me the key to your house and tell me where they are. I shan't snoop, I promise."

He seemed quite honest about all this. His expression changed, and he took Tillie in soberly for a few moments.

"You'll forgive me for prying about one thing, darling, because I'm interested," he said, changing his tone as he took a new tack. "But your marriage is definitely over, isn't it? To that snark who talks double talk? What's his name — Pete?"

"Yes, I guess it is."

"Right. Now I shall proceed to astonish myself. Why don't you take a whack at it with me? You could do worse. Indeed you already have." He turned his head again to give her his sidewise, how-could-you pout, and instantly resumed. "I've never married, for fear of becoming a real person. Not for lack of opportunities. I've had several proposals in my time. I'm exactly your age, to dispose of that, and ready to settle down. I'm healthy, solvent, and amusing. I shall never beat you — I'm not that interested in women. I'm domestic as a plate. Yes, that's from Millay, as I'm sure you know. My conversation is studded with literary allusions of that sort, but I'll never identify another for you. You'll be strictly on your own as to that. A sort of game between us, you on your mettle, me on mine. Mainly I'll be your protectress, not just provider. Because I'm a match for any woman you can name, and it's what you need, because you're not. You don't bat in this league, darling, and Gertrude's faction will be laying for you after this. You don't know what sensitive claws women have. Or at least you don't know how to defend yourself. I do. They'll be out to get you. They'll hound you out of town, unless you leave it on your own and go back to the city, where you'll find them even deadlier. And chicer. And that's the thing. I shall make you chic. You'll find me a good Pygmalion, because they respect me, knowing I'm better at their own game than they are. They need me and they know it. They need me to decorate their silly houses and to run their silly balls. You need me. I'll dress you from head to foot, do something with your hair. I'll make you over, because you do have possibilities. Yes, you can be chic, if you'll but say the word. We'll see all the shows, read all the poets, we'll spend a lifetime together trying to identify each other's literary allusions. Because you see my slant on all this sex war business is this. Men and women should be rivals, not enemies. There'll never be a dull moment. I want to build a new house on some hill acreage I already own, a snug little place where we can sit by the fire and watch the Traffic Column for everyone's age, meanwhile not driving our own Mercedes over twenty-five miles an hour. What else? Travel."

He rose and began slowly to pace the floor in those meowing shoes.

"Abroad once a year, and between times little side trips to like Lake Louise or Sea Island, always eating at least as well as at home, because flanking my cookbooks is a shelf of eating guides, beginning with the Michelin."

"Pete called them Belly Baedekers."

"Please! Not while I'm proposing. That dreadful four-letter word. Where were we? Travel. The main thing is that, wherever we've been, we'll always be glad to get back, whether it's our little nest out here or the apartment in town. In either place you'll find everything a woman can reasonably expect in this world. Food, clothing, shelter, amusement, friends, parties — and a husband to see you through the disillusionments of marriage. Oh, there's your mother. I knew there was something else to dispose of. I met her only once, but I felt instantly I'd known her a lifetime," Jimmy said, sitting down again. "She seems all right of her kind, but as you know, she's on her way to becoming one of those little old ladies who are taken to *Hamlet* and then say that it's all quotations. And she'd vote for Ronald Reagan for President because anyone who had both legs amputated, as he did in that old movie they keep reshowing, and then went on to become Governor of California deserves our admiration. No, she'll have to go, along with that block-front chest-on-chest you have in your alcove. Darling, how could you? You see how you need me. Well, I guess that about wraps it up."

This time he rose to go.

"Done and done. Goodbye for the present then. Now I must go and prattle about us."

"Couldn't we make it a secret for the time being?"

"Of course. Else what would there be to prattle about?" He stood in the doorway with a finger upraised. "But don't you breathe a word. One busybody in the family is enough."

For a long time after Jimmy had gone, Tillie sat with her heels on the chair, hugging her knees, her cheek reclining on them. She could already hear Gertrude explaining to her "faction" the nature and frequency of such marriages. "Men of that sort are notorious for liking women who are, oh, not dowdy, I won't say that, but not feminine smashers who pose a threat to their anti-women concept." Tillie wanted to cut her throat. So that was the set in whose league she did not bat! How cannily Jimmy had stated her need for protection against them; how persuasively put the case for his ability to get her in. She saw herself holding a teacup on the society page of the *Times*, snugly incorporated into a committee planning a fashion show for which he had designed something or which he would emcee. What an adroit chatterbox he was in the limelight. She would be dressed in anything but the tweeds that made her the sort of striding-on-the-moors type to which such men theoretically gravitated. So her only defense against gossip of the sort her marriage to Jimmy Twitchell would arouse was to marry him. Very interesting. Life was endlessly amazing . . . But could he really succeed in making her chic? She had changed no spots on the leopard she'd married. Maybe Jimmy would have better luck . . .

Tillie lay down for her afternoon nap, stretching out with a sigh. Not that she could sleep, or even remotely wished to. She just wanted to lie there and think about her fortune with no immediate regard for whether it was good or bad. That she had the option of an answer was the pleasure in which for the moment she luxuriated. She did not think; she merely lay afloat in a sea of vague considerations among which there was no hurry to choose, lapped by pros and cons themselves in no urgent need of sorting out or evaluation. Their contradictions themselves constituted the repose in which her tired mind drifted. Even the fatigue was a kind of volitionless suspension. She had arrived at the eye of her storm, and the inertia was pleasant. The glow in which she lay was not unsuffused with the sense of flattery normally adhering to any proposal. A line of Eliot's bobbed into her mind. "Teach us to care and not to care. Teach us to sit still." She bet Jimmy couldn't place that.

There was a rap on the door and the nurse again thrust her head in.

"There's a telephone call for you, Mrs. Seltzer. You can take it in the lobby booth."

Tillie was dressed, but she drew on a wrapper anyway before going down. She descended the stairs like someone somnambulating, and in that mood sat in the booth for a moment before picking up the receiver. When she did, it was with the same hazy deliberation.

"Hello."

" 'Tis I. Well, you don't look as bad as I expected."

It was Pete, though it took her a moment to recognize his voice.

"I hear they've locked you up with all the Aunt Sukeys."

"Hello, Pete. How are you?"

"All right. Whuh hoppened?"

"Oh, not now. I don't even know for sure. Keeping busy?"

"Oh, sure. We're test-marketing an odorless cologne. Hey, wake up. Remember the end products we used to make up? How did we miss that one?"

"That's a good one. High time somebody developed it, too. How are things there?"

"Oh, you know New York this time of year. Crawling with Americans. But look, why the hell didn't you get in touch with a man? I had to find out through some friends in the C.I.A."

She suddenly realized something about Pete just then. It struck her all of a heap. You tried for years to put your finger on what was "wrong" with him, what his "faults" or "flaws" were. Now it came to her. He had no faults at all. He was just hopeless. Of how many people could you say that, and then go on to add, at least to yourself, that that was why you had married them? Was, indeed, what you "saw" in them.

Her spirits began to rise. In fact, she thought she might be going to cry. But she smiled to herself as she said:

"What does C.I.A. mean, Pete?" She put the question to him in the old teasing, catechism manner he had never resented, quizzing him on current events. "What do the initials stand for?"

There was a blank silence at the other end, fully conveying his bafflement.

"I'll be damned. I don't know. Something Intelligence, obviously. What is it?"

"Central Intelligence Agency."

"What would I do without you? Which brings me to . . ." He cleared his throat, clearly wretched in the way he was when forced to something personal, or sentimental — or confronted with the crisis of having to call Mrs. Shilepsky something. How long ago that all seemed now! A lifetime ago.

"Look, this separation isn't working out," he said, weaseling out of the sentimentality again. "People sometimes can't make a go of them either, you know. And all this expense. I can't pay your bills there on top of everything else. It's no good. Why don't we sell the house in the country and move back into the city?"

"We don't own it."

"There's that. I was just using the cliché of the moment — people are doing it in droves now. I don't like this pad. I know of a bigger one for not much more money. In that new west side neighborhood they're redeveloping."

"Is it protected by the Mafia?"

"What?"

"That old joke you used to have about the flat where you first seduced me. I don't know what got into me."

"I can tell you if you're interested. And I've still got it."

"You always were lubricious, Pete."

"You don't have to flatter me. But I'm sick of this — this — whatever it is," he brought out in a flustered rush.

"My plumber tells me that pursuit of women is flight from woman."

"What does that mean?"

"How the hell do I know? Call me Alfie, but you find it isn't satisfying, these one-night stands at the Everlasting Arms. I've come to realize that when you reach a certain poosenstock things are apt to get a little ribbiquacky."

"I know just what you mean."

"And you haven't heard the best part. I've got a job lined up for you. I've got spies in the — Christ, I can't remember the name of this either, but it's got something to do with the state welfare department. Fred Crandon works in it and he's got charge of some section of it. You'd be a case worker, investigating families with problems, broken homes and stuff. Didn't you take a lot of sociology in college? Don't tell me I flapped my lip too soon."

"Some. In case I didn't knock them dead on Broadway. Look, are you doing all this because you feel sorry for me?"

"Yes, and myself too. Twinkletoes called me into his office the other day and laid it on the line that I can't go any higher in the firm, though I can bank on what I've got. So we can use a second income. There couldn't be a better time for things to get shambly for both of us. So look. Why don't I come out tomorrow to see you? How's that, me proud beauty?"

"This is all great, Pete, and I'd damn well like to try again. But there's one snag. I promised Jimmy Twitchell I'd marry him."

"Is that what you're in for? Why did you go and do that?"

"He brought me a box of candy. Nobody's ever done that before. It's five pounds."

"I'll bring you ten, if you can let me have five bucks till Saturday. So I'll pick you up at the foolish farm then around seven. I've got a new secondhand car. A Ford that's as good as new except for some fluckage in the rebrifuge or something. Will they let you out?"

"I think. I'll see you then. And skip the candy. I'd rather the money went for a good bottle of wine."

"Right. And keep your chin up. We all have to do that, especially when we begin to get two. That's life. And so in conclusion, I say to you what I have always said. When the consofrinkles seem at their greemest, that's the time to stermify your happaphoids. And if you do this with faith, then all will still be ragasocky. And if you think I'm lying, you can go and look it up for yourself."

"I believe every word of it."

She had planned to cry, but now she didn't. Her tears would keep. She felt the same exhausted calm, but, beneath its surface, a hint of new excitements brewing, as of slowly heaving seas. She was needed. Here it was again, the eternal second chance. She suddenly thought, from left field, "Redemption Center," and laughed aloud, a little unstably. It was a family joke. That was what the Green Stamp place past which the three of them had so often driven called itself, and they would laugh as they went by, imagining a file of white-robed souls turning themselves in for salvation and the life everlasting.

"So you see I'm with you still," she said, nearly aloud as she left the telephone booth. "Always thinking about you no matter what else I may seem to be doing at the time. I'll walk the streets of the city with my raving heart, dreaming of my demolished faun. But I'll be on my way to work, the day dedicated to you. This life too, whatever I can still make of it. Oh, my brave, bright, still seedless boy."

Perhaps, once over the first grief, you could come to share the memory. "Hey, Pete, how's this? Haircuts while you wait. Pete?" She could see him look up from his homework to call over to his idol. She thought of all that as she slowly mounted the stairs to her room, at the same time wondering what she had to wear tomorrow night. She was determined it would be a gay evening. There would be problems to brace herself for, but they would keep too.

She paused, her hand on the rail, to smile at another particular memory. Pete had once said she must excuse him from listening to any more Shostakovitch, as he always laughed in the wrong places. What she was saying, she supposed, was: "Thank God I've got Pete Seltzer to see me through the disillusionments of marriage."